TRAPPED

Trapped

ERIC KRUGER

Space Monkey Press

The Benjamin Drake Adventure Series

Hauler

Bounty

Trapped

Alone

| one |

The impact of the pulse bullet took the young man by surprise. He always expected a pulse wound to burn, but instead, this was a dull throb. He looked down at his arm to find the source of the pain. Blood was seeping out of a wound high on the back of his arm. He twisted his arm around to see better and regretted it immediately, as the throbbing pain transformed into the searing pain he'd expected it to be. He let out a scream.

"Keep your mouth shut!" Corporal Shadburne, smeared with blood, rushed over to his side. She grabbed his arm and inspected it.The pain intensified again, and he did everything he could to stifle the scream that wanted to erupt from his lungs.

"It looks worse than it is. Brad! Fix Provost's arm."

"Yes ma'am. Let's have a look." For the third time in as many minutes, the young man's arm was twisted around, igniting the pain.

"Sorry. Good news is it looks to be a clean wound." Brad pulled a device from his backpack. "Hold still as much as you can."

A bright blue light shone from the device, and Brad held it close to the wound. It felt warm, but not painful. Relieved, Provost relaxed.

It lasted a second.

Brad's grip on his arm increased, and the warmth of the light became a scorching fire.

"Get it off! It hurts!" Provost protested, pulling on his arm.

Brad held firm. "One more second . . ."

Provost took a deep breath and braced himself to break free. This pain was ten times worse than that of the pulse bullet. He'd rather take his chances with the wound.

"All done!" Brad said, letting go of his arm and switching off the light.

Provost breathed out. He carefully turned his arm and peered down at the wound.

It had almost completely disappeared.

Instead of open muscle tissue and blood, a scabbed-up dent sat there. The wound looked a few weeks old, not a few minutes.

"Another week, and it should be gone," Brad said as he got up.

"Thanks!" Provost yelled after him.

The pain was now barely noticeable, and Provost grabbed his pulse rifle, which lay on the ground next to him. He hurried toward Shadburne.

"Good to go, ma'am."

She gave him a quick nod before resuming firing her pulse rifle through the broken window of a burned-out hydro vehicle. The returning fire fell short, and a cloud of red dust covered them. The corporal wiped most of it off her helmet's visor and looked at Provost.

"Soldier, we need to move over to that rock formation. Another squad's pinned down there. Brad!"

Brad came running from behind another wreck. "Ma'am."

"Head count?"

"Seven KIA. Four wounded. Nine operational."

"Okay, gather them up. We're moving out."

"Yes, ma'am. And the wounded?"

"We'll come back for them," the corporal replied. But Provost knew they were as good as dead.

Brad returned with the remaining soldiers and Provost recognized some faces.

"We thought you were dead!"

"Just a flesh wound," he replied, turning his arm for everyone to see.

"Show-and-tell is over. You four group up with Brad. The rest of you are with me," Shadburne said. "Our target is the rocky formation due west. Brad, fall back behind what's left of the convoy and flank our movement. My team will make for a straight approach."

"Okay, you heard her. Buddy up and check all your e-suits and weapons. In three minutes, we move out," Brad ordered.

* * *

Corporal Shadburne would have preferred the armored hydrogen vehicles to have still been intact. But they weren't. The moment the vehicles had pulled out of the shuttles, pulse fire had erupted all around them, pinning them down. It was an ambush. Their intel had suggested the landing zone was safe, but like most intel, it was flawed. Now the only purpose the burned-out wrecks served was as cover.

Corporal Shadburne slowly moved forward, staying as low as possible. Pulse rounds ricocheted off the wrecks and others send dust flying up in front of the team. There was no time to hesitate or second-guess herself, so she pushed on. The rocky formation was only a few meters away now.

She reached the last hydro wreck and turned back to make sure the rest of the team was still there. They were. The easy part was behind them, and the hardest part lay ahead. Next, she had to get them across to the rocky ridge with no more cover. She called two soldiers over.

"Okay. I need you two to lie down suppressing fire. The rest of the team will cross. Once we find suitable cover, we'll take over and you two cross. Copy?"

"Yes, ma'am!" Provost and his teammate replied.

"Good. Okay, let's go!"

Provost and his teammate popped up and fired nonstop in the enemy's direction. Corporal Shadburne and the rest of the team ran as quickly as their e-suits allowed them toward the rocky outcrop. They reached it unscathed and found the trapped team members.

"Who is in charge?" Shadburne yelled at the scared faces looking at her.

No one answered, and everyone just exchanged glances.

New recruits.

"Okay. I'm Corporal Shadburne. You are with me and my team now."

Everyone turned their heads as Brad's team rushed around the corner.

"Sorry we're late," he said as they all huddled down.

Corporal Shadburne had worked with Brad for only a few weeks now, but they'd clicked immediately and understood each other. She didn't have to spell things out for him. Once she'd explained what she needed, he was off, and soon she heard his team's pulse rifles firing.

If they ever wanted to get off this barren planet, she would need Brad to stay alive.

Provost and the other soldier jumped over a rock and fell to the ground next to Shadburne. The firing continued, but with less intensity.

"Okay, our next target is toward the convoy of vehicles north of us. We'll have to lay down fire from our position, as there is no cover between us and them. Make sure you have sufficient cover before attacking. Questions?"

No one did, but multiple scared faces looked back at her.

"Trust your training," she reassured them. "Listen to our commands. You'll be fine."

* * *

Officer Provost hunkered down behind a big rock and reflected on the corporal's words. *Trust your training.* A two-week crash course on how to survive on Mars and combat drills. War was all but forgotten on Earth, but suddenly they had to prepare for one. On Mars. They were all trained Penta Security officers, but going into battle was not the same as upholding the law. And doing it on another planet made it even harder. What had convinced him and everyone else here to go was the credits. Not a crazy amount, but they all knew it was just a matter of time before Penta started drafting people with no extra incentive. So, Provost, like everyone else around him, jumped at the opportunity to have a paid space adventure. They were told a show of force should be enough to convince Santo to surrender. The first fleet Penta sent went too quickly and with no training at all, and Santo had destroyed them. This time, they would have superior numbers, and Santo would realize they would not stop sending people until he surrendered. Provost, along with every other officer, had believed it would be over in minutes once they arrived on Mars.

They were all wrong.

Two hours ago, the cargo hold had opened, and they'd marched out onto the Martian soil. Provost barely had time to take in the alien landscape when the officer in front of him collapsed with a giant red flower spreading out on his back. It took Provost a second to realize it was blood from a pulse wound spreading across his e-suit. The air filled with the crackle of pulse bullets flying past them. Provost fell to the ground, a move that saved his life, as a pulse bullet whizzed by overhead. People started running around, trying to find cover. Some of the more experienced officers ran back into the shuttles and retrieved the armored vehicles. They stopped in the line of fire and signaled for people to jump in. Some made it to the vehicles and jumped in, finding safety inside. But the safety only lasted seconds, as pulse cannons opened fire on the hydro vehicles, blowing them up. Provost, still on the ground, had looked on as most of the senior officers and all their armored vehicles went up in flames. He'd sat up, unsure what to do next, when a pulse bullet hit him in the arm.

Now, arm treated, hunkering down behind a rock, Provost readied himself to attack. He peered over the rock at the armored vehicles, where the gunfire was coming from. The enemy hid themselves well, and he struggled to spot any. The ambush continued, and he tried his best to locate where the pulse bullets originated. After observing the vehicles for a while, he could make out figures behind the vehicles. The reason they were so hard to spot was their uniforms. It was the same color as the red soil and made them invisible. Provost aimed his weapon at a spot he believed had an enemy and fired. He kept looking through the scope on his rifle, and saw something fall backward, hitting the ground. One down. He refocused and scanned the vehicles for the next enemy. A pulse bullet smashed into a rock near his head and fragments bit into his visor. Flinching, Provost only took a second to asses the damage, as he knew someone had him in his sights. He had to retaliate, quickly. He popped back up and fired a few blind shots, then focused on where he thought the enemy was and waited. People were yelling orders and obscenities. Pulse rifles boomed and threw dust in the air. Yet Provost kept his calm and focused on the one spot. Right over the hood of an armored vehicle. He didn't allow himself to be distracted by all the noise and dust. Then a head slowly peered over the hood of the vehicle, just enough for Provost to squeeze the trigger of his rifle and make a big mess of it.

* * *

"Cease fire!" Corporal Shadburne's command carried over the noise and was echoed down the line.

Silence came instantly, like some higher being had pressed pause.

Corporal Shadburne locked eyes with Brad and nodded. He nodded back and ran off, grabbing two officers as he passed them.

"Cover our guys," Shadburne instructed her squad.

Everyone switched their Augmented Retinal Projectors on and tagged Brad and his team. This way they would stand out from the enemy, and the squad's pulse weapons would not fire at them.

The squad watched with their fingers on their triggers as Brad's team shuffled across the open space toward the enemy's vehicles. They reached the first vehicle and crouched down next to it. So far, so good. Brad peered over the vehicle. Corporal Shadburne held her breath, expecting the worst, hoping for the best. Brad crouched back down again and led the team around the front. Shadburne switched her ARP over to a first-person view of Brad's ARP, allowing her to see what he was seeing.

What he saw was carnage. Bodies littered the dusty ground. About thirty-two dead or severely wounded. Brad inspected one of the enemy soldiers, rolling him over. A cracked e-suit visor and mangled face greeted him. Brad scanned the rest of the body.

"Are you seeing this, ma'am?" He knew she was.

Corporal Shadburne looked at the logo on the enemy's uniform, via Brad's ARP.

The logo that was supposed to be a golden Z was instead a tiger's head.

The writing underneath it said Shangcorp Tactical Force.

"We need to call HQ," she said. "Right now."

Three hundred and ninety-four million kilometers away from Earth, war was about to break out.

| two |

"... and we expect this afternoon's announcement from Shang-corp's board of directors to be just that—a declaration of war."

Benjamin Drake turned toward Jimmy Something, but Jimmy kept staring at the Data Display Unit. The special broadcast had interrupted the steady stream of advertisements usually displayed on the enormous screen high above the street, enlightening the masses below. They, like Jimmy, had stopped to watch and were still staring at the screen, ready to be told what to think next.

"Jimmy!" Drake tapped him on his shoulder.

"Wow, ya know?" Jimmy slowly turned away from the DDU that was now back to selling hydrocars.

People started walking again, and soon everything seemed to go back to normal. The familiar, unique aroma of the Shangcorp white box meals filled Drake's nose. Hydrocars whizzed by, and shoulders bumped shoulders as people passed on the crowded street.

"I can't believe Santo is still holding on to Mars," Drake said.

"I thought they'd get him for sure this time, ya know?"

Most people did. After Penta's first blunder, sending a small and underprepared force to Mars, they'd sent a bigger and stronger force to oust Captain Raymond Santo. They failed again. This time, it wasn't Santo or the elements who beat them. Instead, they'd faced something they were yet again unprepared for: Shangcorp.

The Penta Security Forces were greeted with heavy resistance on Mars. Shangcorp forces, who barely beat them to the red planet, had ambushed them. Captain Santo had watched from the safety of his compound as the two forces took each other out. With only a handful of soldiers left, both forces retreated in defeat.

The mission to take Mars back from Santo had failed again. Relations between Penta and Shangcorp had always been tense, and the battle on Mars had escalated it to new heights. War seemed inevitable.

"If they close the borders . . ." Drake knew it was pointless to state the obvious. They were already stuck in Shangcorp. Closing the borders would only make that official.

"Do you wanna make a run for it? While we can, ya know?" Jimmy asked.

"We can't. I can't—"

"Yeah, don't reckon I could either." Jimmy saved him from saying it out loud.

They still had a mission to complete in Shangcorp. Leaving now was not an option.

* * *

Drake and Jimmy arrived at the jobsite and put their hard hats on. They walked over to the site supervisor, who greeted them with a nod and a swipe on his Human Interface Console. They knew what to do and didn't need any instructions. As long as they showed up and got signed in, they were good. Not that the supervisor actually signed them in. Like Drake and Jimmy, most of the workers on-site were there illegally. Management didn't care, in fact, they preferred to hire them. Illegals worked for less and didn't need insurance. And there were no investigations when one died—something that happened regularly.

Management handed every illegal worker they employed a Human Interface Device, or HID. Unlike HICs, which were surgically implanted into the forearm, HIDs were handheld units, primarily used by kids whose parents didn't want to spend money every year upgrading their outgrown HICs. Drake and Jimmy were now the proud owners of brightly colored HIDs with cartoon characters on the back.

Receiving the HIDs was a blessing. Now Jimmy and Drake could earn credits, and spend them on food and necessities, without fear of their Penta Corporation HICs setting off alarms. Shangcorp was corrupt to the bone, and most people lived in poverty. Deals were always there to be made and blind eyes were turned at every corner. People distrusted the authorities and were happy to bend the rules. No one blinked an eye if you had a functioning HIC but preferred to use a HID.

"Man, I'm sweating balls already," Jimmy said.

"I hear ya, buddy," Drake replied, wiping the sweat off his brow.

The work they'd found was hard. Huge, automated machinery came in and demolished the old buildings, leaving piles of rubble behind. Neither machines nor robotic workers could navigate the rough and unpredictable mounds, so humans had to break down the rubble into more manageable pieces. It was hard, dangerous work, but easy to get. Shangcorp was always erecting new buildings, increasing their infrastructure, rebuilding where old buildings stood. It felt to Drake like they were trying to erase their past as quickly as possible. The quicker they replaced it, the more likely people would believe it.

Drake lifted his sledgehammer and brought it down, breaking a piece of concrete into pieces. It was hard work, but also satisfying. All the anger and frustration of the last few months—hell, even years—came to the surface as he swung the hammer. Every memory of the recent past fueled his blows. The concrete didn't stand a chance.

"I think it's break time, ya know?"

"Have you even broken a single piece yet?" Drake asked him. All the surrounding concrete seemed untouched.

Jimmy dropped his jaw, demonstrating his level of disbelief.

"I'm still working out which way best to approach this, ya know? Some of us prefer to use our brains and not . . ." Jimmy gestured toward Drake.

"Not what?"

"Our muscles," Jimmy mumbled.

Drake looked at the scrawny figure sitting in the rubble. Not having enough food growing up took its toll on many New Franconians, and Jimmy was no exception. But what he lacked in size, he made up for in determination.

"That's okay. All I have is my muscles and good looks. At least you have options," Drake replied.

Jimmy smiled. "That's why we make an excellent team, ya know?"

* * *

For the rest of the day, Drake broke up the bigger pieces, and Jimmy then smashed the smaller ones. Drake had to admit Jimmy was right. They made an excellent team.

A siren blared, signaling the end of the day. Although Drake enjoyed the physical activity, he was glad to have a break.

"You boys having a quick one?" a redheaded woman, clearly not a local, asked them.

"Maybe."

Jimmy had been staring at the redheaded woman smashing rocks since they got there. Every day for the last few weeks, Jimmy would find them a spot to work on that was near her. They would acknowledge each other with a nod in the mornings, and again when they left at night. Drake couldn't recall them ever saying one word to each other.

"What do you say, partner? Drinks?" Drake asked Jimmy.

"Um, sure, ya know. Might be nice," Jimmy said, stumbling over the words.

"Me and the girls are heading to the bar on the corner, across from the gate." The rest of her friends caught up to her and they headed toward the gate.

"Seems you got yourself a date," Drake teased.

"Huh? What you mean?"

"Don't play dumb with me," Drake replied.

"Whatever. We better sign out before Shithead leaves, ya know?"

Drake agreed and grabbed his things. They received their wages daily, as there was no payroll or any paperwork involved. Most workers lived a day-to-day lifestyle, earning credits and then immediately spending them again, forcing them to return the next morning.

A man of few words, the manager barely acknowledged their presence as he scanned their HIDs and transferred their daily wage.

"Same time tomorrow?" Drake quipped as they left.

"Why would we show up at another time?" Jimmy asked.

"I was just being silly."

"So, we are going back at the same time tomorrow?"

"Yes, Jimmy."

"Okay. Thought I missed something, ya know."

Drake and Jimmy found the bar packed with laborers unwinding after a long day. Not a clean shirt or a fresh pair of boots in sight.

"You boys made it!" the redhead said as they approached.

"Had to drag this one kicking and screaming," Drake said, tilting his head toward Jimmy.

"Bullshit! I walked next to you, ya know," Jimmy replied quickly.

"I'm Drake, and this one goes by Jimmy."

"I'm Dina. You'll get to know the rest as you go."

No one objected or seemed to care about the way Dina introduced them.

Everyone got along great, and soon a few after-work drinks turned into a lot of after-work drinks. Jimmy tried his best to keep up with the girls, but he seemed to struggle. He was barely able to stand up on his own, clutching at tables, chairs, and people to stay upright. He seemed to be having the time of his life.

Drake took a sip of his own beer. It was only his third one for the night. Unlike Jimmy, he needed nothing or no one to hold him up. He was having fun, enjoying the company of their new friends, but two things were pressing heavily on him. Two things that kept him up at night. Two things that stayed with him when he worked. Two things that prevented him from having too much fun.

The first was not unique to him: war was coming. The DDUs behind the bar showed that all the news coverage was about when, not if, the declaration would happen. It had been coming for months now, ever since he helped Jacob McKenna send Captain Santo to Mars. The latest Penta failure to oust Santo had a bigger impact than anything Drake's generation had ever seen. War. It had been decades since a war had broken out. The previous war had brought an end to governments controlling countries and had ushered in the new era of corporation-owned territories. Now the two biggest corporations were on the brink of starting the first ever post-government war.

It was a crushing thought. Both sides had undisclosed secret mega weapons that could wipe humanity off the face of the Earth.

But of the two things that haunted Drake, this was not the biggest.

The thing that really crushed him, that kept him up, prevented him from eating and occupied his thoughts every waking moment, was not the war.

It was the news article that Jimmy had shown him a month ago about a Jane Doe in a minimum-security holding hospital right here in Lan-noi.

The article had a picture.

He knew her as Lily Wells.

| three |

Eugene Davis looked at the sign on the door. The door led to a small office, nothing big or fancy, but it was still an office. No more shared cubicles for him. He focused on the first four letters on the sign: CAPT. He had been a lieutenant for so long that he'd given up on ever ascending through the ranks. So he'd looked for other opportunities to enrich his life. Opportunities that revealed themselves daily to security officers. And once he figured out who the other like-minded officers were, life became very profitable indeed. Sure, they had rep for being dirty, and some Penta officials had tried their best to get rid of the corruption in the security forces, but somehow, Eugene always evaded any career-ending catastrophes.

Then things improved tenfold.

Captain Raymond Santo, a career security officer with an outstanding record, had asked for some favors. From then on, Davis was untouchable. Whatever Santo needed, he provided, and Santo made sure Davis never faced internal review. Davis was living the dream.

Then everything almost came crumbling down.

He'd known Santo was up to something big, but as always, Santo had outsmarted everyone. He caught them all by surprise when he occupied Mars. Davis did not know Santo was planning it, although he inadvertently played a part by doing a string of illegal favors for Santo. One favor led to him being harassed by that nosy, stuck-up woman, Wells. How he hated her. She always did whatever she pleased, and everyone, even Santo, would allow it and only focus on the results. Davis despised nothing more than overachievers.

Luckily, she was so obsessed with catching Santo that she'd let Davis slip through her fingers. He made sure to stay out of her way, but he also realized that Santo had left a huge vacuum behind. One that needed filling. Davis made sure he slipped into Santo's shoes, taking his place as one of Penta's most corrupt officials. And if there was one thing that Captain Santo had taught him, it was to stay under the radar. Keep things small, but lucrative. Don't attract too much attention or get greedy.

So he did. He kept his finger on the pulse of most of the corrupt dealings happening at Penta and only got involved in the ones that seemed low-risk and high-return. Life was good.

And then it got even better.

Someone had thought it beneficial to promote him to captain. Of course, it had a few strings attached and a side of blackmail, but no officer in Penta uniform could deny him his rank.

Captain Eugene Davis.

He didn't give a rat's ass how he'd achieved it, only that he had. All that mattered was the result. And now that he had even more power, he could get rid of a little problem that haunted him.

A little problem called Lily Wells.

* * *

"Time for lunch. Try to sit up," the nurse said, and propped some pillows behind her back before setting a white box meal in front of her. "Make sure you eat it all, you hear?" She smiled and left for the next bed.

A metallic noise reminded Lt. Lily Wells that she still had only one arm at her disposal. An electronic cuff sat snug around her wrist. Although slightly different from the ones she'd used at Penta, it functioned the same. Usually a detainee would wear two cuffs that clung together electromagnetically. Sometimes, like hers, one was enough, and the cuff anchored itself to the bed railing. She could slide it up and down the rail, but not away from it. She relaxed the arm and used her free arm to pull the meal closer.

The fragrant aroma of the white box meal brought everything back into focus. She was in Shangcorp, in a hospital, apparently. Or jail, going by the cuff around her arm. There were three more beds in the room; two of them occupied. One of the patients also had an electromagnetic cuff around their arm. The beds, floor, and machinery all looked old but clean and well maintained. The voices, signage and people confirmed she was in a Shangcorp territory.

When she woke up the first morning, she'd felt confused and lost. She quickly figured out where she was, but it took a few more days before her memory of the last couple of weeks caught up. There were still some blanks, but she had a rough idea of what had gone down.

She remembered chasing Drake and Jimmy Something across the ocean and into a Shangcorp territory. There, the pursuit continued deep into Shangcorp's main territory until she almost caught up to them. Then she collided with Sammy Sanders. She'd underestimated him, mistaking him for a small-time hustler, when indeed he turned out to be much more ambitious. She remembered a physical altercation with him, and then waking up here.

She had bandages all over, but the biggest discomfort came from a wound on her chest. The location of the wound made it very difficult to move around. A pulse wound? She couldn't recall getting shot. Her cuffed arm had also taken a beating, and her HIC was busted. She tried several times to activate it, but it would not respond. That was probably why she was a Jane Doe. With no way of accessing her Human Interface Console, the authorities couldn't identify her.

Not that they hadn't tried.

With every interaction she had lying in bed, someone would prompt her and asked her about her identity. Some of the nurses had given up, but most still tried. Wells played dumb and just shook her head. If they found out she worked for Penta, they would lock her up in the highest security level building. She'd also overheard the nurses and staff talking about the war that was about to break out. She heard of the conflict between the Penta and Shangcorp soldiers on Mars, and how they had both taken heavy losses.

War was coming to Earth, and a Penta officer in a Shangcorp territory was a terrible thing to be. So she kept her mouth shut and bought herself the time she needed to plan her escape.

Wells finished her white box meal and leaned back into the pillows. The other patients, or inmates, were still eating their meals. The woman next to her had jet black hair, cut just above her shoulders, and two injured arms. She seemed to have adjusted to the setback, and Wells looked on as she ate her meal with no difficulty. The other person, a middle-aged man with barely any hair at all, showed no visible injuries. When she'd woken up the first day, there were three different people in the room, but over time they'd left, and the woman next to her and the balding man took their places. They had been here for a few days now but had not said a word to her or each other.

Wells knew the longer she stayed there, the higher the risk of getting caught. Chances were they had already done a facial recognition scan on her. If they ran it with default filter settings, nothing would appear. Only a competent officer would know how to dig deeper into the scan to get a result. Unless they suspected her of some wrongdoing, there would be no reason for such a scan.

She also knew that she'd need help to get out. Not only did she have multiple injuries, but with her HIC being broken, she did not know what city she was in, nor could she try to scan anything or anyone to gain some information. She was flying blind.

Except for the electromagnetic restraint on her wrist, there didn't seem to be any other security measures in place. This was either a very low-security holding facility, or a security section in a normal hospital.

Wells looked over at the man across from her bed. He had typical Shangcorp facial features and the same slight build. He sat propped up in his bed and seemed to be asleep. Wells kept studying him, trying to figure out whether he could be a useful accomplice. Wells reckoned she could most likely lift him overhead and throw him across the room if she wanted to. But maybe he made up for it in smarts. She scrapped that idea as drool dribbled out of his open mouth. Nothing about this man appealed to her.

Wells turned her attention to the woman.

She also had the local aesthetic, sharing the same facial features as the man and the same slight build. She also had two injured arms. Wells feared she'd have to look elsewhere for help.

"My name is Aranya," the woman said without making eye contact.

Wells felt guilt for staring and judging her.

"Hi. Um, I'm . . ." Wells froze. Playing dumb and not saying anything was easy. Coming up with a new identity on the spot was much harder.

"That's okay. You can tell me later," the woman whispered.

Wells shifted her weight, making the cuff clang against the bed rail. She noticed her broken HIC and reflected on the woman's arms, both in carbon casts. A broken or severely injured arm would surely mean a broken HIC. So how could they understand each other? Even if her ARP was still functioning, it would be worthless without the processing power of her HIC. Yet she understood every word the woman said.

The woman smiled. She pointed to Wells's neck. "It's old, but still works."

Wells put her hand on her neck and felt the strap sitting snugly around it. She immediately recognized it as an old translator unit, used before ARPs became widespread. The first units had earpieces connected to them, but this model seemed to communicate directly to her ARP. The hospital must have put it on her to help with communicating.

"Clears that up," Wells said.

Having a translator strap around her neck made her stand out like the foreigner she was, and Wells knew it would have to go once she escaped from here. It would draw too much attention to her.

"Is this a hospital or a prison?" Wells asked Aranya.

Aranya looked perplexed. "Why, it's a hospital, of course."

Wells felt relieved. Her chances of getting out had just gone up significantly.

The cuff rattled against the rails again.

"Oh, I see why you asked," Aranya said.

"I'm not sure how I got here or why I have this on," Wells said, shrugging. No point in divulging too much yet. "And he has one too."

Aranya glanced over at the bald man.

"Well, he is obviously a thief," she said.

Wells studied him, but couldn't see why Aranya had made the assumption. "Care to tell me how you know?"

Aranya didn't make eye contact when she spoke again. "You were asleep when they came in to dress his wounds. His back is full of welts."

"So?" Lt. Wells needed more proof than that.

"Lan-noi has lots of people and not enough security. If someone gets caught stealing or breaks some small law, the shopkeeper or person affected usually doles out punishment themselves. The security turns a blind eye, as it helps them out. This man has been whipped many times."

Wells couldn't imagine a world where everyone in New Franco took the law into their own hands. The lower sectors would become even more chaotic, and the inner sectors would be a constant fight between neighbors complaining about nonsense.

"It doesn't seem like a fair system. What about evidence? A review process?" Wells asked.

"You are not from a Shangcorp territory, are you? Things work different here."

The man snored loudly and smacked his lips. Aranya seemed to pull back into herself again.

"If I may, what happened to your arms?" Wells asked, trying to keep her engaged, but also curious.

"It was an accident. I work in a factory. Robots do most of the work, but there are still some things only a human can do. Something got jammed in a machine and they sent me to fix it. I found the problem and as I tried to repair it, I caught my arms in the machine and it crushed them. It really was my fault. I should have been more careful."

It was a horrible story, but Wells wondered why this woman had ended up sharing a room with two people cuffed to their beds. Aranya's version of events made it seem like she was a victim.

"I wonder why they put you here with us, then."

"My boss accused me of stealing right after the incident and fired me. Now he doesn't have any responsibility for me and can hire someone to replace me."

Wells's job exposed her to many violent and horrendous things, but she always retreated to the safety and comfort of her unit. The people she left behind after her work was done, people like Aranya, kept living through it.

Wells felt terrible for her. Losing her job and most likely the use of her arms. It sucked. But it also meant she was vulnerable and would be easier to manipulate into helping Wells get out of here.

A staff member came back into the room and removed the remains of their meals. The man slept through it all. Once they were alone again, Wells turned to Aranya.

"What are you going to do once you get out of here?"

Aranya looked at her lap. "I'm just trying to heal, for now. Besides, I can't leave. I'm still suspected of stealing."

Wells assumed the staff hadn't restrained her out of sympathy for her injuries. Besides, Aranya did not strike her as the type to cause trouble.

Another nurse came into the room and went from bed to bed, studying the DDUs mounted above each bed. She ticked off a series of boxes, showing everything was in order with the room and patients. As she left the room, she dimmed the lights, implying it was time to sleep.

Wells stared at the ceiling. She still was no closer to getting out, but tonight she had learned a lot. This was only a hospital and not a security facility. Once she healed, she assumed that would all change. She'd also started to build a relationship with Aranya. The other woman seemed quite frail, but Wells sensed an inner strength in her. Wells didn't know enough about her yet, but planned on finding out.

Wells closed her eyes, ready to rest, knowing that she was taking back control.

| four |

One of the biggest benefits of becoming captain was the higher clearance level that came with the title. A level that allowed Davis to access files and information he could never have dreamed of as a lieutenant. The downfall was that it was almost too much information. He quickly learned what was useful and what was not. Then he figured out how to use it to destroy Lt. Wells. First, he made sure that she received all the dangerous, life threating cases. He was not her immediate supervisor, but by now he knew how to work the system so she'd do the cases he wanted her to. He'd hoped she would be another statistic before long. But as always, Wells had come through. Instead of getting bogged down by her caseload, she solved the crimes no one else could and plunged into the next case. So when Hector Delgado, the notorious sector leader, went back on a deal he made with Davis, he'd orchestrated for Wells to investigate him. Davis had insider information on Hector's next move, so it had been easy to get her involved. Hector was ruthless, and Davis hoped Wells would be out of his life soon.

Except she gathered enough evidence to have Delgado detained, leaving Davis and others to scramble around, hiding evidence and erasing any tracks leading back to them. And then she vanished. No one knew what had happened to her or where she'd gone. The last communication showed her in the northern part of the main Penta territory, chasing that idiot Benjamin Drake; a name he thought he'd never seen again. Davis struggled to find the reason for her being on his trail, except for a very weak link to Delgado. But why would one of Penta's best chase a witness and then disappear?

It made no sense to him. But at least if she'd disappeared, she could not cause him any more trouble.

To be safe, he put feelers out to Penta assets he controlled, and patiently waited for something to turn up.

* * *

Jimmy's hammer barely made a dent in the block. He lifted it up again and let it drop under its own weight. Same result. Drake looked on as Jimmy lifted the hammer for another attempt.

"How's that block going? Getting it smaller?" Drake asked.

It was still early in the morning, but the sun was already warming their backs and making them sweat. Drake started on the pile of rubble they'd left yesterday. He found the biggest pieces and broke them in half, and some of those pieces he smashed again into quarters. He then gave the pieces to Jimmy, who made sure not to break them at all.

Jimmy's contribution to their daily workload was minimal on a good day, but today it was even less. Drake had to carry him home last night, and this morning he'd almost given up trying to wake him. Jimmy had had the time of his life drinking with

Dina and her friends, but the look on his face this morning was one of regret.

The hammer slowly swung down and barely made a sound on impact. From the sweat on his face, one would think the little guy had been breaking block after block.

"Haven't seen your girlfriend this morning," Drake said.

Jimmy stood up and let the hammer drop to the ground. He looked like a thawed out corpse.

"I'm not so sure I want to see her again, ya know? Not sure we clicked."

Drake knew it was the hangover speaking, not Jimmy.

"It looked like you had a great time. You know she's invited us out again tonight?"

Jimmy dry heaved. "Sure. I mean, I don't know if we should waste all our credits like that, ya know?"

"Don't wanna be rude, though," Drake kept going.

Jimmy sat down on his untouched pile of concrete.

"Drake, I think I made a mistake, ya know?"

Drake could feel his stomach muscles tense up, preparing for a laugh.

"I think Dina might just be"—Jimmy kicked at some pebbles in front of him—"too much for me, ya know?"

Drake burst out laughing. He couldn't help it anymore. Seeing Jimmy suffering from his self-induced pain, and now confessing he'd underestimated the drinking abilities of his crush, was too much to bear. Chances were, Dina wouldn't even remember them.

Jimmy looked like a shell of himself, sitting on the pile of rubble, dust clinging to his clammy skin.

"How about you have a nap in the shade over there, and after lunch, you can help me again?" Drake offered.

Jimmy smiled and dragged his feet over to the shade.

"Thanks partner. I promise to make it up to you, ya know," he said as he shuffled past Drake.

"I know, buddy," Drake said, smiling at the pitiful figure in front of him.

* * *

Sweat poured down Drake's face as he smashed another concrete block into pieces. He stood up and wiped his forehead. People were walking around in groups and chatting. No one seemed to be working. Drake looked at his HID and noticed it was lunchtime. Jimmy was still fast asleep in the shade, so he let him be. He opened his little cooler box and took out a white box meal he'd brought for lunch. Years from eating on the road had made him immune to eating white box meals cold and unheated. He opened it up and took a bite.

"Care for some company?"

Drake looked up from his meal and saw Dina standing over him. She looked dusty and sweaty, like Drake, not clammy and colorless like Jimmy.

"Sure. Grab yourself a block." Drake pointed to some unbroken pieces of concrete next to him.

Dina sat down on a block near Drake and opened a white box meal of her own.

"Looks like your little mate had too much fun last night," Dina said, pointing toward Jimmy with her head.

"He tried his best to keep up with you guys. Seems that was a bad idea."

Dina snorted. "We work, then drink. It's all we do. Same as our parents before us. Few people can keep up with Slavors."

Drake had met plenty of people from the Slavor region in his time as a hauler. Although it was a Shangcorp territory now, people from the region still referred to themselves as Slavors, refusing to accept the Shangcorp rule. The Slavors were hard-working people, living in an unforgiving part of the world. To call them hardy would be an injustice. Drake had never met a Slavor he didn't like. Stoic, mischievous, and hardworking, all of them. Then there was the drinking. No one could drink like a Slavor. Looking at Dina, he wondered how he hadn't picked up on the Slavor characteristics earlier.

"You Slavors should really warn people before you invite them to drink with you," Drake laughed.

Dina smirked. "I guess."

Jimmy grumbled and rolled over, but kept sleeping.

"Your little friend said you were looking for someone," Dina said.

Drake hadn't heard Jimmy say that last night, but then again, he wasn't keeping track of him the whole time. "Sort of."

Dina seemed like a decent person, from the two conversations they'd had, but Drake couldn't be too careful. He was still a Pentacorp citizen hiding in a Shangcorp territory. Although war had not officially started, all the borders were on high alert, and getting in or out was almost impossible. Then there was the carnage that Sammy Sanders had left behind. That had their names connected to it too. Best to trust no one and keep a low profile.

"What did he say?" he asked.

"Not much, just that you were bounty hunters and looking for someone," Dina said.

"We're not fucking bounty hunters." Drake stared at Jimmy, who snored softly. He really wished the little shit would stop telling everyone that.

Dina gave him a look that said calm down.

"Sorry. We chased a bounty, but it's all done," Drake said.

"So who are you chasing now?" Dina asked.

Drake wondered how much of this was a friendly chat and how much of an intel operation. Was Dina a bounty hunter? Did she work for Shangcorp Security Intelligence? Shangcorp did not operate the same way Pentacorp did. Their dealings were always a bit more underhanded and sinister. At least to outsiders.

"We are not bounty hunters. Actually, we're—" Haulers. But were they? Drake tried to recall when last he sat in a truck and hauled cargo. They were couriers for a while then, in theory only. Bounty hunters. But haulers? Not for months. Soon it would be over a year since he'd had a legitimate hauling contract.

"I used to be a hauler," Drake finally said.

Dina nodded and took a bite of her meal. "So, you're not looking for a person then, Mr. ex-hauler?" she asked through a mouthful of food.

Lunch time was almost over, and a drone came flying over toward them and sat hovering above the workers. No one dared take a minute too long, in fear of having an entire hour deduced from their pay for being late back to work. The drone didn't tell them to get back to work, but simply recorded the moment any break was over. It just sat in the sky, silently turning people in for being human.

Drake looked at his HID. They had two minutes left.

"We are, but it's complicated, and it could get them and us in a lot of trouble if someone found out we were here," Drake said.

Most people on the site walked around with HIDs, and Drake was confident most of the workers had something to hide. That included Dina. He hoped that the shared secret would make a bond between them and not be used as leverage.

"It's none of my business, but I've been here for a long time now," Dina stated. "If you need help, I could be very useful. At a price, of course."

Her honesty put Drake at ease. If she'd offered to help him as a friend, he would have been very skeptical. He barely knew her, and she had no reason to help a stranger with an illegal activity. But being upfront about doing it purely for credits was transparent and put everything in the open.

Drake looked at his HID again. Break time was over.

"Best get back to it," he said.

Dina stood up and grabbed her things.

"If you decide you need help, let me know," she said, and walked over to her friends.

* * *

Jimmy finally woke up. His timing was impeccable. There were only a few minutes left of work.

"How's work?" he asked as he stretched himself out.

Drake stopped swinging his hammer.

"It's going great, thanks. In fact, about the same as every other day," Drake replied.

Jimmy missed the insinuation. "That's good, ya know. Man, I feel so much better."

Drake felt the weight of the hammer in his hands. If it had been anyone other than Jimmy Something, a workplace incident would have occured.

"I'm glad, Jimmy. How about tomorrow I sleep all day, and you break concrete?"

Jimmy pursed his lips, indicating a high level of thinking.

"Nah, not sure it would be as efficient, ya know?"

If it was anyone else.

"Dina came over to chat," Drake changed the subject.

"Oh yeah? What did you tell her?" Jimmy sounded nervous.

"Not much. She said you told her we were looking for someone and she offered to help."

"Oh, okay. That's good, ya know?"

"What did you think we talked about?" Drake asked.

"I thought that maybe, ya know, she, uh, asked about tonight. Drinking again."

"No, Jimmy, she didn't, but I think you're missing the bigger problem here?"

"Oh, yeah, what's that?"

"That you told her we were looking for Lt. Wells. You put us and her at risk, Jimmy."

Jimmy sat down again and put his head in his hands and mumbled to himself. He looked up at Drake.

"I'm sorry, partner. I must have gotten drunk and—" Jimmy tried to explain.

Drake saw nothing but regret in the face staring at him.

"It's okay, buddy. She didn't mention any names, and besides, she offered to help. So, I guess, it worked out for the best, really."

"That's what I thought would happen, ya know?" Jimmy never missed an opportunity. "That's why I told her."

"We could use some help, to be honest," Drake admitted.

They had been pounding concrete and debris for weeks now, barely making enough credits to live on. The plan was to save up, buy an old junker, and then somehow free Lt. Wells and escape Shangcorp.

A rock-solid plan.

Except that they were broke and the impending war would guarantee the borders were closed permanently. They were no closer to rescuing Lt. Wells than when they arrived in Lan-noi. Maybe it was time to enlist a local.

"What do you reckon?" Drake asked Jimmy.

Jimmy didn't hesitate for a second.

"If it will help to get the lieutenant out and back home, then I say yes!"

Drake could have kissed him.

| five |

"... but so far, neither corporation has made a declaration. Both sides are keen to avoid a war that will most likely spill over to the rest of the world. For now, the negotiations are at a stand-off, with neither group issuing any statements. Some insiders believe that Penta Corporation has already armed its security personnel and is preparing to defend its territories. Shangcorp officials refused to comment. For now, all we can do is speculate about what will happen next."

The nurse changed the DDU back to displaying the vital functions of the bald man sleeping in the bed underneath it. He gave Wells a *what can you do?* look. Wells just smiled.

She was glad neither side had declared war yet, as getting out of Shangcorp was going to be hard enough without having to escape a war zone. The longer the corporations twiddled their thumbs, the better for her—and everyone else.

Aranya was also awake, and she smiled at Wells.

"Seems things are about to get crazy," Wells said.

"Things have always been crazy in Shangcorp," Aranya replied softly. "I don't think our lives will change much."

Wells had grown up in a middle sector of New Franco. She'd had food and enough credits to go to a respectable school. She knew from a young age that many people had it worse than her, but still wished for a better life. So she'd worked hard to make sure it happened. Aranya's words reminded her that not everyone had the opportunity to work themselves into a better position.

Leaning forward, a sharp pain reminded Wells of the wound in her chest. It felt better but still hurt when she moved. Her arm was also feeling much better.

The nurse walked over to her bed.

"Ready for some exercise?" he asked.

Wells had hated her walks in the courtyard the first few days here. Her body was broken, and she was confused and wanted nothing but to rest. But the staff was adamant that she had to get out of bed every day and go for a walk. Escorted, of course. She hated them for making her shuffle down the corridors toward the center of the building, where a beautiful courtyard welcomed visitors. She also knew they were right. It wasn't just that her body needed to move. Her mind needed to get out of bed too. Seeing unfamiliar faces, hearing conversations, and experiencing different areas of the hospital lifted her mood.

Wells was looking forward to today's walk, but not for the usual reasons. The last few walks had been less about exercise and mental well-being and more about reconnaissance. She'd set her mind on getting out, so now she had to prepare. It was only a hospital, and people could just walk out if they wanted. But the electromagnetic cuff on her wrist meant that option was not available to her, as her arm was continuously attached to a metal rail on the wall. As they walked down the corridors, multiple cameras followed her progress. Privacy, like most basic human rights, was not a given in Shangcorp. Even the patients' rooms had cameras monitoring everything 24/7. If she somehow broke free and left via the front door, her face would appear on all the local security forces' DDUs as a person of interest. She would go from a Jane Doe to an All Persons Beware. If she wanted to get out, she would have to do it quietly.

Wells and the nurse passed the nurses' station. Every floor had one, roughly in the middle of the building, leaving an equal number of rooms on either side of it. Data Display Units sat on desks, and some had staff working on them. Behind them on the wall, more DDUs displayed the views from the cameras she saw. They rotated between the hallways and the rooms, showing a few seconds of each view. Aranya was sitting on her bed on one DDU, before it switched to another room. Wells saw herself on one too, standing in the corridor, before it too changed. The nurses didn't seem to take too much notice of it, but Wells was sure it got saved to a central location and kept for a set time. If something happened, they would access it and study it. The nurses only glimpsed at it occasionally, making sure nothing appeared out of the ordinary.

Wells didn't want to linger too long and raise suspicions, so she kept walking. A cleaning bot almost bumped into her before it corrected itself and swerved out of the way, cleaning the floor as it went. She lost sight of it as it turned a corner.

They reached the end of the corridor and stopped in front of an elevator. As the doors opened, the nurse gave her a look: *Don't do anything silly.* The nurse pressed a command on his

HIC and the magnetic cuff disengaged from the wall rail. They stepped inside and Wells's arm floated up to a new rail as the nurse reactivated the cuff. The nurse selected the ground floor, and the doors slid shut. Wells casually looked around the small space. Besides the small DDU mounted next to the door, she also spotted a camera mounted in one corner. Wells's room was on the fifth floor and the ride down was brief. She had never gone up and did not know how many floors were above them. The DDU in the elevator only showed the current floor on its display. The nurse always blocked the screen when he entered the destination, and Wells could not see how many floors were available to choose from. Having the option to get to the roof would be great, but not essential.

The doors opened, and they exited. Unlike her floor, and presumably most floors, the ground floor had no patient rooms. Instead, it was a more open design, with administration offices on one side and a cafeteria on the other. Beyond them was the courtyard. Wells had noticed before that the exit and entrance to the hospital was not located here on the ground floor. Or at least, not here where they walked. It had to be here somewhere. She'd find it.

Reaching the courtyard, the nurse scanned her palm on the DDU at the door, and it slid open and then shut behind them. The courtyard was the only place where the cuffs got turned off. Wells kept up appearances and walked a lap of the courtyard, as she always did.

The courtyard seemed to be in the middle of the building, as walls surrounded it going up multiple stories. Wells realized all she had to do was count the levels to figure out how many stories the building had. She counted the levels and squinted as the sun got into her eyes. Walls surrounded the courtyard but it had no roof. Seeing the blue sky was usually the highlight of her day, but today she barely noticed it. Wells finished her count. Twelve floors. She had no plan yet, but needed all the logistical information she could get.

Plants filled the courtyard and there were plenty of benches to sit on. Wells rested enough lying in her bed, so she always walked in her allocated exercise time. Doing another lap, Wells noticed some cameras hidden behind the plants. Not surprising, consider patients could fall into trouble out here. It seemed that every inch of the building was being monitored, or at least recorded.

The nurse came over to Wells.

"Ready to go back up?" he asked. Wells knew it was more of a polite instruction than a question.

"Yes, thanks," she replied.

They left the courtyard the same way they'd come in and used the same elevator to go back up. Soon she was back in her room.

Aranya was sitting upright in her bed, but Wells noticed the other bed was empty.

"Hey. Where's the bald guy?" Wells asked Aranya as she walked over to her own bed.

"They took him," she replied in her soft tone.

"Who?" Wells asked.

"Security," Aranya replied.

Wells took a deep breath. She must have missed them by only a few minutes. She knew they weren't looking for her, but she still felt relief at not having to deal with them.

"Did they say anything? About me? Or you?" Wells asked.

Aranya shook her head.

"No. They walked straight over to this bed and took him away. He looked terrified."

"Do you know where they took him?"

"No. But there were three security officers, all armed, so I imagine it's the last we'll ever see of him."

Penta territories had their own issues and a fair share of corruption, but Wells feared Shangcorp was on a level she had never seen. Taking someone to some hellish lockup facility for simple theft was pure intimidation. It sent a powerful message to everyone contemplating a crime. Wells shuddered to think what a corporation who ran its territories with terror would do to someone it considered a spy.

Her time was up. She knew it. She would have to get out of this hospital and the territory as soon as humanly possible.

"Aranya, we need to talk," Wells said.

Aranya nodded her head slightly.

"My name is Lily," Wells started. "And I need your help."

"Hi, Lily. I'm glad to meet you."

Wells hoped her gut, which she always blindly trusted, was right to trust Aranya.

"I need to get out of this place, and I'm not sure how. I do know that I'll need help."

Wells focused on every small facial expression Aranya made. Not that there were many. Aranya's face hardly moved or changed at all when she spoke. Still, Wells knew every human had tells when they lied, felt stressed, or were hiding something.

Aranya sat patiently, waiting for Wells to continue.

"I remember more than what I have led the staff to believe. I'm afraid if they found out who I was, that I might be in trouble."

Aranya didn't move a muscle.

Wells wondered if she might have overestimated Aranya's value. If she'd had more time, she could have tried to befriend a nurse or another staff member, but that might take days, if not weeks. Aranya was practically in the same boat as her; injured and in trouble with the law. They already had a common ground. Forging an alliance, if not a friendship, should be easy. And yet, Aranya seemed disconnected from her.

"It's just a matter of time before they declare me fit enough to call security. Once that happens, I'm done for."

Wells hoped that Aranya's silence was her taking in and processing the information she received.

Finally, Aranya looked at her and spoke.

"I think we are very much alike, Lily. But for me to trust you, you'll have to trust me."

" Okay. Yes, you're right. If we are to work together, there needs to be trust."

Although she believed every word, she had never actually put all her trust in someone. She had always been a leader, which isolated her from her peers. From her early days in the security force, she'd had to rely on herself, not others, making trust a very hard thing to have. Now, it was second nature to distrust everyone.

"Mutual trust. You got it," Wells said. "How do we start the process?"

"Honesty," Aranya replied. "In my culture, honesty means everything. Unfortunately our leaders have forgotten this, and the corporation is even worse. Honesty is part of what makes us human."

Aranya's ideology fell on deaf ears, but from a practical point of view, she was right. They needed to be honest with each other to build trust and a working partnership.

Wells knew she would have to take the plunge and tell her who she was and who she worked for. Shangcorp was littered with spies and informants, making it the last place on Earth one should be honest with anyone. Aranya might believe that people in Shangcorp were honest people at heart, but Wells knew the truth. She had seen all the files and data gained from spies and assets working for Penta. She knew that anyone in Shangcorp could turn her in at any moment. Even sweet Aranya.

But she had no choice.

She was badly injured, had no working HIC and no resources. She needed help, and local help would be even better.

If Aranya was after honesty and trust, then that was what she would get.

Wells looked into her eyes one more time, and let her gut guide her.

"My name is Lily Wells," she whispered, "and I'm a lieutenant in the Penta Security Forces."

She kept eye contact with Aranya, waiting for her to yell for help or draw attention to the room.

Aranya didn't.

Instead, she smiled at Wells.

| six |

The short message made Captain Davis's day.

Potential lead. Will confirm and report back.

It was only a few words, but it made him smile from ear to ear. If they'd found her in some remote town in Shangcorp, he could get rid of her and have no trace back to him. People disappeared in Shangcorp all the time.

This was as good an outcome as he could have wished for.

* * *

Drake and Jimmy's shared living unit in New Franco had been small, musty, and always cold. The walls needed paint, the flooring had to be ripped out and burned, and the ceilings had inexplicable stains on them. There were no windows in sight and the climate control was stuck on a temperature that made it too hot in the summer and too cold in the winter. There really was nothing to love about it.

Except that it was better than this place.

When they had arrived in Lan-noi, they'd had limited options. They knew they couldn't use their HICs to access any credits. They'd fled a major crime scene only days before and had been living under trees and bridges. Drake knew he'd have to rely on Jimmy's criminal skills to get them through. They had run out of white box meals and needed food.

Drake had found an abandoned hydrocar he claimed for their house and Jimmy set off to do whatever Jimmy did. Drake would sit alone for hours in the hydro, thinking about Lily Wells and what he could have done different. He knew he was to blame. She'd followed him because he refused to go back to New Franco and help her take down Hector Delgado. He was the reason she'd crossed the ocean. She'd risked her life to do the right thing.

One night, a few days after they found the hydro, Jimmy had come back empty-handed but beaming from ear to ear.

"No luck?"

"If finding us jobs that pay daily and turn a blind eye to official paperwork is what you call having no luck, then I guess I have no luck, ya know?"

Drake climbed out of their converted hydrohouse.

"You'll need to be a bit more specific, buddy?"

Jimmy's smile didn't waver. "Construction. Actually, the opposite. What is the opposite?" The smile disappeared, and a frown replaced it.

"I don't know, Jimmy. You're the one who got us this construction that's not construction job."

Jimmy kept frowning and thinking. "Whatever," he said, giving up. "I got us jobs demolishing buildings!" The smile returned.

"Demolition. That's the word." Drake said.

"That's what I said, ya know?" Jimmy replied.

"Yes, but that's the word you were looking for. Demolition. I'm just saying you found it."

"Huh?" Jimmy frowned again.

"Never mind," Drake said, knowing they were about to get way off track. "Tell me about the job."

Jimmy told him how he'd walked past a building that was being torn down and started a conversation with one worker. One thing led to another and the next thing he was in the office, signing them up.

Jimmy pulled two HIDs out of his pocket.

"He also gave me these."

Drake grabbed Jimmy and hugged him. "What would I do without you?" He let go and looked at Jimmy. His eyes were shiny with tears. "So, when do we start?" Drake asked, not wanting to make Jimmy any more uncomfortable.

"Tomorrow. Did I do the right thing?" Jimmy asked.

"You did great, buddy. In fact, you might have just saved our lives."

Jimmy's eyes sparkled even more and his face beamed with pride.

* * *

They'd tried their best to make the hydrocar livable. All the windows were intact, and the doors worked. The locks were busted, so they couldn't lock their house when they left. Which, considering they owned nothing, wasn't a big deal. They found some insulation at the work site and brought it home.

They ripped the front seats out and set them next to the hydro, then jiggered the back seat so it was more like a double bed. After work, they could enjoy their meals and a beer on the outside seats before crawling into the small cabin for the night.

Living like this was almost unbearable, but the day Jimmy showed him the article of the Jane Doe with Lily Wells's photo, everything changed. All of this—the job, the car, everything—was temporary. The only sure thing was getting her out of the hospital and back to Penta.

After Dina had offered her services, Drake and Jimmy discussed it and agreed to take her up on her offer. They couldn't talk at work, and Jimmy didn't want to go to a bar with her ever again, so they invited her over to the hydro.

"Maybe we should go to a bar. I mean. Look at this place." Drake said to Jimmy.

"No. I can't, Drake, ya know. I just can't. Besides, what are you worried about?"

Drake thought it absurd that he had to point it out. "We live in a wreck, Jimmy. We're homeless."

"Yup. So what? This is where we live, and this is who we are. No point in pretending anything else, ya know?"

Drake tried to think of a comeback but couldn't. Jimmy was right. This was who they were. Two guys who'd lost everything after helping the most infamous person on Earth steal Mars, and who now had to live in a hydro while they planned to rescue someone who'd probably shoot them on sight.

Drake felt a weight pushing on his heart. His breathing became more labored. Things were falling apart. He could feel it. Nothing was going their way.

"You okay, partner?" Jimmy asked.

Jimmy needed him. Now was not the time to give in to the world.

"Yes, just a bit nervous about what Dina has to say is all. Who knows with these Slavors, right?"

Jimmy looked shocked.

"Just a joke, buddy." Drake laughed.

Jimmy shook his head.

"Slavors, right?" It was not Jimmy's voice.

Drake spun around and saw Dina standing right behind him.

"Uh, sorry, Dina. I was just trying to cheer Jimmy up and made a poor joke," Drake smiled his most charming smile. He couldn't tell if it was working.

Dina seemed to have already forgotten the slight. She made herself comfortable in one of the torn-out hydro seats and looked around her, taking in the desolate scene.

"Nice place," she said in her monotone Slavoric accent.

Drake couldn't tell if she was being sarcastic.

"Thanks. We love it. We really made it a home, ya know?" Jimmy answered. He sat on the hood.

"So, tell me more about this person you're looking for," Dina continued.

Drake still had some reservations. "Dina, why are you willing to help us?"

Dina shrugged. "I told you. For credits. And fun. It's been a while since I did something fun."

"And how is it you think you can help?" Drake asked.

A Hydrocomet thundered across the bridge overhead and Dina waited a few seconds before answering. "From what I gathered from your little friend the other night, you need to break someone out of someplace. And I've broken a few people out of a few places before. I've seen the two of you at the site, and I would bet a week's credits that neither one of you has ever done anything like that before. Am I right?"

Drake wanted to tell her she was quite wrong. He wanted to tell her about evading a squad of Penta Security Forces and bluffing their way into a top secure facility, working with the same forces they'd tried to outrun. How they'd chased a bounty and encountered—and defeated—many bandits. He wanted to tell her their whole resume and how capable they were, but he stayed quiet. Because all those things, they did for themselves. This time, they were doing it for someone else, and they could not risk screwing it up.

"No, we haven't," he finally said. Jimmy looked a bit perplexed but luckily kept his mouth shut.

"So then, tell me who we're after," Dina asked again.

Drake was keeping his cards close to his chest for now. "An old friend who we recently found out is here in Lan-noi."

"And where is this friend?"

"A hospital. Under security, we believe."

"You believe? Why would they be under security?"

Drake thought about how much he was willing to share.

"They did something that might get them into trouble. I'm sorry, Dina, but I really can't divulge too much. If you want to help, then great. If not, that's fine too."

Dina shrugged again. "I really don't care what they've done or who they are. But the more I know, the easier this will be. And I'm not *helping* you. You are paying me."

There was something reassuring about Dina's honesty and transparency.

"So, is it doable?" Drake asked.

Dina sat for a while, looking at Drake.

"Sure," she said. "For a thousand credits."

"Fuck," Jimmy blurted out.

A thousand credits were a lot, and it would take them weeks to save up for it. No more nights at the bar and they'd have to work extra shifts. A lot of planning had to go into getting Dina her credits.

Planning that Drake did not have time for.

"Deal. When can we do it?" Drake's mouth beat his brain to the punch.

"How about we go in three days? That's should give you enough time to get me my credits and prepare."

Three days was an impossible timeframe. But Drake stood up and held out his hand to shake on it.

"That's cute, but Slavors drink to complete a deal." Dina produced a small container, presumably full of some homebrewed liquor.

Jimmy slid off the hydro, trying to escape.

"Where are you going?" Dina called out. "You are part of this too."

Jimmy dragged his feet over to them.

"To a successful partnership!" Dina took a big swig of the liquor.

Drake was next. He took the container from Dina, lifted it into the air, and took a sip. Whatever it was burned all the way down his throat and set his lungs on fire.

Jimmy reluctantly took his turn, and the container made it back to Dina, who started a fresh round. Drake realized that only an empty vessel was going to end this. Luckily for them, it was only a small bottle and after a few rounds, it ran dry.

"Okay, boys. Speak soon." Dina pocketed the empty bottle and left.

"Glad she only brought a small bottle, am I right?" Drake said to Jimmy once he was sure she was out of earshot.

"How the hell are we going to get a thousand credits, Drake?" Jimmy asked.

Drake felt lightheaded, and the world was swaying slightly. But Jimmy's words were as clear as a bell. "I don't know, Jimmy, but we need to get to Lily as soon as possible. I'll figure it out."

| seven |

Lt. Wells's chest still hurt like hell, but she couldn't wait any longer. She needed to get out. After the disappearance of the bald man, she knew it was just a matter of time before they came for her. She felt sore and weak, but knew her determination would get her through it.

She was not a quitter.

And it seemed she had an accomplice now.

A mischievous sparkle appeared in Aranya's eyes.

"My turn for honesty," she said. "My name is Aranya Kai. And like I said, I'm here because of a workplace incident. Except it happened a little different from the story I told you before."

Aranya paused as a nurse came into the room to check on them. She scrolled through the DDUs above their beds, making some notes on her HIC, and checked Wells's cuff.

Once the nurse had left, Aranya turned back to Wells.

"Machines crushed my arms, like I said, but it was no accident." She looked down at her lap.

Wells waited for her to regain her courage again. No point in rushing or pushing her.

Aranya took a deep breath and continued. "My boss, an evil little man, put my arms in the machine. He didn't do it himself—I would have fought him off. He used two of his guards to do it. They held me down while the machine turned the bones in my arms into dust."

Tears trickled down Aranya's cheeks. She wiggled her fingers, as if to confirm they were still there and working.

"That's awful," Lily said. She meant it. If this had happened in a sector where she worked, Aranya's boss would be the one in the hospital with broken arms. "Just because you stole from him?"

Aranya wiped the tears away. "I didn't steal from him, Lily. Things in Shangcorp are ... Well, it's complicated. The corporation claims we are all equal and treated as such, but the reality is quite different. There is a huge divide between the rich and the poor. Most of the people in Shangcorp territories are struggling just to survive, while the few at the top get richer and richer, walking all over us. Even pathetic men like my boss, who has little power and just a moderate amount of credits, do their best to suppress their poor workers. He fines us for anything he sees fit. Suspends us without pay. He does all these things, while he takes the credits for himself. Power is everything in Shangcorp."

Wells had seen all of this before in reports they received at Penta, but hearing it from someone directly affected by it felt different. It was hard to be indifferent when the victim was standing right in front of you.

"It all sounds horrible, Aranya, but it doesn't explain how your arms ended up in that machine," Wells said.

An alarm went off in a room down the hall and footsteps hurried toward it. It happened so frequently that Wells had stopped reacting to it.

"Remember how I told you that things won't change for most of us if war comes? It's because, for most of us, war is already here. Shangcorp will never admit it to the other corporations, especially Penta, but we have been close to civil war for decades now."

Wells had so many questions, but didn't want to sidetrack Aranya, so she kept quiet and allowed Aranya to get her story out.

"Although the people are not very well organized, we have started to fight back. Small groups, doing small things. Burning down buildings, sabotaging factories. Hacking worker bots. Little things to make the rich and powerful uncomfortable."

"And you did something at your work, didn't you?" Wells guessed.

The smile on Aranya's face was pure pride.

"Yes. I led a small group of workers, and we sabotaged some machines at work, halting production and costing the company thousands of credits every hour."

Wells would never have thought that the tiny person in front of her could be the leader of a resistance group.

"What were your demands?"

Aranya looked a bit surprised. "You don't understand. We don't want anything from them. We want to destroy them." Everything Wells had presumed about Aranya seemed wrong.

"So, he found out your plans and made an example out of you."

"Yes. He gathered everyone in a warehouse and demanded to know who the leader was. No one spoke up. So he grabbed the first person he saw, a young girl, maybe fifteen or sixteen, and had his guards put her arm in the machine. I knew it wouldn't stop with one. We are used to being abused, Lily. Everyone would stay quiet and have their arms mutilated. No one would ever turn one of their own over to the elite. I guess there are some that would, but no one there did. Not my people. Anyway, I handed myself over before they could hurt her. He showed no mercy, as I expected, and he had them crush my arms in front of everyone."

"Once you're healed, then what?" Wells asked, but she already had a good idea of what lay ahead for Aranya.

Her face would already be in every Shangcorp Security database. Every time she swiped her HIC at a shop, it would flag her as a traitor. She would have to live off the mercy and kindness of others. She could never work again. She would be an outcast.

"If I'm lucky, I'd go to a jail for a few years. But I fear the moment I'm healed up, they'll send me off to a worker camp, where I'll stay until I die." She said it with no emotion. Just stating a fact. Nothing to be done about it.

"I'm so sorry, Aranya." Wells said. And she was. She forgot that other people also had problems to deal with, most of them bigger than hers.

"Don't be," Aranya said. "Meeting you might just save me after all."

"How?" Wells asked.

"Well, Lieutenant, it seems you are not the only one who needs to get out of here."

Wells was used to leading and being obeyed. Not collaborating. Security forces were not democracies. Everyone didn't have a say in what happened. The leaders made decisions and the rest followed. That was what she was used to.

Wells had set off looking for someone she could manipulate into helping her get out of here. What she found was not an asset to be used, but an ally. An equal. Someone with as much at stake, who was after the same thing.

Escape.

"Do you have any family here, Aranya? Someone who will start looking for you if you go missing?" Wells asked.

"No." She offered no more explanation, and Wells didn't see the need to pursue the point any further.

"What about your fellow workers? You said they wouldn't turn in one of their own. Wouldn't they come looking for you?"

"They know I'm captured. By now, they have already mourned my death."

So she was all alone. Wells pitied her, but also felt relieved.

"Do you have any experience in breaking out of anywhere?" Wells asked. It was great to have an ally and a partner, but she needed to figure out how best to use her. What her strengths were. What she brought to the team.

"I feel it's time for more honesty," Aranya said.

"Okay," Wells said tentatively, wondering if Aranya was inferring that she was hiding something.

"The people at my work were not the only ones I had doing illegal things. I have been organizing and leading attacks against the corporation for some time now, Lily. I guess from your viewpoint you would refer to me as a terrorist."

"I guess so," Wells said. Anyone who attacked their own corporation and tried to hamper its running of their territories was a terrorist. There was no other word for it.

"Maybe I am. But that's just a word to me." Aranya shrugged it off. "Anyway, I have some connections and people who will help us here in Lan-noi and in the neighboring villages."

Wells took in everything Aranya had said. Working with criminals was part of her job. Criminals turned on each other quicker than she could transfer credits to them and using informants was part of her day-to-day. Aranya wasn't an ordinary criminal, but she was a self-proclaimed terrorist, and Wells didn't know how trustworthy that would make her, especially once they broke out of the hospital. For now, that was the mission, and Wells pushed everything else aside to focus on it.

"I think we need to prioritize," Wells said. "My main goal is getting out of Shangcorp, right? But the first hurdle is simply leaving this hospital."

A nurse came in again and went through the same ritual of checking DDUs and cuffs.

"We'll be dimming the lights in a few minutes, so try to rest," she said in a friendly but rehearsed way. She gave them a courtesy smile and left.

"Do you have anyone that can help us get out?" Wells asked once she was sure the nurse was far enough away. She still had her doubts about Aranya. Her story seemed plausible, but there was no way to validate it, and there were a lot of gaps to fill before she could trust it. Not that Wells ever trusted anyone completely anyway.

"Yes. I think so. But what is the plan?"

What was the plan? Wells hated being rushed, but she also detested procrastination. She knew she had to get out, so why wait? She had a willing partner ready to go. No point in putting it off.

She sat up, and a pain shot through her chest, numbing her arm, and making her feel dizzy. For a moment, she had forgotten about her injuries. And Aranya's. They were in no shape to make a run for it. If they encountered any physical resistance, it would stop them dead. Wells had the skills and confidence to take on almost anyone one on one. But feeling the pain course through her body and almost knock her out made her realize that even the weakest adversary would knock her down.

"How are your arms, Aranya? Can you move them? Or pick anything up with them?" She knew Aranya could see her discomfort, and she didn't try to hide it. Honesty, right?

"They are much better than the doctors think," Aranya replied. Proving her point, she lifted an arm and wiggled the fingers to Wells. "I've been trying to buy myself some time by exaggerating my pain and discomfort."

Just like Wells. This gave Wells more hope that they were on the same page.

"That's clever. So you can move them, but can you use them?"

"It's difficult with these casts on," Aranya said, lifting her arms. Carbon fiber shells sat snugly against her arms, keeping everything in place. She got up from her bed and walked over to the chair that sat in the corner for the visitors that never came. She looked around, making sure no one was watching, then lifted the chair up. Wells saw her grimace.

"You okay?"

Aranya put the chair down again. "Yes. I didn't think I could move it, let alone pick it up. I got a bit carried away." She smiled.

"Did it hurt?"

"A bit, but not much. Caught me by surprise, is all."

"This is great, Aranya!" Wells lowered her voice. "This will help us a lot!"

Aranya's face did not match Wells's enthusiasm.

"What's wrong?" Wells asked.

"My arms. They feel great, and soon the staff will realize it. I can only fool them for so long," she said. "Any slip up from me and they'll know. And once they know—"

"They'll call security and discharge you."

Time was running out.

| eight |

Like most news stories, this one had little substance and barely any details at all. Authorities had found a severely injured person near a crash site that included an armored vehicle. There were three casualties. The three dead were all in the same uniform and worked for a local private security group. It was unclear, but unlikely that the survivor was part of the security group, as she did not have the same uniform. Attached to the article was a picture of the survivor. Although she looked pale and had medical machines attached to her, her athletic body and piercing eyes were unmistakable.

Lt. Lily Wells.

Only, they called her Jane Doe.

Capt. Eugene Davis took a sip of his whiskey. Real whiskey, none of that synthesized crap for him anymore. Moving up in the world had its privileges, and this was one he enjoyed tremendously.

Please confirm identity.

His newest asset in Lan-noi had turned out to be worth every credit they charged. Having someone in the same town as Wells was going to make this so easy. He didn't like to micro-manage, so he didn't put any pressure on the asset to get it done quickly. They had already proven themselves more than capable, so he would let them decide when to strike.

Davis swiped the message away and typed in his reply.

Identity confirmed. Proceed at your discretion.

The ice made a delightful sound as it hit the sides of the glass. The amber liquid filled his mouth and warmed his throat.

No one belittled him and got away with it.

* * *

"But as it stands, neither corporation has made any declaration. The standoff continues, but sources have revealed large-scale movements of what they believed to be Shangcorp Security forces toward its main borders. Are they readying themselves for defense or attack?"

Jimmy looked up from his HIC. It took him a few minutes to battle through reading the news bulletin that had been automatically sent to everyone. His throat clenched up and all the spit in his mouth disappeared. His heart raced. He had never been good at reading, and reading in front of everyone was giving him an anxiety attack.

Most people at the site only had HIDs or had their HICs turned off in fear of getting tracked on them. The ones who had working HICs had old, outdated ones, like Drake's, that were barely legible. Though Drake and Jimmy used their company-issued HIDs more often, Jimmy's HIC was the newest model, a souvenir from their escapades working for Jacob McKenna, and Drake had volunteered him to read aloud to everyone.

"That's all it says, ya know," he finished. They all looked at him as if he should say something more. "Sounds like things are about to go down." They kept staring.

Luckily, Drake realized that was all there was to it and stepped in. "Thanks Jimmy. Seems it's about to get serious. Anyone sticking it out?"

As the crowd murmured, discussing Drake's question, Jimmy looked at their faces. Most of them looked out of place here in Lan-noi. If Shangcorp got serious about protecting its people and borders and tightened their already strict laws, it would be easy for the people around him to get into trouble. People in Shangcorp had no qualms about turning in their friends and neighbors for any suspicious behavior. In fact, they were encouraged to do so. Jimmy despised that. Most people he knew in New Franco would never ever trust the corporation, let alone hand people over to them. He could not grasp why anyone would want to do such a thing.

He knew that life would get very difficult for everyone standing here once Shangcorp declared war. They stood out, and they would be easy targets for scared people.

Jimmy wasn't surprised to see faces filled with fear. But he saw even more faces that showed defiance.

Dina was one of the latter.

"Most of us have nowhere else to go," she said. "We'll just have to run and hide, I guess."

People talked among themselves, pondering Dina's statements.

"I'm taking the hyperloop back to my family tonight," a voice in the crowd said. "They're in a small independent territory south of here."

"I'm staying," said another.

Everyone started talking at the same time. Some were staying, some were going. Some made plans to travel together, and share resources. Everyone knew they had to prepare, regardless of whether they were staying or going.

It was the beginning of the end.

* * *

Jimmy stood in the middle of chaos, bombarded on all sides. Seeing the look of panic in his eyes, Drake elbowed his way through and grabbed him by the arm.

"Let's go, buddy."

Jimmy blankly stared at Drake as he let himself be dragged away.

Once they reached relative safety, Drake let go of Jimmy's arm.

"You okay, buddy?" Drake asked.

Jimmy nodded. "Yea, yea, I'm good. Just a bit overwhelmed, ya know?"

The group broke off into smaller groups and dispersed. A lone figure came toward them.

"You boys running or staying to save your friend?" Dina asked.

Drake looked at Jimmy, who nodded. "Staying."

"Good. Me too. I suggest we get this shit show going."

By now, most people had left the site. The workday was over, and everyone had some big decisions to make.

Including Drake.

"What's the plan, Dina?" he asked.

"I've made a few inquiries. It seems the local security uses the hospital they hold your friend in regularly. They've upgraded it to help them."

"Help them?" Drake asked.

"Yes, they've added things like additional DDU and camera surveillance, electromagnetic cuffs, and possibly some drones. So they can manage the people they hold there remotely."

These were things Drake could have gone without. "So, it's a jail then?"

"Not quite," Dina replied. "It's still just a hospital. There are no security personnel working there, but like I said, they have eyes on the place."

Breaking in and out of such a highly monitored place would be extremely difficult.

"But you have a plan, right?" Drake asked.

Dina looked over at Jimmy and sized him up. "Sure."

"Okay then, let's hear it."

"I'll need to see those credits first."

The sun had set, and streetlights now bathed everything in a yellow glow. Hydros filled the roads with people rushing to get home or away.

"I don't have it yet, Dina, but I'll get it. Can you please just tell me the plan?"

Dina shook her head. "No credits, no plan."

Drake was wasting his time. Until they could come up with the credits that she demanded, they were on their own. Time was running out fast, and he had no idea where to get a thousand credits from.

"Is there a problem, Drake?"

"No. Well, to be honest, Dina, I don't know where to get the credits from. I thought we had more time, but with the news of war and people panicking—"

"All things that are not my problem."

Frustration had him balling his hands into fists. He felt powerless. Lily was being held captive just a few kilometers away, and he could do nothing about it. Dina could help them but was only in this for the credits. There was no use in trying to appeal to her softer, emotional side. If she had one.

"I'm not sure if I'm staying or going yet," she said, "but I think having a hydro might help me either way. You boys get me one, and I'll consider you paid up."

Dina had just thrown them a lifeline. Drake looked over at Jimmy.

He had a smile a mile wide.

* * *

"If you get caught, then everything is over. We'll think of something else."

"Relax, partner. This is what I do, ya know?" Jimmy almost laughed at Drake's concerned face.

Jimmy had boosted his first hydro when he was twelve years old. Well, he counted it as his first. He almost got away with it, but at the last minute, the owner showed up and dragged him out of the cabin. Gave him a good beating too—Jimmy couldn't eat for a week. But the next time he tried, he used a lookout. After that, it was almost a weekly occurrence, stealing hydros. Sometimes to sell, sometimes just for a joyride.

"A thousand-credit hydro has the worst firewalls and security. I could steal one of those with my arms tied behind my back, ya know."

"It's not worth the risk," Drake persisted.

"Huh? Not even for the lieutenant?" Jimmy knew it was a low blow, but sometimes it was the only way to get through Drake's stubbornness.

"Hey now, that's not what I meant," Drake said, backpedaling.

Jimmy had to keep the momentum and keep Drake on the back foot. "Okay, now that it's settled, we need to figure out a few things. Do you want to go tonight and get it done, or wait a day and hope no one declares war?" He was on fire.

"Tonight, I guess. Are you sure you can do it so quickly? I mean, when last did you steal a hydro?"

Drake was a hauler and used to living on the fringes of the law. Jimmy had seen firsthand how Drake's moral compass shifted as the situation called for it. He was no angel. Nevertheless, whenever they had to do something overtly criminal, like stealing a hydro, he always had some inner turmoil. Jimmy didn't get it.

"We need Dina's help. She needs a hydro. It's pretty simple what needs to be done, ya know?"

Drake nodded. Clearly, he had fought his inner demons and given in, yet again. They had to be quite small for him to always defeat them so easily, Jimmy thought.

"So what's the plan?"

"I dunno. We walk around, ya know, until we see a hydro. And steal it."

Why did Drake always have to overthink things so much?

* * *

Walking the streets of Lan-noi, Drake could sense the change in the air. People were loading their hydros, getting ready to leave town. Shops were full of people panic buying white box meals and bottles of water. Nobody alive had ever been through a war, and none of them knew what to expect. He wondered where everyone was fleeing to.

The only person who looked relaxed was Jimmy.

He was in his element, scoping out hydros and locations. They'd been wandering for hours. Was Jimmy ever going to pick one?

"No need to rush, ya know? Plenty of hydros around, and look,"—Jimmy pointed to a couple loading their hydro—"everyone is scared shitless. This will be a walk in the park."

They crossed the street and as they reached the curb, Jimmy grabbed his arm.

"This way," he said with urgency.

Jimmy guided Drake down the smaller street and then he led him down an even narrower alleyway. It was poorly lit and there were no people in sight. A lonely hydro sat staring back at them a few meters away.

"Let's go." Jimmy set off toward the hydro.

Drake felt his heart racing. He switched on his Augmented Retinal Projector and scanned the area. No thermal traces. No movement. They were alone. He ran to catch up to Jimmy.

When Drake reached him, Jimmy rounded the hydro and crouched behind it. Drake followed. Jimmy activated his HIC and searched for something. Drake kept an eye out for any movement.

"What's the holdup?" Drake asked.

Jimmy kept scrolling through his HIC. "Aha!" He swiped on something on his HIC, and the hydro's door popped open. He smiled. "Keep a lookout. We should be out of here in two minutes." Jimmy jumped into the cabin.

Drake peeked over the roof of the hydro. He did another sweep with his scanner. Nothing.

He peered through the hydro's window and saw Jimmy pulling wires out from underneath the dash and reconnecting them to other wires. He then did something on his HIC before swapping some wires around again.

Drake tapped on the window.

Jimmy jerked his head up and bumped it against the steering wheel.

"Shit! Ouch! Damn it!"

Drake moved away from the window.

"Sorry," he whispered.

"It's okay, ya know," Jimmy said, rubbing his head.

Drake felt useless. All he was doing was slowing things down. "Sorry," he whispered again. "How's it going?"

Jimmy crawled back under the console. "Almost there. Just . . . got . . . to—"

A whooshing sound passed by Drake's head, making him flinch. He instinctively stepped aside, and a rusty metal pipe hit the roof of the hydro with a loud clang. Drake followed the pipe back to the hand holding it, and the person that hand belonged to.

He didn't like what he saw.

| nine |

Lan-noi security had disabled Aranya's HIC the moment they took her from her workplace. She had no way of contacting her fellow freedom fighters. Wells couldn't even offer her the use of her own HIC, as hers had taken heavy damage in the fight with Sammy Sanders, and it didn't want to switch on. Aranya had contacts on the outside, and maybe even inside the hospital— people who were willing and waiting to help—but she couldn't reach them. She told Lily she had hoped someone would show initiative and come visit her, but she feared that without her guidance they were too afraid to do anything.

"We need to reach them, Aranya. It's critical that we do," Wells said, stating the obvious.

If they could get word out to one of her contacts, they could get the supplies they needed to plan their escape. They didn't need much, but what they did need was critical.

One thing that was crucial was an electromagnetic pulse blanket—a palm-sized device that transmitted a signal that would disturb any electronic devices in its vicinity. If you wore an EMP blanket, ARPs couldn't scan you. Cameras and DDUs showed a pixelated blur. Drones' sensors made inaccurate readings and would fly right by you. It was the closest you could get to being invisible.

It was also only available on the black market, and extremely illegal.

Wells knew Penta had the technology to bypass EMP blankets, but she doubted a small security force in the middle of a nothing Shangcorp territory would have the budget for it. And even if they did, they would not have it installed at the hospital, where they only occasionally held prisoners.

Wells was confident that if they could get a couple of EMP blankets, they could escape the hospital unseen and with no collateral damage.

They needed to contact Aranya's people, and fast. If a nurse caught wind of her injuries' progression, they would alert the local security force. It was only a matter of time.

The cuff clanged on the bedrail. Wells looked down at it. Another hurdle they'd have to cross. An EMP blanket's signal was not strong enough to disengage an electromagnetic cuff. But looking at the cuff sitting over her broken HIC reignited a memory.

A memory of another device covering her HIC. An older, disgusting HIC, sitting on her skin. A HIC that was not connected to her or Penta.

"Aranya, where do they keep our belongings?"

"When I arrived, they had me take off all my clothes and put on these." She pinched her hospital clothes. "They put them in a box, together with some of my jewelry, and took it away."

"Do you know where they took it?"

Aranya shook her head. Wells thought for a second.

"What time is your walk?" Wells asked.

Just like Wells, Aranya had an escorted daily walk to the courtyard. Unlike Wells, she had no cuff connecting her to a rail the whole time. She had slightly more freedom, and Wells figured since she had never tried anything with this freedom, no one saw her as a threat.

"In about twenty minutes. Why?" Aranya replied.

Wells figured this was the only floor, and maybe even the only room set aside for Lan-noi security prisoners. If so, she reasoned, their personal items would also be stored on this floor, to keep things organized and simple. It would also make sense from a logistics point to have it close to the nurses' station. Logical, but not guaranteed.

The plan Wells came up with was simple, as most successful plans are. When Aranya went on her escorted walk, she would plead with the nurse to retrieve a personal item from her stored belongings. She would do this as they passed the nurses' station. If the nurse agreed, she might take Aranya with her and make her wait outside the room while she retrieved it. Then they would know where their stuff was kept and call it a day.

If she told her to stay at the station, Aranya would try to monitor her movement on the wall of DDUs and see which room she entered. Either way, the most important part was Aranya's ability to convince the nurse to retrieve the object. Seeing which room held their belongings would be easy.

Wells explained the plan to Aranya.

"Do you have any item that is small enough that they might allow you to keep it at your bedside?" Wells asked.

Aranya didn't hesitate.

"Yes. A necklace from my grandmother. To be honest, it would be a relief to have it back."

Footsteps announced Aranya's escort.

She sat up, grimacing as she pushed herself off the bed. As she walked past Wells, she gave her a knowing look.

Wells watched her leave, hoping her gut was still working the way it used to.

* * *

When Aranya returned, she walked past Wells's bed, making no eye contact. She shuffled over to her bed, and since the nurse was still there, struggled to get back onto it. The nurse waited until she seemed settled and left, giving Wells a cursory smile on the way out.

Wells turned to Aranya, ready to be debriefed.

As always, Aranya seemed drawn into her own world and needed some coaxing.

"So?" Wells whispered loudly.

The familiar faint smile and bowed head appeared.

So did a fine gold chain with a small pendant attached to it.

* * *

Aranya explained to Wells how they'd left the room and turned left, as they always did, and walked down the corridor toward the elevators. On their way, they passed the nurses' station, and Aranya stopped. She explained to the nurse escorting her how she really missed her family and that they'd taken the only item she had to remember them by when she arrived. The nurse seemed sympathetic to her pleas and agreed to help her. Which turned out to be quick and simple. The nurse walked a few meters past the station and opened a door. She entered a code into a small DDU mounted on the wall, and the door slid open. It was not a door to a room, but a shallow closet. Aranya could see a few boxes and folded clothing. The nurse pulled a box down and opened it. Inside were all of Aranya's personal effects.

"Damn, that was easier than I thought," Wells said.

"I know. I think the security relies more on the threat of surveillance and drones to keep us here."

Wells had to agree. There were no guards or officers to be seen, but there were plenty of cameras. Drones would surely be deployed if they just walked out the front door. Lan-noi security would be informed the minute it happened and the drones would track down the escapees in minutes. No need to have over-the-top security here, as they could take care of things remotely.

"Did you see the code?" Wells asked.

"I memorized it."

Wells felt a tiny surge of adrenaline as her plan started to fall into place.

The next phase would be to get to the closet and retrieve the old HIC she'd acquired when she arrived in Shangcorp. With all the surveillance, it would be difficult. The logical move would be a distraction.

Wells looked at Aranya, who appeared so fragile and harmless. Who could walk around with no cuffs and get away with staff opening locked doors for her. Who no one would suspect of anything. Diminutive Aranya, who also lead people in a revolution.

"Okay," she said, "here's what we're going to do."

* * *

"You ready for your walk?"

Wells was sitting on her bed, ready to go. She had been ready for some time.

She nodded to the nurse. The less she said to him, the better. If she got lost in a conversation with one of the staff, she might let something slip that could aid them in identifying her.

Wells stood up, and the nurse swiped his HIC to disengage the electromagnetic cuff. Freedom lasted till they reached the door, where a metal rail attracted the cuff again. Wells walked slightly slower than normal, giving her some extra time to locate the locker. As they passed the nurses' station, she saw it. The locker was slightly narrower than the other doors that led to rooms. She saw the DDU next to it and kept walking. It was not her job to open it.

Wells counted ten steps and stopped.

The nurse didn't realize, at first, and walked on for a few steps before turning around.

"You okay?"

Wells liked this nurse. He had the facial features and small build of most people she had seen here in the hospital, and he was always friendly to her. She regretted that he'd been the one to come fetch her for her walk, and not one of the more obnoxious staff members.

"What's wrong?" he asked again as he approached her.

"This stupid cuff! I can't have it on anymore! Take it off!" Wells yelled. She yanked and pulled on her arm. Pain radiated from the center of her chest, but she kept going.

Two more nurses came running out from the nurses' station to see what was happening.

"Okay. I can see it is causing you some distress," the nurse offered. "Maybe we can come up with a solution."

Wells knew he was just buying time before another nurse injected her with a sedative.

"No! Just get this off!" Wells kept tugging at the cuff.

She heard a commotion behind her and then footsteps. The other nurses coming to the rescue.

"Just calm down before you hurt yourself," the nurse pleaded.

Wells felt a pang of guilt as she braced herself and kicked the nurse harder than she planned on, sending him flying across the hallway. The footsteps behind her stopped.

"Get this thing off me!" she yelled again, making sure she kept all the attention on herself.

Doors opened on all sides of the hallway and heads poked out to see what was happening. A few brave souls even stepped out into the hallway for a better view.

"Please, I can't take it anymore!" Wells wailed.

The nurse stood up and nodded to the other nurses to show he was fine. In a show of unity, they all stepped closer to Wells. Behind them, Aranya quickly moved past the nurses' station and stopped at the slightly narrower door. Then, behind their backs, she used the DDU to gain entry. The door silently slid open, and Aranya grabbed something out of the dark space. The door slid shut again, and she disappeared.

Wells fell to the floor just as the nurses reached her and sobbed.

"I'm so sorry. I'm so sorry," she repeated. She offered no resistance as she felt the sting of a needle introducing sedatives to her nervous system. She welcomed the warmth it filled her with and fell into the arms of the nurses.

Faces around her became blurry, and she floated back to her room.

She saw Aranya sitting on her bed. Mission accomplished.

Wells closed her eyes and let the sedatives take her to another world.

| ten |

"Stand still so I can hit you!" the enormous man yelled.

Drake ducked down just in time to see the thick, rusty pipe make another dent in the hydro's roof. The man growled at Drake and lifted the pipe up again. He was bigger than most people, but not as huge as a moon miner. Though he did have the aggression and temper to be one, Drake thought, as he lifted the pipe and swung again.

"Slow down, buddy!" Drake yelled. "We made an honest mistake, okay?"

A man of few words, the man swung yet again, smashing one of the hydro's windows.

Jimmy crawled out of the hydro, arms covering his head.

"What the hell, Drake?"

Seeing the new target, the man tried to swing at Jimmy's head.

"Hey! Watch out!" Jimmy yelled as the pipe barely missed.

Drake saw an opportunity and jumped on the man's back. With one arm around his neck, he started punching his ear with his free hand.

"Yeah! Get him, Drake!" Jimmy cheered.

"How about some help?"

The man bucked underneath Drake, trying his best to shake him off, but the only thing that went flying was the rusty pipe. Drake kept punching the man's head as Jimmy jumped from one foot to another, readying himself to hopefully do something.

"What the fuck are you doing?" Drake yelled.

"Just waiting for an opportunity, ya know?"

Drake's arm could no longer hold on, and the man threw him off. Drake felt the air leave his lungs as he hit the ground hard. He rolled onto his belly and got onto all fours, trying to get his breath.

A rib cracked, and Drake felt himself lifting off the ground as the man's boot connected. He hit the side of the hydro and slid to the ground, breathing now almost impossible.

Jimmy decided that was his cue to jump in.

Picking up the discarded pipe, he ran up to the man from behind, bellowing a war cry.

The man turned around just as Jimmy swung. The sound the pipe made confirmed solid contact with its target. Clutching his groin, the man toppled over. Jimmy ran over to Drake and shoved him into the hydro. Drake cried out in pain. Jimmy jumped into the driver's seat and sped away as quick as he could.

"I'll kill you!" the man yelled after them, still curled up in the fetal position.

* * *

Once they were far enough away, Jimmy pulled over.

"You okay, partner?" he asked Drake.

"Not really," he admitted. Every shallow breath he dared to take hurt like hell.

"Do you want me to take you to a hospital?" Jimmy asked.

Drake had considered the option, but decided against it. Lannoi only had one hospital, and it was the one where they were holding Lt. Wells. If they went there, they would have to sign in, and even if they used aliases, the system would capture their faces—Drake's for the admission, and Jimmy's on all the surveillance cameras. And then they'd be recognized before they could get anywhere near her.

"We can't risk it, buddy," Drake said.

"Hang on." Jimmy typed away on the stolen hydro's DDU. Though the hydro was old and the DDU outdated, it still worked.

"Okay," Jimmy said after a few minutes. "There is a clinic nearby. It's the one the demolition company uses when one of us gets hurt, ya know? So I reckon they'll be less picky who they let in."

Drake had never been there, but knew the place. "That hack shop? I'd rather shoot myself." He had seen their work. It wasn't pretty.

"Don't be so dramatic. We're going." Jimmy started the hydro back up.

Drake wished he had the strength to slap him.

* * *

Jimmy's driving was even more painful than the kick he'd received. It seemed he couldn't decide which pedal to use, so he alternated between hitting the accelerator too hard and stomping on the brakes. Drake slammed against his seat belt, and then back against the seat again. Jimmy took the corners at full speed, all his concentration on the wheel. Drake braced himself against the door and prayed for a swift death.

Jimmy stomped on the brakes one last time, tires squealing, and shut down the hydro.

"Here we are. Let's go, partner," Jimmy said and jumped out.

Drake gingerly unbuckled himself and climbed out of the hydro. It looked like Jimmy had swerved to avoid hitting another hydro and mounted the sidewalk in doing so, barely missing a lamp post. Seeing no other hydro nearby, Drake realized this was just Jimmy's interpretation of parking.

The clinic was as dirty and rundown as Drake had feared. As the doors squeaked open, they revealed an overly lit waiting room. The bright lights hurt Drake's eyes, and he had to squint for a few seconds until he adjusted to them. A few benches lined the walls, framing a sticky floor. A station in the middle of the floor housed four DDUs on each of its sides. Jimmy dragged Drake over to the DDU station.

"Okay," Jimmy said as he read the information on the screen. "Seems all basic, ya know. Name, address, occupation, employer details. Usual stuff."

Drake groaned in response.

"You sit down. I'll take care of this, ya know?"

Drake didn't argue. He knew Jimmy was more than able to come up with an alias and fake details to get them through. To be honest, between the two of them, he was better suited to it. Drake found a bench, plopped himself down on it, and proceeded to feel sorry for himself.

It didn't take Jimmy too long to complete the admission forms.

Besides the benches and the DDU station, the only other feature was a door that slid open every few minutes to either let people through or send them back out. Drake saw no improvement in the people leaving.

A DDU above the door announced the next victim.

"I think I'm feeling better. Maybe I should just go home and sleep this off." Drake could not wait to get out.

"No one knows your body better than you. So, if you want to go—"

"Yes! Please. Take me home, Jimmy."

"Your body, your choice, ya know." Jimmy elbowed Drake in the side.

Drake tried to gasp for air so he could yell at Jimmy like he had never been yelled at before, but the pain was so immense, he could hardly get any air in, let alone out.

"Fuuuuuuck." He quietly expelled the little air he had.

"Oh, crap! Sorry, Drake," Jimmy said.

Drake glared at Jimmy and couldn't believe the face of innocence that looked back at him. Had he really just elbowed him by mistake? Was it really an accident and not a ploy to keep him here? Drake took another shallow breath, readying himself to let Jimmy have it.

"Dale Goodyear!" a synthesized voice called over some PA system, and the name flashed on the DDU above the door.

"That's you buddy." Jimmy smiled at Drake.

"Huh?"

"The alias. That's you. C'mon, let's go." Jimmy held out a hand.

As Jimmy helped him up, Drake muttered, "Of all the names in the world, you picked *that*?"

Jimmy shrugged and led Drake to the automatic sliding door. The hospital was rough and worn down, but this side of the door, things were at least cleaner. They had entered a short hall with multiple doors. A DDU stood in front of them. On the screen, Drake's alias and a number appeared, corresponding to one of the numbers on the doors. Through that door sat a dark-skinned man in another brightly lit room.

"What's the problem?" he asked bluntly. it took a moment for their ARPs to detect the language and translate it.

"We think he's broken a rib. Maybe a few." Jimmy answered.

The doctor waited a second for his ARP to do the same.

"Sit there." He pointed to the only bed in the room.

"I got it," Drake said, as Jimmy escorted him over. He sat down on the bed, and the doctor grabbed a medical scanner. He ran the scanner over Drake's abdomen, sides, and chest. He returned to his small desk and looked at the results on his DDU.

"Left number five and six ribs appear to be damaged. Take off your shirt."

Drake tried to lift his arms to take his shirt off, but all he could do was make agonizing sounds. Jimmy jumped up, ignored Drake's protests, and swiftly had him out of it.

The doctor placed a graphene sleeve over Drake's torso, and fiddled with some kind of device. An electric pulse ran through the fabric, and it constricted, contouring to Drake's body and becoming much more rigid. Immediately, Drake could breathe again.

"Come back in six weeks," the doctor said, returning to his DDU. The door slid open. Drake looked at Jimmy and shrugged.

"Thanks," he said as they passed the doctor on their way out. Once the door had shut behind them, Drake smiled at Jimmy. "Not much of a people person, but damn if I can't breathe again."

"Had me worried there, partner," Jimmy said, and turned away. Drake saw him wipe his eyes before turning back.

"I'm not going anywhere, buddy."

As they exited into the waiting room, Drake glanced at the new faces. Most of them were dirty and malnourished. Drake left as quick as he could. He didn't understand Shangcorp. Most of its citizens were starving, yet medical care was free. Not that things were better in New Franco, where Penta handed out Basic Income, then left everyone to fend for themselves.

* * *

Drake felt much better, so much so that he'd insisted on driving the hydro to Dina. The graphene mold was rigid but offered him enough maneuverability to drive. Besides, he did not want to risk breaking another bone thanks to Jimmy's driving. As they pulled in, they saw Dina and another woman leaning against the wall, with a large duffel bag slung over her shoulders.

"What is this?" Dina said as Drake and Jimmy climbed out of the hydro. "It's a piece of crap!"

"Ah, but it's now *your* piece of crap." Drake slapped the roof. Glass fragments fell to his feet. "I'm confident that is still worth over one thousand credits," he added.

Dina looked unimpressed. She shot a look at her friend, who stifled a laugh and said, "You can't be serious. It's all busted up."

"I reset the whole operating system," Jimmy said. "And once you log in, she's all yours."

"It's a *she*?" Dina's friend said.

"Well, ya know, it's how people talk." Jimmy looked at Drake for backup.

"You have your hydro, Dina. Now tell me the plan."

Dina looked the banged-up hydro over once more before facing Drake.

"We're leaving town in two days, so it must be tomorrow, and we only have one shot. I'm making no guarantees, and whatever the outcome is, I keep the hydro."

Drake knew it was nonnegotiable. Dina held all the cards and could make all the rules. He and Jimmy had to go along with it.

"Sure. So, what's the plan?" he asked again.

"Ziggy, will you do the honors?"

Dina's friend opened the bag and stepped back so Drake and Jimmy could peer into it.

A couple of pulse rifles and a few pulse pistols filled the grinning bag.

"This is the plan," Dina said.

| eleven |

"I don't like it, Drake," Jimmy said.

The windows of their hydrohouse were fogged from their breath. Jimmy opened a door to let some fresh air in, and with it, the sounds of Lan-noi waking up. Hydrocomets shook the bridge above them, while smaller hydros filled the roads down below. There was more traffic than usual. People who had stayed one more night while planning for what lay ahead. Trying to consider every scenario and contingency for when war broke out. It seemed, judging by the exodus, that being in a big city was no one's first choice.

Drake got out to stretch his legs. The hydro kept them safe and warm, but it was not spacious. Drake relished the feeling of uncurling every part of his body. Jimmy stood watching him, all nervous energy.

"I don't like it either," Drake said, "but what alternative do we have? Look around you. Everyone is leaving. Soon it's going to be chaos. We need to do this while we can."

Jimmy inspected his shoes for answers.

"I have no intention of shooting anyone, okay?" Drake's voice was softer now. "We'll set all the pulse weapons to nonlethal. I promise. No matter what Dina says."

"That's not it," Jimmy said.

"What is it then?"

"I'll shoot anyone holding or hurting the lieutenant. It just seems very risky, ya know?"

A row of shops lined the street across from them. Drake and Jimmy sometimes bought white box meals from one, and the others sold used goods, alcohol, and surplus security clothing. Most mornings, their lights were on as Jimmy and Drake made their way to work. Today, only the security surplus store seemed open. At first, Drake assumed the other shops were closed for the day, but as he studied the buildings, he noticed their windows were missing. He flipped his ARP on and zoomed in.

Broken glass littered the pavement in front of the shops, and a few items, things usually found in the shops, were strewn between the broken glass. A few burned-out security drones also lay upside down on the ground. The shopkeeper of the surplus store was outside his shop, sweeping away the neighboring shop's debris. Drake wondered why this shop had been spared until he saw the pulse rifle slung over the owner's shoulder. A woman came out of the shop, also carrying a pulse gun. They both had black rings around their eyes—souvenirs from a night of no rest, as they protected their store from looters.

Drake switched his ARP off.

"We have no choice, buddy. People are losing their minds. Soon, injured people will overrun the hospital. Who knows where they'll send Lily then?"

Jimmy nodded.

Drake looked back across the road. The shopkeeper had finished sweeping and went back into his store to begin the day. Drake wondered if he'd see him again tomorrow.

* * *

Drake suggested they go to work. It was a workday, and since they'd received no message on their HIDs telling them if they were still operating or not, he assumed the site to be open. Not even a war would prevent the greedy companies from trying to squeeze everything out of their workers before it was too late. This suited Drake. He needed to keep his mind and body busy, and not sit around ruminating on what they were about to do. He knew that counted double for Jimmy.

When they arrived at the site, the manager was sitting in his small office, working on a DDU. "Seems some people have a work ethic," he said. "Didn't figure it would be you two."

Drake ignored him and scanned himself in. Jimmy did the same.

"Almost no one showed up. But I guess that's what you get for hiring a bunch of—"

The manager stopped himself and sucked air through his teeth. Drake made a mental note to remove some of those teeth whenever he had a chance.

As they headed to their spot, Drake looked around but could not see Dina or her usual group. At this time of day, the site was normally buzzing with activity. Hammers smashing concrete, autonomous carts running around, drones buzzing overhead. Now the hammers were leaned on, and the carts empty. Small groups had formed and people were doing more talking than working. Drones hovered above them, but today no one seemed to care.

This was not where they were supposed to be.

"Fuck it," Drake blurted out. "Let's go."

Jimmy jumped up from the concrete block he'd just sat on. "Go where?"

"I think it's time to rescue the lieutenant."

* * *

Drake knocked on the door. The DDU next to it had a cracked screen and sat dormant. It fitted in nicely with the graffiti and litter lying in the hall. He waited a few seconds and hammered on the door again. This time, shuffling noises came from within the unit. The door slid open.

"It's those two idiots from the yard," Ziggy called loudly. She turned around, leaving them standing in the hall.

Drake shrugged at Jimmy, assumed they could enter, and stepped inside.

The room was bigger than most places Drake had ever lived in, but still nothing special. Like most places he called home, the carpets were threadbare, the walls needed paint, and the whole place had a lingering, musty smell.

"Lovely place, ya know," Jimmy said behind him.

"Thanks." Dina was sitting on an old couch. She moved over to make room for Ziggy, who took the spot next to Dina and put her leg over hers. Dina put her hand on it.

"Are you guys together?" Jimmy thought out loud—the only way he knew how.

"Yup," Dina replied.

"Oh, cool," Jimmy said.

Drake knew Jimmy had a thing for Dina, but as always, the moment a door closed for Jimmy, he moved on. Drake saw the smile on his face and knew he already had.

"Dina," Drake said, "things are falling apart out there. I'm afraid the hospitals will be overrun soon and that they will move Lily out to who knows where. I think we need to go today, not tomorrow."

Ziggy gave Dina a nod.

"Sure, we can go today."

"So, what now?" Drake asked, slightly taken aback that there was no resistance.

Dina gently shifted her girlfriend's leg from her own and leaned forward.

"This will not be a stealthy operation. Ziggy and I used to be security in our hometown. We are used to working together and to close quarter combat. I wouldn't think any less of you two if you wanted to stay behind and let us girls find your friend."

"Not that you could think any less," Ziggy muttered.

"No. The deal was for you to help, not take over," Drake replied. "Either we go, or it's off." He was not about to leave Lily's fate in the hands of these two, who were practically strangers to him.

Dina gave Ziggy a look. Ziggy stood up and left the room. When she returned, she had the bag with the pulse guns in her hand. She used the bag to swipe old white box meals off the coffee table and set it down, then rejoined Dina on the couch.

"This will be an offensive rescue. Meaning, we will go in, guns blazing, and grab your friend. It's a hospital, not an actual holding facility, so I think the noise and confusion will benefit us. I don't expect any resistance, but we might encounter some drones."

Dina looked at Drake and Jimmy, as if to gauge their understanding.

"Got it. One question," Drake said. "I'm all for going in *guns blazing*, but could we switch all the pulse weapons to stun, or at least to low damage? I don't see the point in hurting hospital workers or any bystanders."

Dina and Ziggy both snorted. "Sure," Dina said through bursts of laughter, "We'll put all the weapons on tickle."

"He's serious, ya know," Jimmy said.

The laughing subsided.

"Fine. We'll knock the energy down a notch or two, okay?"

"Thanks."

Dina pulled the bag closer to her and opened it up. She took two pulse guns out and removed the cartridges holding the pulse rounds. After inspecting the chamber to ensure there were no rounds in them, she switched on the safeties and laid them on the table next to the bag.

"Have you ever used these?"

Drake looked at the two weapons. One looked similar to the weapon they'd taken off the bandits when they were chasing Bob Turner, and the other one he'd seen hundreds of times. Jimmy bent down and looked them over.

"Sure do, ya know."

Grabbing the one that looked familiar to Drake, Dina held it, muzzle pointing to the ceiling.

"This cutie is a PF-AR3. It's a third-generation pulse assault rifle made by your industrious Penta Corporation. Its street name is Artie."

"Artie. I like it," Jimmy said.

Dina handed the weapon to Jimmy and grabbed the other one.

"That one is a Shangcorp Arms Close Range Scatter-gun," Ziggy said. "The name is quite stupid, and it's not even their own design. It's a copy of the PF-SC12, which, as you might have guessed, also comes from the world's most violent territory, Penta Corporation."

Dina turned it over a few times. "But despite the name or its heritage," she said, "it packs a punch at close range and never misses." She smiled as she admired the implement of death in her hands.

Dina threw the scatter-gun to Drake, who fumbled it, but held on.

"Great hands," Ziggy chirped.

Drake looked at the weapon. Scatter-guns were quite popular with haulers and most of them carried one in the cabin of their trucks. Drake had always preferred the compactness of a pulse pistol himself. But feeling the sturdiness and heft of the scatter-gun, he could see the appeal. It had the same grip as a pulse pistol, but the barrel was twice as long and twice as big. Drake held it up and stared down its barrel. Jimmy's head popped up in front of him, putting the gun's sights right between his eyes.

"Looks good on ya, ya know," Jimmy said.

"Fuck sakes, Jimmy! It could've been loaded!" Drake yelled as he lowered the barrel.

"Nah, I saw Dina take out the cartridge, ya know."

Ignoring Jimmy, Drake studied the weapon further, familiarizing himself with the safety switch location, the cartridge release button and the energy pulse setting knob. He experimented with them, getting a good feel for them, figuring out the best position to have the gun in to make changes on the go. He lifted it up to his eyes a few times and did a few practice fires, with some practice switch operations thrown in, too. Within a few minutes, it felt like second nature to him.

"Jimmy, you comfortable with that one?" Drake asked.

Jimmy twirled the gun around its tactical sling and made pew-pew sounds. "What ya reckon?"

Drake shook his head. If he hadn't seen Jimmy in action before, and knew he could handle himself, he'd have backed out on the spot.

"Okay, Dina. Anything else in that bag we might find useful?" he asked.

It was a rhetorical question. Drake could see other guns and unidentifiable items in the bag. He wanted to see what Dina was willing to share.

"No, not really. Just some guns for me and Ziggy. You guys good with those?"

"Oh, yeah!" Jimmy said, lifting it up and shooting imaginary bad guys.

Drake eyeballed the bag straining at the seams with things Dina wasn't willing to share with them. Then he caught Ziggy watching him.

"Sure, we're good. It's not our first fight. We've got this."
Drake said.

He looked at the bag again.

Jimmy was right.

Something felt wrong.

| twelve |

Dina led the way, Drake and Jimmy followed, and Ziggy brought up the rear. They went down a few flights of stairs and entered an underground parking lot. It was almost completely empty. At the far side of the empty expanse sat the smashed-up hydro. As they approached, Dina swiped on her HIC. Nothing happened.

"Piece of shit," she mumbled. She swiped again, but still nothing. "Last time I ever accept any goods from you guys. This thing is junk."

She bent down and fiddled with something underneath the rear bumper. The trunk popped open.

"Had to rig it myself." She shot Drake a look, but he knew best not to reply.

Ziggy loaded the weapons bag into the trunk and slammed it shut. The doors were all unlocked, and everyone got in. Being the guests, Drake and Jimmy took the back seats.

Dina ran the pre-drive start-up program, and once everything was online, she floored the accelerator, slamming everyone back into their seats. She hardly slowed at all as they exited the building. Jimmy and Drake crashed into each other as she made a hard left turn. Dina regained control and sped down the road. Drake braced himself for the inevitable pain from his cracked ribs, but the graphene cast had absorbed all the force.

"Nice neighborhood," Drake said. Burned-out hydros were scattered around. Some were still alight. Most shops had broken windows. This was not the best part of town, but things were clearly worse than normal.

They drove on in silence.

A few drones were out surveilling the streets, but Drake didn't see any security forces out patrolling. Maybe they were busy elsewhere, or if things were the same here as in New Franco, they would be hovering around the inner sectors, protecting the rich minority.

Two smoking wrecks blocked the road ahead, and Dina slowed down.

"Looks like we'll need to find an alternative route." She started to turn the hydro around.

Another hydro shot out from a narrow laneway, blocking the path behind them. Its doors were flung open and four people jumped out, armed with pipes and iron bars. Drake didn't see any pulse weapons.

"What now?" he asked.

Dina turned around in her seat to have a better view. "You two sit still and stay out of the way," she ordered.

Dina gave Ziggy some abbreviated instructions that Drake couldn't follow, and they opened their doors. The two women kneeled next to the hydro, pulse rifles drawn.

"Stop right now," Ziggy yelled. "Turn around and leave. One more step and we'll open fire. I repeat—one more step and we'll open fire."

The four pipe-wielding assailants stopped as the supposed leader lifted his hand.

"You are making a big mistake, darling." He whistled loudly.

Behind Dina and Ziggy, Drake and Jimmy saw three people jump over the wrecks that blocked the road. Dina motioned with her head, and Ziggy spun around.

"Three bogeys. No weapons," Ziggy said as she observed the new players.

The new arrivals also carried makeshift weapons of pipes and metal, but clearly Dina and Ziggy did not see them as a threat.

"Seems we have you outnumbered and trapped. So what do you say, darling? How about you give me that big gun before you hurt yourself?"

"Dina, how can we help?" Drake yelled at her.

"Stay put and out of my way!" she snapped back. Drake did as he was told.

The leader's patience lasted less than a minute. " Get them!"

Both sides started moving in, swinging their weapons and pulling their scariest faces.

"Engage!" Dina ordered.

Drake barely had time to cover his ears before it was all over. Short, two-shot bursts rang out, and with every burst, a body hit the ground. Bap, bap, thump. Bap, bap, thump. Quick, accurate, and efficient as hell.

"Report!" Dina yelled.

"Clear. No hits."

"Copy. Clear and no hits."

They both stood up and went over to their individual piles of bad guys, making sure no one was still stubbornly holding onto life. Then, satisfied they'd eliminated the threat, they headed back toward the hydro. Ziggy grabbed Dina around the neck and kissed her.

"Idiots," she half laughed.

They got back into the hydro. Drake and Jimmy gawped at them, wide-eyed.

"Wow, you guys are badasses, ya know?"

"What he said."

"I know." Dina turned back to the hydro's controls. "Now, let's find a way around this mess."

* * *

The rest of the journey was less eventful. A few people were running around scrambling to get out, but as they entered the better areas of town, things had calmed down a bit. As always, the wealthier people believed someone would come and save them, so they stayed put. The super-rich were paranoid and powerful enough to have escape plans in place and had left days ago.

Drake did not know how far away the hospital was and didn't want to ask Dina. Things might have calmed down a bit, but he could see she was still in fight mode.

A mode he didn't know she had. When she'd offered her services, Drake had assumed she was a small-time criminal, like Jimmy when he met him, and that she had some contact at the hospital. He'd thought she had some easy and quick way to get in and out and make some credits along the way. Then she'd pulled out the bag of weapons and played coy about most of the contents. She and Ziggy had to be more than just a couple of retired security officers. The way they handled themselves reminded him of Lt. Wells, who was anything but an ordinary officer. They'd clearly had some serious tactical training. Drake wanted to interrogate Dina further about her past, but he was also relieved to have her on his side. If things went south, it would be good to have her and Ziggy around. He could ask her about her past later, once Lily was safe.

They rounded a corner, and Dina slammed on the brakes. Drake peeked around her seat and saw a big, gray, uninspiring building a few hundred meters away.

"There it is," Dina said.

The hospital loomed over the other buildings around it, a landmark in the area. They stopped well short of it and followed Dina's lead as she exited the hydro and walked to the front of it.

"Does your ARP still work?" she asked Drake.

"Yup."

"Okay, everyone, switch on your ARPs and scan every area and corner of that building. We only have one side to look at, but it is the front, so should be sufficient."

"What are we looking for?" Jimmy asked.

"Literally anything. Cameras. Drones, deployed or passive. Look at the windows. Can we see any security personnel? Check the roof, balconies, the ground level outside. We'll take ten minutes and go from there. Questions?"

There were none.

Drake zoomed in to his ARP's maximum setting and scanned the building. Having the ARP zoomed in so much meant he had to make small head adjustments or the entire picture would move away and he'd have to start over.

"So, you and Ziggy used to work together?" Drake asked as he scanned.

"Yes, security."

No drones were visible flying around and patrolling.

"Special division?"

A hydro pulled up to the front of the building and a person got out and walked into the hospital. The hydro pulled away and disappeared.

"Just security."

From this distance, it was impossible to say if there were cameras mounted outside.

"Slavor must be a well-protected region," he pushed, "if the ordinary security officers are as good as you and Ziggy."

Drake felt movement next to him. He switched his ARP off and saw Dina staring at him.

"What do you want?" she asked.

"Nothing. It's just that back there, you and Ziggy—I mean, you guys went into full kill mode. You were so clinical and efficient."

"So?"

"I mean, it looked like you were more than just normal security, that's all."

"This is riveting, but we need to move closer and do another scan. I can't see shit from here," Ziggy interrupted them.

"Yeah, I was thinking the same, ya know," Jimmy joined the choir.

"Okay, let's move in and do another scan." Dina turned her back to Drake.

Everyone jumped back into the hydro, and they drove in silence toward the hospital. About one hundred meters out, Dina stopped again.

"One more ten-minute scan, same parameters as last time, then we regroup."

Everyone jumped out and switched on their ARPs again. Everything seemed the same, almost. Everyone saw it, but Jimmy spoke up first.

"There! At the front doors. Cameras. I see, one, two, three . . . Um, six. Six cameras."

Drake counted and came to the same number.

"Is that a problem?" Drake asked.

"Nah. It's expected. We'll cover our faces. If they're serious, they can still use gait recognition. We'll move in a crouched position to throw them off, and Ziggy will disable the cameras as we approach. They might get a few seconds of footage, but nothing to worry about."

Dina's confidence gave Drake hope that the mission would succeed.

It also scared him.

"Listen up. We're on foot from here. Follow me and listen to my commands. They are not suggestions, they are orders. Understood?"

Drake nodded.

"Yes, ma'am," Jimmy replied.

"Good. Stay behind me and use your heads."

"Can we make sure all the weapons are on stun? I noticed the guys back there leaking a lot of fluids," Drake reminded Dina.

Dina frowned for a second, then smiled.

"Sure. Everybody, confirm weapons are on stun."

Jimmy flicked his Artie over to stun. "Confirm."

Drake did the same on his scatter-gun. "Confirm"

"Confirm," Ziggy said.

"Confirm. May I continue?"

Drake tried to steal a glimpse at her rifle to see the position of the switch, but the selector was on the other side of the pulse weapon and hidden from view.

"Yes, of course."

"My source told me what floor they normally hold the security patients on and which room. I have a schematic on my HIC and will move directly to the target. Keep up. If you fall behind or get lost, it's on you. We shouldn't encounter any resistance, as it's mainly hospital staff, but there may be some security. If all goes to plan, we should be in and out in under twenty minutes."

Dina looked at Drake and then Jimmy.

"If you do something stupid and get shot, or lost, or whatever, try to get out and don't come back to the hydro. This is Ziggy's and my escape vehicle. Once we're outside the building, you're on your own. Questions?"

"You could at least take us back home, ya know?"

Drake stopped him. "It's fine, Jimmy. We'll think of something."

It was only a hospital, with minimal security, but Drake took no comfort in that. They were storming a building, armed to the teeth. Things could still go pear-shaped in an instant. Neither he nor Jimmy had any training in tactical assaults. They could each hold their own shooting a pulse weapon, but bursting into a building full of people—almost all of them civilians—was on another level. He dared not even think of what would happen if things went wrong in there. Dina and Ziggy could clearly handle themselves, but was that a good or bad thing? He couldn't shake the feeling that they were total overkill for this venture. It was only a hospital. With minimal security. Surely he and Jimmy could just walk in and grab her.

Drake felt his stomach shrink and his throat close.

He looked at the scatter-gun in his hands. It looked even deadlier out in the bright sunlight.

"Dina, I'm not so sure—"

Dina brushed past him. "Okay, here we go! Stay close!" She started off at a jog and Ziggy followed close by.

"Fuck," Drake mumbled.

"I know, right? Do we really need to run, ya know?"

| thirteen |

"Drake! Drake, slow down," Jimmy said through labored breaths.

Drake slowed down a bit, and then some more, realizing he could walk at Jimmy's jogging pace.

"What is it?"

Seeing Drake walking, Jimmy grabbed the opportunity to walk as well.

"I'm nervous, ya know?" Jimmy said, keeping his eyes down.

"Me too, buddy, but luckily we have those two."

"They scare me."

Drake almost laughed. Not because it was funny, but because he felt the same. "They are a bit intimidating, I'll give you that."

Ziggy looked over her shoulder and Drake gave her a thumbs-up.

"Keep up," she whispered loudly.

"C'mon buddy, let's pick up the pace." Drake broke into a jog again.

"Why are people always running?" Jimmy grumbled.

* * *

Dina stopped and held her hand in the air. They were about twenty meters from the hospital's fence. It was more decorative than functional and only stood three feet high. There was no gate, and people could just drive in. In front of the hospital was a sizable parking area for hydros. Drake couldn't see a lot of options to provide them cover.

"Shit! Get down!"

Dina and Ziggy dropped to the ground and rolled down into a gutter next to the road. Drake did the same and found Jimmy already at the bottom of it.

"What happened?" Drake asked.

Dina put a finger in front of her mouth. Everyone stayed still, awaiting her orders.

"Ziggy, go check it out," Dina said after a few minutes had passed.

Ziggy crawled on her belly to the edge of the road. Everyone else stayed put.

"Clear!"

Dina stayed low and scurried over to Ziggy. Drake and Jimmy followed.

"What happened?" Drake asked again.

"An ASV. Ziggy saw it just in time."

Drake was familiar with them. About half the size of a normal hydro, the Automated Security Vehicles were all over New Franco, patrolling the streets and carrying drones which operators could deploy remotely. Some of them could even disperse tear gas to deter crowds or use long-range acoustic devices to scare them off. Mostly they just drove around sending footage back to HQ, who then analyzed it and looked for anything out of the ordinary.

"That's the first time I've seen one in Lan-noi," he said.

"Shangcorp doesn't like to waste money, so they usually only patrol—how should I say this? The nicer areas."

Drake knew that tune very well. New Franco was the same. Penta did everything it could to keep the inner sectors safe and happy, but gangs and crime bosses ran the poorer outer sectors. Penta did the bare minimum to keep its most vulnerable citizens safe. They were halfway across the globe, but some things never changed.

"Do you think they saw us?" Drake asked.

Ziggy shook her head. "I think we got out of the way in time. But now is as good a time as any to put these on."

Dina reached into her jacket pocket and pulled out four identical black squares. She handed them out. Not knowing what to do, Drake watched as Dina, Ziggy and Jimmy each grabbed a corner and shook it out, unfolding it into a tubular sock. They each pulled it over their heads until it covered their faces. The material was semitransparent, and Drake could still make out Jimmy's face.

"Uh, guys, I don't think these will work very well," he said, holding his black square up.

"These are great, ya know," Jimmy said. "We used to use them all the time when we robbed—" His enthusiasm faded.

"It is made of a magnetically charged material," Dina said. "Our faces will show up as a black spot on any electronic device. See for yourself."

Drake looked at the small folded square in his hand before switching on his ARP. Dina, Ziggy, and Jimmy's heads were missing. In their places were just black holes. Drake switched off his ARP and everyone was back.

"Wow," he said.

"Now put the damn thing on," Dina said.

"Okay," Dina said once Drake had covered his face. "We're going to stay low and make for the first hydro over there. We'll go one at a time. Now!"

Ziggy went first and moved quickly toward the hydro, keeping low. Once she got there, Dina tapped Jimmy on his shoulder. "Go!" In seconds, he was crouched next to Ziggy.

Drake got his tap and sped off as fast as he could. As he took his position next to Jimmy, he saw Dina coming over.

"Good job. Remember this system. We might have to move like this once we are inside."

Jimmy and Drake both nodded.

Drake swiped his hands over his thighs as he realized how sweaty they were. Just meters away from him was the building where Lt. Wells was being held. He struggled to swallow and tried to breathe deeply to control his heart rate. A dull pain went through his chest as he sucked in the air.

"I'm so nervous and excited I might pee my pants," Jimmy said.

Ziggy cringed. Drake was glad to hear he wasn't the only one.

"Two more runs, and we should be ready to enter. Ziggy, at the next one, take out the cameras."

Ziggy nodded and made for the next hydro, this one much closer to the entrance. Jimmy got his tap and ran, so did Drake. Once they all grouped up, Ziggy screwed a silencer onto her

Artie and took aim at one of the cameras. A soft crackle emitted from the rifle and the camera exploded.

"Keep shooting. Jimmy, Drake, follow me."

Dina took off, still crouching, toward the entrance of the hospital. She swerved to the side and squatted against the wall a few meters away from the entrance.

"Just saw a drone approaching," Ziggy said as she joined them.

"Okay, let's get inside. Drake, Jimmy, fall behind us and stay close." Dina didn't wait for a response.

Drake and Jimmy had to jump to their feet to keep up. They followed Dina into the hospital.

* * *

All four froze as dozens of people blocked their way. People filled the entire entry hall to the hospital, standing shoulder to shoulder. Everyone was trying to get their loved ones out before they fled the city. People were yelling and screaming, trying to get someone's attention to let them in. This was not good. Two security personnel manned the door to the hospital interior, and they looked scared as hell. Back up would surely be on its way.

"We need another way in," Drake said.

"Follow me," Dina ordered, and went back outside.

Two suppressed crackles went off next to Drake's head. He turned to see Ziggy looking over her barrel into the sky. He followed her gaze and saw the smoking drone spiraling to the ground.

"On me," Dina commanded again, and sped off.

She rounded the corner of the hospital and signaled to Ziggy. Two fingers pointed to her eyes, and then she pointed them to a spot on the wall meters in front of them. Ziggy moved slightly forward and let out a two-shot burst. Camera down.

They were on the move again.

A wall met up with the building, and with no words exchanged, Dina leaned against it with one shoulder. Ziggy stepped into Dina's cupped hands and hoisted herself over the wall in one fluid movement. Dina turned and looked at Jimmy. "Let's go!"

He ran and put his foot in her hands. He tried to lift himself up with his legs but failed. He put his hand out on Dina's forehead and pushed off again. This time, he almost got up high enough. Dina saw he needed more help and grabbed his ass and shoved him over. A loud thump announced his arrival on the other side.

"Drake!"

Drake walked over to Dina, who stood up to face him.

"You need to swing one leg over and sit on the wall, then reach down and grab me. Can you do that?"

It had been a while since Drake had done any of the body-weight exercises he used to do religiously, but pounding concrete for weeks had kept him in shape. Besides, he knew he had no choice.

"No worries," he said, and readied himself to jump over.

Dina braced herself, and Drake set off. He timed his jump perfectly and placed his foot in Dina's hands as he lifted off the ground. He felt her boosting him, and he grabbed the edge of the wall, pulling himself up. When his hips reached the wall, he swung a leg over and sat upright. It surprised him how well the graphene protected his ribs. He'd barely felt a thing.

"Ready?" he called down to Dina.

Dina backed up a few meters and made a run for the wall. She jumped and extended an arm, which Drake caught. As he pulled, he felt all her weight and almost fell off the wall. Pain shot through his side as he pulled. Biting down, he tried his best to not yell out and pulled with all his strength. Dina grabbed the wall with her other arm and pulled herself up next to Drake.

"Thanks," she said, and slid down the other side.

Drake followed her, hugging himself, and saw Jimmy lying in the fetal position.

"Shit, Jimmy. You okay?"

Jimmy rolled over onto his back and pulled his pants leg up. Blood streamed down his shin.

"It's broken! I broke it! It hurts, Drake! It hurts!"

Drake bent over, exhaling loudly as the pain hit him again, and inspected Jimmy's leg.

"Anyone got a water bottle?"

Dina handed him one.

Carefully, Drake washed Jimmy's leg. A big gash smiled at Drake, a few centimeters under Jimmy's knee cap. Drake cleaned it a bit more before leaning back.

"You'll be fine. It's just a big cut."

"You sure? It hurts like hell, ya know."

Drake nodded. "Stand up and put some pressure on it."

Jimmy groaned loudly and grabbed onto Ziggy to pull himself up. She tried to shake him off, but he held on and got himself up. Pulling excruciating faces, he wobbled around and tested out the leg.

"I dunno, Drake. Feels broken to me, ya know," he said as he walked around in a circle.

Drake bit his tongue.

"Just try your best, buddy."

"I'll try. For the lieutenant."

Dina shook her head. "You two done?" She started for the next corner of the building.

Drake took a shallow breath, which didn't hurt too badly, and followed. Jimmy hobbled behind.

Dina lifted a hand, and everyone stopped. She peeked around the corner and came back to face them.

"As I expected. The loading bays. Two cameras and one guard. Ziggy and I will move first. Ziggy, cameras. I'll take care of the guard. You two stay close, but don't get in the way. Clear?"

Everyone nodded.

Dina stayed in a crouching position and moved forward. Ziggy followed, gun ready. In unison, they both fired short bursts, only Dina's was much louder, not having a suppressor attached. Drake pulled Jimmy along, and they followed. As they passed the security guard, Drake noticed he wasn't bleeding.

A small set of stairs led to a door, which Ziggy had already breached. Dina stood outside, covering Drake and Jimmy. They hustled inside. They were in.

| fourteen |

Once they entered the back entrance of the hospital, they moved in silence and encountered no more security, not even a hospital worker. They moved quickly, still hunched, and came to another door. Dina nodded, and Ziggy breached it.

That's when the noise made Drake jump.

It was Ziggy's suppressed pulse rifle that broke the silence. The absence of any other noise made it seem louder than it was. It took Drake a second to find the reason for the shooting: a security camera mounted high on a wall. Smoke poured out of it and it hung limply.

Doors lined the hallway, but it was clear their target was the elevator at the end of the line. Dina and Ziggy made their way forward. Drake and Jimmy followed, mimicking their movements.

At the end of the hallway, Dina held her hand up again. They all stopped, and Drake braced himself against the wall. His breathing was still shallow but getting better. The graphene sleeve was doing its job well, but pulling Dina up and over the wall had aggravated the injury again and made breathing and moving very difficult. He tried his best to hide it.

"Okay, we're using the elevator to reach the floor where they keep detainees. The doors to the fire escape stairs will most likely be locked and only open in an emergency. So, if the elevator doors open on any other floor, we'll have to improvise, which means shooting. If that happens, all bets are off, and we're shooting our way to your friend. Questions?"

"Yes! So many. That's a shit plan, Dina. We can't be shooting our way up the building."

Dina looked Drake over.

"You have any better ideas?"

"I can hack the elevator's DDU, ya know, and prevent it from opening."

Everyone turned to Jimmy.

"It'll be easy."

Dina nodded. Jimmy shuffled past everyone and popped the DDU next to the elevator doors. Drake couldn't see what Jimmy was doing, but even if he could, he wouldn't understand it. The elevator doors slid open, and Jimmy jumped in. Drake followed and saw he was doing the same to the internal DDU. Dina and Ziggy stood outside, guarding the perimeter.

"Good to go!"

Dina and Ziggy got into the elevator.

"Just punch in the floor number, and it will take us there, ya know, uninterrupted."

Dina did, and the elevator made its way up. Shortly after it began, it stopped, and the doors slid open.

Dina and Ziggy stayed put and observed the area over the barrels of their guns. Another long hall, with multiple doors. Halfway down the hall was a break in the wall, and some sort of activity. Dina lifted her arm and brought the schematic of the hospital up on her HIC.

"Down the hall, on the left, is the nurses' station. It will be occupied, and we'll have to restrain whoever we see there. Then four doors down, on the right, will be room S5B. That's our target. The extraction route will be the same as the entry one. Questions?"

Drake's heart was beating against the graphene sleeve. Lily was only a few meters away now. He'd left her for dead, thinking he would never see her again. And now he was about to. He figured she would not share his enthusiasm for their reunion, but they could talk later. Right now, it was about getting out of here. And out of Shangcorp.

"Move out!"

Staying hunched over, hoods still in place, they shuffled forward. Whenever someone walked by, Dina held her hand up, and they froze. Soon they were upon the nurses' station. Everyone seemed busy with their work. No one noticed the four armed people squatting down a few meters away.

Then a door slid open across from the hall and a nurse walked out, looking straight at them.

She froze, her brain unable to process the scene.

Ziggy did not. Her brain was firing and wired for these situations.

The suppressed crackle superseded a thump as the nurse fell to the ground. Another nurse saw the commotion and came over to investigate.

Ziggy swiftly sent another burst of pulse cartridges down the hall. The second nurse fell, almost on top of the other one. This time, four more nurses showed up.

Ziggy and Dina fired, sending two more nurses to the floor, but the other ones ducked out of the way just in time. Not being suppressed, Dina's rifle made much more noise, attracting people from both ends of the hall. Doors slid open and inquisitive heads popped out. One nurse made it back to the station and pressed the alarm. A loud, deep buzzing sound penetrated their ears and red flashing lights filled the hallway.

"Let's move! Only engage if you see weapons."

No need to crouch anymore. Everyone ran full steam ahead to room S5B.

They were meters away from Lily.

An enormous block of a human stepped in front of them, blocking their path. He had no weapons on him, but he was intimidating nonetheless. He wore a nurse's uniform but would have looked more at home in dirty miner's overalls.

Everyone came to a grinding halt just short of the mass of flesh blocking their progress.

Dina lifted her pulse rifle to meet his gaze.

"Move it, Big Boy."

Big Boy shook his head.

"Have it your way," Dina said, and slipped her finger onto the trigger.

Faster than logic would allow, Big Boy grabbed the rifle and threw it over his shoulder. With his other arm, he grabbed Dina by the elbow. He lifted her clear of the ground and smirked. As he balled his free hand into a fist, red spray covered his face. He held onto Dina for another moment before they both dropped to the floor. Dina held her arm where he'd gripped her. Big Boy held the stump where his arm used to be attached to his body. Drake turned to see Ziggy still aiming at the big man.

"Damn!" Jimmy yelled out.

Big Boy sat up and shuffled back until he sat against the wall, defeated and out of their way.

Ziggy helped Dina up as she went past her. "Drake, get her Artie," Ziggy yelled.

Drake ran and retrieved the rifle and handed it back to Dina.

He wanted to ask Ziggy if she had switched her rifle back to stun, but the look on her face stopped him. Instead, he fell in line and followed them to the door of room S5B.

All the doors had shut when the alarms went off, and it was up to Jimmy to get them in. He made his way to the front and worked his magic on the DDU.

The door that held Lt. Wells captive slid open.

* * *

Four beds, two on each side, filled the room. Above each bed, a DDU displayed different numbers and data. Each bed had a person in it, and each person had a cuff around their arm attaching them to the bed. They were in the right room, except—

"It's all dudes, ya know?"

Drake walked over to each one to make sure, but none of them looked remotely like Lt. Wells.

He turned to Dina.

"It must be the wrong room."

"According to my source, they only have one room set up for detainees."

Drake scanned the room again, confirming he hadn't overlooked something.

"It's the wrong room."

"Drake, it's not. Maybe they transferred her?"

The alarm was still vibrating his chest, and he knew they were in a race with time. The security officers would be here at any moment.

Drake pushed past Ziggy and Dina and went back into the hall.

"Drake!"

He turned left and walked up to the big nurse, who was still holding onto his stump.

"Where is she?"

Big Boy looked confused. "Who?"

"The woman that you were holding in that room! She had a chest wound."

Big Boy looked less confused. "The Jane Doe?"

"I guess."

A look of defiance washed over Big Boy's face. "Good luck with that. No way I'm helping you *waiguoren.*"

The noise of the alarm and the flashing red lights made everything tense and surreal. Drake looked at the nurse's injury and kicked it as hard as he could. The man screamed in pain.

Drake raised his scatter-gun to the man's face. "Last chance, stubby. Where is she?"

All the fight had left him. He shook his head, mouth in a twisted snarl. "She left."

Drake felt the urge to kick him again.

"Did you find her?" Jimmy yelled.

Drake turned his head and saw Jimmy, Dina, and Ziggy next to him. He shook his head.

Drake turned his scatter-gun sideways so the nurse could see what he was doing, and flipped the selector over to full power. He pointed it at the remaining arm. "Where is she?"

The man swallowed hard. "She left. With another woman. Yesterday. I'm sorry. Please don't shoot me."

"Drake, if she's not here, we need to go," Dina said.

"I'm not leaving without her!"

Dina looked at Ziggy and shrugged. "Suit yourself. We've done what we could." Dina and Ziggy made for the elevator. Drake watched them get in and disappear as the doors slid shut.

"Drake! What now?" Jimmy yelled over the noise.

Drake recalled passing the nurses' station and seeing a wall of DDUs lining the one wall. They would have a recording of every movement of every patient in every room. If Lily had left, they would have a recording of it.

Drake grabbed Jimmy by the arm and dragged him over to them. On them, every room, every hall, every corner of this floor of the hospital appeared.

"I'm on it!" Jimmy said, not needing to be told what to do.

All the nurses had fled by now, except the few unconscious nurses and the big man.

"Can you see if you can do something about—"

The alarms stopped, but the lights still flashed.

"Pretty annoying, ya know." Jimmy kept working away on the DDU in front of him.

The silence felt tangible after the constant droning of the alarm.

"There!"

On the DDUs mounted on the wall, Drake saw Lily Wells lying in her bed. His heart skipped a beat. Jimmy had the playback on four times the normal speed, and everything moved with an erratic motion. Lily rolled around, and it looked glitchy and broken. She sat up, and so did the person next to her. They appeared to talk to each other, and the other person got out of bed. She walked over to Lily and handed her something. She then did something, and Lily's arm disconnected from the bed. Lily got up, and they both made for the door. Drake couldn't make out what they did, but the next camera angle, from outside the room, showed the door of S5B opening and closing.

"Where are they?" Drake yelled. "What happened?"

Jimmy smiled. "They put blankets on. Look." He walked over to the DDU that showed the door of S5B. "See here? It's a bit fuzzy. Pixelated. That's them."

Drake didn't bother to ask what blankets were. Instead, he focused on the fuzzy part of the DDU. It was impossible to follow it from one screen to another, so he watched the DDU that showed the elevator. Nothing happened. He kept looking at it, focusing, making sure not to look away for even a second. Then the doors slid open, and he saw a faint blur of motion before they shut again.

"Follow the elevator!"

Jimmy worked the DDU in front of him, and multiple images of the elevator appeared, each from a different floor. The last image, showing the floor where they'd entered with Dina, showed the doors open. Drake moved closer, but couldn't be sure if he saw a blurry motion this time. Without telling Jimmy, the cameras changed to show all the angles available on that floor. Drake kept an eye on the door to the loading dock. The same door they'd used to get in. The door opened, and a man appeared. Suddenly, two figures appeared next to him. One was Lily. They spoke to the man and then stepped outside.

Another camera showed all three of them get into a hydro van and leave.

Lily was gone, again.

| fifteen |

"Lily. Lily, wake up."

Her eyelids felt almost too heavy to open. Wells had to talk herself into not giving up and opening them up. It felt like someone was pulling them down harder than she could push them open. She wanted to give up, but the voice kept urging her.

Finally, she forced them open and, after taking a second for them to focus, saw Aranya standing over her.

Aranya smiled kindly. "I've never seen anyone sleep so deeply. I have been trying to wake you up for hours."

Wells needed a moment. She recognized Aranya, but everything else felt foreign to her. She tried to sit up, but a pain in her chest forced her back.

"I can see you're confused," Aranya said. "They gave you a heavy dose of sedatives that knocked you out. You've been asleep for almost a day."

Wells relaxed her body and let her mind wander. She took a deep breath, letting the process happen naturally. Slowly, it did. Memories became clear. Sammy Sanders, standing in front of her, then the road close to her face. Another memory of her arm being attached to the bed. Then one with Aranya in it. One where Aranya stole something. Nurses pinning her to the ground. She stole something they needed. Something that belonged to her. But not hers. Something old.

"The HIC!" Lily blurted out.

Aranya looked around and lifted a corner of her shirt. "Yes, the HIC. I have it, Lily."

Wells looked at the old tech with the leathery skin framing its edges. "We need to charge it."

A look of accomplishment shone on Aranya's face. "You were asleep for so long that I had enough time to figure it out and get it charged."

"You are quite resourceful, aren't you?"

"I have also contacted someone who can help us with the EMP blankets."

All their planning and conversations came back to Wells. "And? Can they get them?"

"Yes. One of my fellow Believers replied. He knows some like-minded people who work in the hospital. They'll contact us soon."

"Believers?"

"Yes, we call ourselves Believers. People who believe we can have a better life. People who believe in a better future. Those of us who believe we can overthrow Shangcorp."

Wells looked at the skinny, frail woman standing next to her bed. She looked like the wind could blow her away and carry her off to a faraway place. But her eyes had a passion and determination that would make the wind stop blowing and wait for her command. There was a fire within her that attracted Wells.

"Do you know who they are? Or when we'll get the blankets?"

Aranya shook her head.

"No, sorry Lily. We'll have to wait it out."

A nurse walked in. Aranya slid the old piece of tech underneath Wells's sheets as the nurse approached.

"Ready for your exercise? Seems your friend has decided to join us again. Feeling better?"

"Yes. Much better. Sorry for my breakdown before. I—"

The nurse waved her off. "No need for that. We're all out here trying our best. You ready, dear?"

Wells looked on as the nurse led Aranya through the door and disappeared.

Reaching down, she pulled the antiquated HIC out from under the blankets.

She swiped the screen to activate it. Unlike her Penta-issued HIC, it took its sweet time to run the necessary background code to fire up the home screen. When it finally did, she swiped to see her messages.

She held her breath for the two seconds it took to display an empty screen.

The breath escaped her lungs.

No one knew of this HIC, and realistically, no one would try to reach her on it.

But hope dies last.

She switched it off to preserve its power and hid it under the covers again.

The pain in her chest had subsided, but there was still a weight bearing down on it. They had made contact, and it seemed they might get the EMP blankets they needed to escape, but then what?

The weight became slightly heavier.

She was still stuck in a Shangcorp territory who knew how far away from the border. Escaping from the hospital was crucial, but it was only the first step in a thousand-mile journey. She had no contacts, no weapons, and no credits. She was putting all her faith—all her trust—in someone she hardly knew. Someone who most likely had their own agenda. If she reached out to Penta, they would have to denounce her. Shangcorp and Penta were about to enter the first war in decades. Any security personnel found within the other side's borders would be considered a spy. If she reached out to Penta, she would cause more problems than she solved, and paint an even bigger target on her back.

She had only one person to rely on: herself.

The weight pressing down on her chest became a little lighter.

Footsteps announced Aranya's return. The nurse left her at the door, as she had no electromagnetic cuff that needed activating. She posed no threat to anyone. But Wells knew better.

Aranya sat on her bed, feet dangling off the side, and straightened her clothes. She kept her head down and talked to herself, making sure all the camera footage would show her as docile as ever.

"They've made contact."

* * *

Aranya told Wells how a nurse twice the size of a normal man had relieved the nurse who usually fetched her for her walk. He'd told the old nurse that she was needed elsewhere and took over, taking Aranya on her walk. As soon as they were alone, he'd told her he was part of the resistance, or as Aranya called them, a Believer, and he was here to help. She told him what they needed, and he told her he could easily find some EMP blankets. He told her he could also organize for transport away from the hospital. He asked for nothing in return, calling her an inspiration. Aranya blushed when she related that part.

"Did he say when?" Lily asked.

"No, but he sounded very confident, and I think it will be sooner than we might expect. We should ready ourselves to go at any moment."

Wells nodded.

"Oh, I almost forgot," Aranya said. "He also gave me the code to unlock your cuff."

The weight on Wells's chest had now almost completely disappeared. Having the EMP blankets, a way to remove the cuff, and transport out of here meant they had everything they needed.

Now all they had to do was wait.

* * *

The nurses did their last rounds of the night, making sure everyone was ready for a night's rest. Wells and Aranya were already in bed when the nurse came into the room to check on their DDUs and Wells's cuff. The moment the nurse entered, Wells saw it was their contact. The man reminded her of all the ex-moon miners she had dealt with lately. He was almost as tall and as wide as the door itself. He walked over to Aranya and discreetly dropped something on her bed. He did all his checks and came over to Wells.

"I wish you all the best," he whispered, as he went through his duties.

Wells gave him a small smile and a nod.

He finished up and left the room. Five minutes later, all the lights in the hospital dimmed.

Wells waited another ten minutes before she whispered to Aranya, "Are those the blankets?"

"Yes. The driver is also awaiting at the loading dock. He gave me instructions on how to get there."

Aranya sat up and went over to Wells. If a nurse watched the wall of DDU's right at that moment, they would see Aranya removing Wells's cuff and giving her the EMP blanket. Having no other choice, they worked as quickly as they could. The moment Wells was free, they made for the door and switched the EMP blankets on.

"Okay. We need to move down the hall, take the elevator down, and then it should be almost a straight run to the loading bay."

Wells nodded. She was used to being the one coming up with the plans and executing them. She was usually the one leading, and everyone else nodding and listening. But she was a seasoned security officer and knew when to listen and use assets to her advantage. Aranya knew this city, had contacts here, and seemed to be a respected leader. Wells knew she would do best following her orders until they were safe.

"Ready to go," Wells said.

Moving as quickly as they could without making a sound, they made for the elevator. Wells waited for Aranya to operate the DDU next to it and kept an eye out for any nurse coming their way. Luckily, no one did, and they entered the elevator. A short ride later, they walked out and followed a narrow walkway, and approached a corner.

Wells stopped and peered around it. At the end of the next corridor, she saw an exit. A man stood next to the door.

"Hold on." She grabbed Aranya's arm. "Is that the driver?"

Aranya squeezed in next to Wells and peeked around the corner.

"I don't know. He fits the description, but to be honest, the description was vague. We have a code word, but if we're wrong, he could sound the alarm."

Their EMP blankets were only good for hiding digitally, and the man would see them clear as day as they walked up to him. They had one shot at this. Wells sized him up. She could take him out one on one easily. She based this not on arrogance but training and experience. She readied herself for what lay ahead and took a deep breath.

A slight pain reminded her of the wound in her chest.

Her confidence eroded.

"If he is not our guy, we'll have to subdue him, Aranya. Usually I would relish the opportunity, but"—she tapped her chest gently—"I'm going to need your help if it comes down to it. Concentrate on anything soft: belly, groin, eyes. Poke, hit, bite— do whatever. Okay?"

Aranya nodded. Her eyes restored Wells's confidence.

They rounded the corner and walked straight toward the man.

With fifteen meters to go, he held up a hand, signaling for them to stop. Wells held her breath.

"The dragon shall rise."

"And so shall we."

Aranya walked up to him, and Wells followed.

"I am honored to help, Aranya. My brother worked with you at the plant," the man said, and bowed his head.

"You look like him. I remember him well."

"This way." He ushered them through the door.

A hydro van sat waiting for them.

"Aranya . . ." Wells grabbed her arm again. "You sure about this?"

The faint buzzing of a drone broke the silence of the night. Wells knew it could be a patrolling drone, or one deployed to look for them. She didn't want to find out, and shoved Aranya into the van. The door slid closed, and the driver took off. Within a few turns, they were driving around the streets of Lan-noi.

"I think so," Aranya finally answered her.

| sixteen |

The standoff with Shangcorp kept everyone busy, even lazy corrupt officials like Captain Eugene Davis. Not only did he have to make sure he did his job at Penta Security to the bare minimum standard, but he also had to make sure not to let any new opportunities in Shangcorp slip through his fingers. War was a very lucrative time for people in charge. He had to make sure he knew of all the dealings being made by his peers and try to stay one step ahead. He had no preference as to who should win the war, but he had to position himself to ensure he aligned himself with the winner.

Then there was the Lt. Wells side project. It had been days since he'd heard anything new from his asset in Lan-noi, but with everything on his plate, it suited him. The chances of her making it out alive were slim, and having someone monitoring her made the odds even better. She was as good as gone already.

All he needed was the confirmation.

* * *

Jimmy had never seen Drake so defeated. They had been through some trying times lately, but this was one setback too many. Drake sat on the ground, legs spread out, back hunched, his arms hanging limp in his lap.

Jimmy had to drag him out of the hospital. All Drake wanted to do was go room to room searching for the lieutenant. Jimmy had to restrain him and had tried his best to talk sense into him. Drones buzzed outside the windows, and soon security would show up. Finally, Jimmy got through to him and Drake agreed to leave.

They'd run a few hundred meters from the hospital and collapsed to the ground.

That was almost an hour ago.

Jimmy constantly scanned the area with his ARP and listened for any sirens or drones, but no one was in pursuit.

"Drake . . ."

In the distance sirens blared, but they kept their distance.

"Drake, we need to—"

The plan had been to rescue Lt. Wells, and then escape Shangcorp. Looking back on the plan, it lacked a lot of detail. They'd handed the rescue operation over to Dina, who promptly left once they learned Lily wasn't there. For her and Ziggy, it was purely business. Drake was so focused on getting the lieutenant out that he'd never even discussed the second half of the plan— maybe the most important part: getting out of Shangcorp. All they had were a handful of credits, a makeshift house, and—

Jimmy looked at the Artie in his hands. He had been holding onto it for so long that he had forgotten about it. Drake still had his scatter-gun too, lying across his thigh. It gave Jimmy hope. They had something. They weren't completely at zero. The weapons would still have plenty of ammunition in them, as

Dina and Ziggy had done most, if not all the shooting. They had something.

"Drake, partner, it's time we go."

The slumped figure didn't move. "I feel so useless, Jimmy."

Jimmy squatted down next to Drake. "You tried, Drake. I know it sounds, I don't know, patronizing or something, but you tried. It's not like you knew she was there and just waited for her to be released, ya know? You tried."

The silhouette remained the same.

"When I left home, I knew I would starve and probably die, ya know, if I didn't join a gang. So I tried. I was the smallest and youngest kid in the sector, and nobody wanted me, ya know? They would throw rocks at me, or pin me down and beat me, and tell me to leave them alone. Day after day, I would try, and every time I would fail. One time they broke my arm. I was always hungry and cold. I slept under hydros in the winter, so I wouldn't freeze to death. But I never stopped. And one day, I found a group who accepted me, ya know. Sure, they used me to steal and get into places no one else could . . . But I never gave up, Drake."

Drake pulled his legs up, placing his arms on top of them, and lifted his head.

"I'm not good at this, Drake. I'm just trying to make you feel better, ya know?"

"I left her to die, Jimmy. And now . . ." He dropped his head again. "I couldn't even save her."

"For what it's worth, I don't think the lieutenant is the saving type, ya know?"

Drake chuckled softly. "No. I guess not."

Jimmy's own mood lifted, seeing Drake's smile. "We've got this, partner. We'll just keep trying, ya know? We'll find her."

Jimmy knew they would. People had chased them and hunted them before. They'd crossed an ocean and traveled across the globe to find someone. And they always made it through.

"We'll find her."

* * *

He couldn't believe they'd missed her by a day. After waiting months, it had come down to hours. He did not know what the next step was. Jimmy kept looking at him, waiting for direction. But he had none to give. She could've boarded a hyperloop or be in a housing unit twenty meters away. There was no way of knowing. He tried sending her messages through his HIC, but they didn't go through.

"We'll find her." Jimmy, forever the optimist, always believing things will work out for the best.

Drake looked at Jimmy's arm, imagining him walking around with it broken but still trying to get into a group. Still trying to survive. He needed to be more like Jimmy.

Drake cleared his throat. "You're right, buddy. We need to get out of here and regroup. I assume Dina and Ziggy are long gone, so no point in trying to contact them. I just need a second to figure this out." He ran his hands through his hair.

"It's a shame we can't ask that big guy at the hospital, ya know? Sounded like he knew who she was."

He had. Thinking about their interaction, Drake recalled him being almost protective about sharing the information he had.

His arm had been shot off, but still he refused to give up the information about her. Until Drake kicked him, that is.

"Jimmy, I think you might be onto something," Drake said. "Maybe we should go back and talk to him."

"Um, you know, I was just talking, right? It would be suicide to go back in there now, ya know. The place will be crawling with security."

Jimmy was right again. Although they hadn't killed anyone, they'd immobilized quite a few people and injured the big nurse. The hospital might even be in a complete shutdown by now. Still, the only lead they had was in the hospital.

"Besides," Jimmy continued, "why would he even speak to us after what Ziggy did to his arm?"

He had a point.

"Maybe he won't, but the fact that he was almost protecting the information about her leaving—it feels like there might be a bond or some connection between them. Maybe if we talk to him . . ."

He knew he was being optimistic, maybe naive, but he had a feeling Jimmy was right. The nurse was the person to talk to. "We're going back to the hospital, Jimmy."

Jimmy stood up and dusted off his pants. "Okay then."

* * *

The first hurdle they needed to clear was their newly acquired weapons. Although the guns could be extremely useful, they could also prevent them from entering the hospital. By now, if the hospital was not in lockdown, it would surely be on high alert. The cameras would run every scan and algorithm to spot any potential threat. If an odd shape or a bulge under a jacket was detected, all hell would break loose. The safest bet would be to stash the weapons outside, but still close by. If the nurse had some personal connection to Lt. Wells, they would have no need for the weapons. If Drake was wrong, they would be in a world of trouble.

They were only a few hundred meters away from the hospital, but it felt like kilometers.

The moment they set off back to the hospital, an Automated Security Vehicle drove by. They both dove into some bushes and watched as it made its way past them. Depending on its equipment and its search parameters, the ASV could easily spot them, even hiding in the bushes. But luckily for them, it kept on driving.

"Think it saw us?"

"I don't know, Jimmy. Hard to say, but I reckon it would have stopped if it did. No guarantee, though."

"Keep going, then?"

"Keep going."

Back on the road, they hid the weapons under their jackets as best they could and walked on the shoulder. A few hydros passed them, and there seemed to be a calmer feeling in the air.

"You've noticed things seem calmer?"

Jimmy swiveled his head and looked around. "I guess. I mean, it's been a while since I've seen any hydros going at breakneck speeds, ya know?"

Drake pushed the thought to the back of his mind. It didn't matter right now if things were quieting down in Lan-noi. All that mattered was getting to the nurse and getting information on Lt. Wells.

The hospital loomed over them as they approached, and Drake pulled Jimmy back. "We need to get rid of these."

Jimmy nodded and pointed out a thick shrub growing close to a building. "No one would see the guns behind that, ya know?"

Drake agreed. Watching out for any ASVs or cameras, they pushed their weapons in behind the bush. Drake stepped back and inspected it to make sure nothing stuck out. "Looks good. Let's go."

The building with the shrub holding their weapons was only two buildings away from the hospital. As they passed the second last building, Drake crouched down, and Jimmy copied him. This was the same side they'd used to get in and out with Ziggy and Dina. The back door was closed but seemed unmanned. The camera above it still hung limply by its wires. Unless a drone or an ASV patrolled the area, no one could see them enter the building.

As Drake moved forward toward the building, Jimmy tugged at his jacket. He turned around to see Jimmy pointing at something overhead. A drone was hovering high up, observing the area surrounding the hospital's back entrance. It sat high enough in the air that no one on the ground could hear the buzz of its rotors.

"How did you know?"

"No way they would leave that door vulnerable, ya know? I just looked around, and there it was."

"Now what? Shoot it down?"

Jimmy shook his head.

"They would watch the live feed, ya know. If it goes down, they'll know something is up and send a squad."

Drake could see Jimmy was planning something and waited it out.

"What if . . . Yup. That's it. Okay, I got it," Jimmy said. "Here's the plan."

* * *

Drake hated the plan, but had failed to come up with a better one. Squeezing himself in behind the same bush that held their weapons, he watched Jimmy scour the ground for ammunition. A few more steps and he would be in the drone's visible range. Jimmy kept moving forward, hunched over, picking things up from the ground. As he entered the drone's line of sight, Drake saw the drone slightly readjust its position. Not much, but just a fraction to secure the perfect viewing angle.

Having entered the target zone, Jimmy stood up and threw the first rock. It missed the drone by three meters. Drake's hopes of this plan succeeding faded quickly. Jimmy loaded up and threw another one. Another miss, but closer. The drone took no notice and held position. Jimmy reloaded and fired. A hit. The rock was too small to cause any significant damage, but then, that was never the plan. The drone repositioned itself and moved a few meters away. Jimmy followed it and threw a few more rocks until he connected again. This time, the drone did what they had hoped it would do.

Most autonomous machinery and robotics had a self-preservation AI module that ensured it would try everything in its protocols to avoid destruction. Everything except hurt a human or destroy another autonomous unit—a caveat Penta and Shangcorp tended to forget when designing security equipment for themselves.

The drone steadied itself, and having identified Jimmy as a threat, set off in pursuit of him. Jimmy had reassured Drake that the drone had no visible weapons, and watching it chase Jimmy, he hoped Jimmy was correct. Jimmy turned around, threw a few more rocks to keep its attention, and set off running again. Drake knew he'd be swearing with every step he took, running.

It was time for Drake to move too. Sliding out from behind the bush, he kept low to the ground, and moved as quick as he could toward the rear door of the hospital. Staying in the shadows, he scanned with his ARP continuously to monitor for any new drone activity. It seemed that Lan-noi security could only spare one drone for the back door, as Drake reached it with no more interference. Recalling Jimmy's instructions, Drake entered the codes into the DDU next to the door. A red screen denied him entry.

"No, no, no, no, no," Drake mumbled.

He closed his eyes and recited Jimmy's instructions.

He tried again. This time, a green screen allowed him to enter the building. Switching his ARP over to call Jimmy, he saw the three white dots dance in front of him in the darkness of the hospital basement. They kept bouncing around, not connecting.

"C'mon, Jimmy. Pick up." Drake hoped it was running from a drone that prevented his friend from answering, and not something more serious.

The dots kept dancing.

Drake gave up and made his way down the long hall.

| seventeen |

The alarms and red lights were no longer activated, and normality had returned to the hospital. People were still sick, and operations had to be performed. War may be coming and a group of people may have stormed in and shot up the place, but a hospital waited for no one. It had to go on.

The elevator door opened, and Drake walked out, heading toward a nurses' station similar to the one they'd ambushed earlier that night. Only this one was two stories down. Although he'd worn the electromagnetic mask earlier, and his face would be unrecognizable on all the captured footage, he saw no point in taking extra risks. Someone might recall a characteristic or even his voice. He assumed that the nurses on different floors would not have been exchanging details about the crazy people ambushing the hospital, only generalizations and exaggerations. Still, he thought it best to not go to the same floor again.

Walking up to the nurses' station, Drake saw two Lan-noi security personnel standing around. They turned their focus toward him as he approached them, and he willed himself to stay calm and act natural.

"Hey, guys," he said as he got closer to them.

They ignored him.

Drake felt a drop of sweat run down his temple.

Both sets of eyes stayed glued to him.

"Can I help you, sir?"

Drake turned toward the voice. It came from a rotund nurse standing behind the counter. She looked annoyed and tired.

"I sure hope you can." Drake flashed every tooth he had.

She replied with a steady, disgruntled look.

"A friend of mine, well, really the son of a friend of my parents, works here and got injured tonight. I was in the area, so they asked me to pop in and see if he was okay."

"Name?"

The security guards lost interest in the babbling idiot looking for a friend of a friend and turned their attention away from Drake. He leaned in toward the nurse and spoke as softly as he dared.

"Benjamin Drake."

The cranky nurse typed it into the DDU in front of them.

"We have no Benjamin Drake listed, sir."

Idiot. Not only had he just put his name in the Shangcorp database, but he now had to give her a name he didn't have.

"Oh, sorry, that's my name." Drake shook his head in exaggerated embarrassment. "Like I said, it's the son of a friend of my parents. I've only met the guy once, and I'm horrible with names."

The nurse looked even more annoyed.

"My parents just want to know if he's okay, that's all. So that they can tell his parents. He's such a big boy, I'm sure he's fine, but you know how parents worry." Drake hoped the little detail about him being a big boy might soften her will.

"I'm sorry to have wasted your time. I'll just tell them to contact the hospital themselves. They have so much to worry about at the moment. I just thought I could help them out a bit. Thank you anyway." Drake smiled and slowly turned around.

The nurse called his bluff and didn't call him back. He walked as slowly as he could, hoping she would change her mind, but knew he'd look suspicious if he kept it up. He fought the urge to turn around and kept his eyes forward. Step by step, he neared the elevator and decreased the chance of getting to the big guy. He reached for the DDU next to the elevator door and felt a hand on his shoulder.

"Come with me, sir."

Drake turned to face one of the security officers he'd seen at the nurses' station. They were of equal build to Drake, and he knew fighting them would be futile. Although out of sight, he knew their partner would come running if anything out of the ordinary happened. He'd have to obey their orders until an opportunity presented itself.

"Okay."

The officer stepped aside, allowing for Drake to take the lead. Drake noticed they hadn't unholstered their pulse pistol yet as he walked past them.

"Where are we going?"

"Just keep going straight."

Drake did as he was told and kept walking. They passed the nurse's station and Drake noticed the nurse wasn't there anymore. He kept walking.

"Turn here."

He did, following the hall around a corner into a similar hallway with doors on either side.

After a few steps, the guard stopped. "In here."

The door had a number on it, but no description. Drake wondered if it was a soundproof room, used for things that could make lots of noise but shouldn't be heard.

The door slid open, and Drake felt the guard urging him in.

It was not a soundproof kill room, as he'd feared, but a normal hospital room, with four beds, two on each side, with DDUs mounted above them. Identical to the room he thought he would find Lily in.

Only one bed had a patient in it. A large patient, missing an arm.

Big Boy looked at Drake with confusion. The last time he saw Drake, he'd had the thin black face blocker on. Although it was see-through, it would still have masked his face to a degree. Drake knew he had only seconds before Big Boy would match his voice to the vaguely familiar face.

"I'm so glad you're okay!" Drake said loudly, confusing him for a second. Drake walked over, leaving the guard at the door. Big Boy shot the guard a confused look, but Drake blocked him with his body.

"I need your help," Drake whispered as urgently as he could. "Your mom and dad will be so happy to hear you are okay."

Big Boy was at a complete loss. Drake had to strike quickly, while he had the upper hand.

Whispering again, he continued. "My friend that escaped. I think you have some connection with her, and I need your help. Please."

The room went silent, and he could hear Big Boy's labored breathing. Some other sounds become prominent too, sounds made by the DDUs and some electrotonic buzzing, most likely from the overhead lights. The security guard's boots squeak as they shifted their weight around nervously.

"Do you know this man?" they asked.

All the noises disappeared, replaced by the rhythmic thumping of Drake's heart.

Drake kept eye contact with Big Boy. "Please."

The guard's boot squeaked again as they took a step forward.

"Yes. I know him. We've met before. Thanks, Jinn."

Drake turned to face Jinn and gave them his best *see-I-told-you-so-now-buzz-off* look.

Jinn huffed and left, shaking their head.

"Thank—"

"Don't. You have one minute before I call Jinn back in." Drake almost laughed as Big Boy had to use his nose to swipe his HIC and activate it, ready to call for help.

"Sorry about the arm. I'm sure the bionic replacement will be great."

Big Boy pushed his nose closer to his HIC. Drake swallowed hard in an effort not to laugh.

"The woman that escaped is a dear friend of mine. Her name is Lily Wells. Like me, she is from a Penta territory. We need to get out of here as soon as possible. We got separated a few months ago, and I've been looking for her ever since. I'm so sorry for the way we handled ourselves earlier, but we're desperate. Please, can you tell me where she went?"

"You sound sincere, but the person I helped was not your friend. I'm sorry, but I can't betray their confidentiality."

Drake racked his brain, trying to figure out a rebuttal.

"Besides," Big Boy continued, "I don't trust those two Slavor friends of yours."

"They're not friends. I paid them to get me into the hospital. They left once they'd done their part."

The feeling of failure and hopelessness came back, crushing down on Drake. His legs felt weak, and he flopped down in a chair. Hands once more in his hair, he tried calling Jimmy again. The dots appeared, but they never merged.

"It really fucking hurt when you kicked me, man. It was so unnecessary."

Drake dismissed the call and looked up. "Yeah, that was not my best moment. Sorry, buddy. I just felt so frustrated knowing she was here, but that we'd missed her. But, yeah, you're right. It was a dick move. Sorry."

"It was a dick move."

The weight still pressed down on him, but he knew he had to get out of there and start making new plans to find Lily.

Big Boy studied his severed arm. "A bionic arm does sound pretty sweet, actually."

"If my friend was here, he would tell you to look on the bright side of all this. I'm sure you'll love the new arm." Drake stood up, ready to leave. "Sorry again."

"Do you know anything about the Believers?"

Drake had heard vague mentions of them at the work site. He had never been a very religious person, but he also knew that no one had a clue what happened when we died, so he tried to keep an open mind. "Not much," he said. "Why? Are you one?"

He wasn't sure how listening to the ideology of a cult was going to help, but he had limited options.

Big Boy looked around, confirming no one had materialized in the room, and beckoned Drake to come closer.

"I am a Believer. So was the person helping your friend," Big Boy whispered.

Things were getting worse by the minute. Not only had he missed an opportunity to rescue Lt. Wells, but now it appeared a cult had kidnapped her.

"So, how does one join the Believers?"

Big Boy shook his head in confusion. "Why? You're not even from here."

Drake felt slightly offended. "Doesn't sound like a very inclusive religion, if you ask me."

"Religion? You really aren't from here," Big Boy shook his head. "It's a resistance group. A group who believes we will be better if we can overthrow Shangcorp and change the system." Drake had to lean in as Big Boy lowered his voice even more. "It's not the name of the resistance, but everyone calls us the Believers."

Drake felt an enormous amount of relief, knowing Lily was not involved in a cult. "Okay, so you're saying Lily and her friend escaped here with help from the resistance and that you are also part of it? A Believer?"

"Keep your voice down," Big Boy snapped at Drake. "Yes, that's what I'm saying. That's why I couldn't tell you who she left with, as you could be a spy."

Drake appreciated that he thought he was clever enough to be a spy. "I can assure you, I am not a spy." He laughed.

"That's pretty obvious."

Drake didn't care too much for Big Boy's new tone. "Okay, so I'm not a spy, and have no intention of derailing your grand plans. But what I want is to find my friend. Is there anything you can tell me?"

"Not really, sorry. We have small cells that work independently. It's not very organized, to be honest. But Aranya is trying to change that. She is the one who will unite us."

"Okay, but who is Aranya?"

Big Boy beamed. "The one who helped your friend."

At last they were getting somewhere.

Three dots appeared on Big Boy's face. They danced before merging and replacing his face with another.

"Drake," Jimmy yelled breathlessly, "you need to get the hell out of there!"

| eighteen |

The taste of blood filled his mouth, and his throat felt raw. His lungs barely held any oxygen before expelling it all again. Luckily, he couldn't feel his legs anymore, but his feet were throbbing.

Jimmy sat down, exhausted. He tried to listen out for the drone, but his pounding heart and heavy breathing made it difficult. He switched on his ARP to help him out. Head bobbing and body shaking, he did his best to scan the area. No drones showed up. He'd figured as much as the last stone took out a rotor, and he assumed it would autopilot back to base. To be safe, he backtracked to make sure that if a replacement drone showed up, it would go the wrong way.

He knew it had been his plan to distract the drone, but he regretted ever suggesting it. Jimmy Something was an easygoing guy, but the one thing he detested was exercise. Drake always tried to get him to work out with him, but Jimmy always had an excuse or fake injury on hand. Chest burning and hands shaking, he wondered if he might take Drake up on his offer next time.

Once he had the drone's attention, he knew he had to keep moving. Stopping to catch his breath every few meters, he would throw another stone or stick at it to keep its interest. Drake tried to call him once, but Jimmy had just set off running again, and he couldn't cope with running and talking at the same time. He promised himself to call back as soon as he could.

Jimmy scanned the area once more, feeling his breath returning to normal and his heart rate slowing. He'd need to circle back to the hospital soon. He almost finished scanning the area when an electronic signal showed up. It was too low to the ground to be a drone, and it moved too slowly to be an ASV. Jimmy monitored it, seeing which way it was heading. It was still too far away to make out what it was, but it seemed to be moving toward him. It was coming from the direction that Jimmy had to go toward. If he tried to go around it, it would take forever, and he might bump into the drone again. He knew he should head back but opted to wait a few seconds longer. If it was a slow moving ASV, it would chase him down, if it spotted him. If it kept going at its current trajectory, it would pass within fifty meters of him and hopefully keep going. Jimmy took position behind a low concrete fence that would give him some protection from a scan.

Having a quick peek, he saw it was only a few hundred meters away now, but he still could not identify it. Surely if it was an ASV, it would show up on his scan already? His curiosity made him stay. He waited another minute and popped his head up again. This time it was close enough to scan and for Jimmy to see it.

He almost jumped over the fence.

A bright orange Automated Service Robot was running toward him. Its four hydraulic legs made it move with short, jumpy strides and gyros kept its black head, filled with cameras and sensors, level and stable. Some ASRs had single arms on them, or even pulse weapons, but Jimmy could not spot any weapons or accessories on this one. Jimmy felt the excitement build up in him as it spotted him and came running over.

The ASR stopped in front of Jimmy and sat down on its rear hydraulic legs. It lifted its head up as the camera and sensors scanned the human face in front of it. Jimmy froze, knowing what it was up to, and feared he'd made a big mistake. The ASR had no names or insignia on it, but Jimmy knew that meant nothing. It could be—and probably was—a unit used by local security. The lack of accessories and weapons didn't mean anything either.

Jimmy studied the ASR as it was studying him and noticed all the scratch marks and dents. This unit had had a tough life. An orange panel hung on by only one screw, and Jimmy could see a small DDU inside. Jimmy had always wanted an ASR, but he had never used or handled one before. He figured the small DDU was the control panel. By the looks of this unit, it had not seen the inside of a workshop for a long time.

Kneeling, Jimmy carefully lifted the panel and inspected the DDU. As he suspected, the small DDU contained all the information to program the ASR.

"Okay, little guy. I'm going to go in here for a second and see if I can see anything."

Hydros, living units, safes—all used DDUs to keep them operating and secure, and Jimmy Something knew how to crack every one of them. This ASR was no different. After spending a few minutes finding his way around the software, Jimmy hacked it. It offered limited options, but he found what he was looking for and, after reprogramming it, he renamed it as well.

Jimmy stood up and looked at the orange ASR, head titled, sensors awaiting a command.

"Okay, Seymour. Let's go find Drake."

The orange ASR jumped up and stood next to Jimmy, ready to go. Jimmy could not be any happier. Together, they set off for the hospital.

* * *

Even before they reached the hospital, Jimmy knew there was trouble.

Blue and red lights lit up the sky. They still had a few hundred meters to go, but clearly security had finally caught up and had come to secure the building. They kept moving forward until Jimmy's ARP could pick up the vehicles. It was slightly better than he had feared. A single hydro blocked the road to the back entrance of the hospital. Inside the cabin of the security hydro, he could make out two officers. He could only assume that another hydro was sitting at the front entrance. Lan-noi security had to be spread pretty thin at the moment, if two units were all that they could spare. Jimmy figured they would be here for a few hours and then move on to whatever fresh crisis showed up.

Only, he could not wait a few hours.

Scanning the area, he tried to find a way in that didn't involve walking past the hydro and getting arrested. There was none. The fence they'd jumped earlier was too high for him to scale alone, and even if he used Seymour as a step, he would fall short. The Lan-noi security knew the only way in was through the gate they now blocked. Another distraction was the only way to do it.

Attacking the drone and making it chase him had worked perfectly last time, so Jimmy decided to stick to what worked. He looked down at Seymour.

"Okay, Seymour, your job is to find Drake and bring him to me, okay? He's my best friend, ya know, so this is very important."

Jimmy found a photo of Drake on his HIC and swiped it to Seymour's DDU. He also downloaded a schematic of the hospital and sent it to Seymour.

"Now, I don't know where he is, ya know, so you need to wait for him at the back door. Once he comes out, you need to bring him to me, okay?"

Jimmy programmed Seymour to be linked to him so no matter where he went, Seymour would find him, as long as he had his GPS switched on.

He sent Seymour off to move closer as Jimmy looked for rocks and other items to start his foolproof plan. Once he had a pocket full of junk, he made his way closer to the security hydro. Across the road, he saw Seymour slowly crawling forward too. He always knew having an ASR would be great, and watching it follow him and mimic his movements confirmed it. He couldn't wait for Drake to meet Seymour.

Once he figured he was in striking distance, he switched his ARP on and gave Seymour its last instructions. He waited until he saw Seymour lay down, out of sight, before he popped up from his own hiding spot.

"Oi, dickheads! Over here!" He grabbed a few stones and pelted the hydro.

The officers' HICs would not have had time to translate what he was yelling. All they saw was a crazy-looking man appearing out of nowhere, yelling and throwing rocks at them. The rocks did not do any significant damage to the hydro, but they were enough to draw their attention.

"Stop and get down on the ground. Now!" a voice belted out over a speaker mounted somewhere on the hydro. Unlike the officers, Jimmy had already set up his ARP to translate the local dialect, and he knew exactly what they were telling him to do. Not that he was planning to comply.

Popping up from behind his cover, he threw more rocks and rubbish at them.

Frustratingly, they didn't move. "Last warning. Stop and get down."

Jimmy grabbed the last of the junk he had in his pockets. Looking at it in his hands, he knew throwing it was futile. These guys would not abandon their post to chase him. He needed to do something a bit more dramatic.

He remembered the pulse weapons they had stashed nearby.

"Raise your hands and make yourself visible."

Scuttling to the building where they'd left the weapons, he stayed low and out of sight. He heard another half-assed command come over the loudspeaker, but clearly these guys were happy to sit in their hydro and not do much. The building was closer than he remembered and soon he held his Artie in his hands. He made his way back to the hydro and noticed that the security officers were still sitting in the hydro's cabin.

"Let's see you sit still now, you bastards!" Jimmy jumped up from his hiding spot and fired at the hydro.

A drone launched from the back of the Lan-noi security hydro and went straight over to Jimmy. Wasting no time, Jimmy shot it out of the sky. The adrenaline had now taken over all cognitive functions. One officer climbed out of the hydro, pulse pistol drawn, and Jimmy opened fire on him. The officer dove back into the hydro.

"That's right, run! Plenty more where that came from, ya know!"

Jimmy half turned, ready for the pursuit, but frustratingly, the hydro sat still.

Down the street, the trees flashed red and blue. Jimmy activated his ARP and saw two security hydros speeding toward them. Backup. Something he hadn't even considered.

"Seymour! Go find Drake."

Jimmy shot another burst into the hydro's windshield, allowing Seymour to run past in the chaos. Once Seymour was clear, it was Jimmy's turn to run.

The officer who dove back into the hydro had regained some of his courage and shot at Jimmy as he ran away. The shots were close too, and Jimmy had to find cover. Crawling, he tried to reach the closest building as quickly as he could. Pulse rounds smashed into the surrounding trees and buildings, making Jimmy scuttle even quicker. He rounded a building and set off on foot again. His lungs and legs were already burning. He swore to himself that next time, Drake could do all the running.

Tires squealed as the backup hydros turned at full speed, changing their trajectory to keep up with Jimmy. They were closing the gap quickly and would be all over for him in seconds.

Activating his ARP, he dialed Drake. The white dots bounced around and quickly merged to show Drake's face.

"Drake," Jimmy yelled, "you need to get the hell out of there!"

| nineteen |

The room was small and mostly empty. A single lightbulb hung from the ceiling, barely illuminating the space. The door had no DDU next to it, but an antiquated key lock instead. Rust covered its surface. A light shone through under the door, occasionally blinking out as something moved in front of it.

Across the room was a thin mattress which had a rumpled blanket on it but no occupant.

Lily Wells sat up. There was a lot of background noise and chatter, but she focused on the voices closest to the door. One of them sounded like Aranya, and she could make out two more. The conversation sounded calm and friendly. Wells switched on the translator on her neck, but its limited range prevented it from doing its job. Before going into the room with the voices, she needed to do an inventory and status check.

Searching through her pockets, she found the EMP blanket. She also had her used HIC with her. She went through all her pockets but found nothing else. She shook her head as she remembered how Aranya's fixer had given them new outfits in the van. They'd fled from the hospital in only their hospital-issued pajamas. Of course, there was nothing in the pockets.

Next, she did a check on herself. Hands and feet seemed fine. Legs were good too, as was her right arm. Her left, containing the busted up HIC, was sore, but functional. She didn't feel any discomfort around her head. The biggest problem came from her chest. Unbuttoning her shirt, she looked at the synthetic collagen-based skin covering the middle of her chest. It was a few shades darker than her normal pale skin but looked to be intact. The pain she was experiencing must have been the muscle underneath it. It was still healing, and she had been putting some unnecessary strain on it. She would ask Aranya for some pain relief meds.

Wells buttoned up her shirt as Aranya walked into the room.

"Oh, sorry, Lily. I can come back later."

"No, it's fine," Wells said as she finished up.

Aranya walked over to the other mattress and sat down.

"We are in a safe house, on the outskirts of Lan-noi. We will be safe here for a few days."

Wells had assumed as much. Aranya crossed her arms, and Wells noticed a new HIC implanted into her arm.

"Thanks, Aranya, for getting me out. I really owe you."

Aranya smiled. "I'm glad you said that, Lily."

"Sounds like you already have something in mind, Aranya." Wells knew nothing was ever free and that every relationship was give and take. She fully expected there to be a price to pay for her freedom.

Aranya stood up and motioned toward the door. "Would you like to meet some of my friends?"

Lt. Wells nodded and got up. Outwardly, she displayed a soft friendly facade, but internally, her security training took over.

She was in a hostile territory, in unfamiliar surroundings, with unknown operators. She would have to assume everyone to be an enemy, even Aranya. Although she'd freed her from the hospital and portrayed herself as a freedom fighter, Wells was deep in enemy territory and knew how the Shangcorp intelligence forces worked. They pitted everyone against each other, making virtual spies out of everyone. Anyone she met beyond that door was a potential enemy and could turn her in at any moment.

She did not dare trust anyone.

"Sure," Wells replied, "I would love to."

* * *

No heads turned as Lily and Aranya entered the room. It was bigger than the one they'd slept in, with DDUs and tables lining two walls. Six people worked with their backs to them on the DDUs. It looked like chaos to Wells, with the foreign text on the screens and the operators talking loudly, on their ARPs. This was more than a simple safe house.

In the middle of the room was another table, with chairs scattered around it. Two people sitting at it looked at them eagerly. Aranya offered Wells a seat, and they took their places at the table. Wells made sure her translator was on before anyone spoke.

"Welcome, Lily. My name is Kay, and this is Miha." He smiled warmly. "We are very glad to have you here."

"Thank you very much for helping us escape, Kay. I am very grateful."

Miha and Kay bowed their heads to Wells.

"Aranya told us about your time at the hospital and your help, so we too are grateful." Everyone bowed again.

Never one to accept a compliment easily, Wells simply nodded.

The operators on the DDUs never stopped for a second, keeping up their noisy work.

"She told us you are aware of our work, and she also told us your role in your own territory."

"Excuse me for playing dumb, but what exactly did she tell you about me?" Wells shot a look at Aranya. What she had told her had been in confidence. It could get her killed.

An uneasy mood settled around the table.

"Only that you worked at Penta Security. Not much, really."

Everyone was a potential enemy.

"Having someone from Penta helping us would give us such a significant advantage, Lily."

"Really? And what would I be helping you with?"

Wells knew her tone was harsher than it should have been, but the betrayal of trust had upset her.

"Lily, please. You sound angry," Aranya said. "I had to tell them you are from Penta, as I was the one bringing a stranger into the group. It was for your own good."

Aranya's words made sense but brought little relief to Wells. Trust was not something she handed out easily.

"As you know," Kay said, moving the conversation along, "some of us believe Shangcorp needs to be stopped. They are the biggest landholders in the world. Over fifty percent of the world is a Shangcorp or Shangcorp-affiliated territory."

These facts were all known to Wells. After the fall of the world's governments and their takeover by companies, Shangcorp had risen as one of the most aggressive corporations, buying up governments and calling in debts as quickly as they could. Soon they held more than half the land on Earth. It gave them an advantage that made Penta very nervous. So they, in turn, became the biggest arms manufacturer in the world.

"In every town and territory," Kay continued, "you'll find people who feel that Shangcorp needs to be stopped. We operate in small cells, independently from each other, but toward a common goal."

Wells sat quietly, patiently waiting for the sales pitch.

"We have been planning a big operation. Something to a scale we have never attempted before. And now, with all this chaos surrounding Mars, and even a war, we feel the time is right to strike."

Wells braced herself.

"Our plan—what we need your help with, Lily—is to take down the hyperloop network."

* * *

Lt. Wells stifled a laugh, but her eyes betrayed her. Kay and Miha looked quite offended.

"The hyperloop network? All of it?"

Kay composed himself. "No. Clearly, that would be impossible. We are planning a large-scale, simultaneous attack. Crucial lines that connect to military facilities and arms factories. A guerrilla tactic. The aim is to disrupt the Shangcorp effort to control Mars and their preparation for war with Penta and its affiliates."

Wells bit her tongue. Looking around at the few people in the room, all dressed in civilian clothes and working on run-of-the-mill DDUs, she struggled to imagine them pulling off anything so ambitious.

The hyperloop was a complicated network of tunnels and tubes stretched all over the globe. It had replaced air travel as the primary form of medium- and long-distance travel. Some people in the bigger cities had never traveled on anything but the hyperloop.

"I'm not too sure how you do things here, but where I'm from, the hyperloop only transports people. What are you planning on achieving by targeting lines to military facilities? Or even pulse factories?"

Miha spoke for the first time. "All those places need people. Engineers, workers, soldiers. They all travel on the hyperloop. Most people live far away from their work, since the hyperloop can get them there in a short time. If we disrupt the workforce, we'll slow down their productivity."

"Okay. So what do you want from me?"

Miha, Kay, and Aranya looked at each other. Evidently it was Aranya's job to seal the deal.

"We need your skills. Someone with experience who can show the rest of the cells how to do this."

The conversation was almost too absurd for Lt. Wells to process.

"Aranya, what are you talking about? My only aim is to get back to New Franco. I think you have a noble cause here, but to be frank, it's got nothing to do with me. I'm sorry, but I don't think I'm interested."

No one seemed surprised by her answer.

"We don't expect you to join us," Kay said, "or believe in our cause, Lily. That would be naive. If you help us, we'll help you get back to New Franco." He seemed to have thought out all the answers.

"I think it might be less trouble if I just do it myself. No offense."

Kay shook his head. "I don't think you have been following the news. Shangcorp knows its people are fleeing the cities to avoid conscription. The hyperloop is under strict surveillance, and so are all the highways. They have also set up roadblocks wherever they can. And believe me, Lily, Shangcorp has no problem using force against its own people. An outsider like you would stand no chance if caught."

Lily hated not being in charge. Back in New Franco, she was the one who came up with the tactical plans and lead their execution. She was used to Penta giving her free rein, and in return, she gave them exemplary results. What Kay was offering sounded more like blackmail to her than an offer. She knew they wanted an answer now, and to get their plan underway, but she had never been one to jump in headfirst.

"You are asking a lot from me, Kay. I'll need some time to think it over."

"Take your time, Lily. But we need to act fast. Shangcorp is readying itself to send more soldiers to Mars and strengthening its fighting forces at home. The world can't afford Shangcorp taking over. Trust me on that."

Lt. Wells needed no convincing of that.

* * *

Aranya, ever the diplomat, excused herself and Lily from the conversation to go have a meal. They left Kay and Miha in the control room and went to another room, which served as a kitchen and dining room.

Aranya grabbed two white boxes from a cooling unit and put them in a reheating unit, while Lily found a table. The smell of the food made her tummy grumble, and she realized how hungry she was.

"Have you ever tasted white box meals from another territory?" Wells asked.

Aranya, mouth full, shook her head.

"I can't speak for all the other territories, but compared to this, the Penta boxes taste like shit."

Aranya had to put her hand in front of her mouth as she snorted.

"The ones back home have almost no taste at all. But the ones here—I could eat them all day."

Lt. Wells took another bite of the aromatic food, trying her best not to think of the decisions that lay ahead.

It didn't last long.

"We really need your help, Lily."

The food would most likely lose its appeal soon, so Wells took another bite while she could.

"We only have one shot at this. If we fumble it, they'll know our intentions and it would be impossible to try again. I believe fate put us in each other's path."

And with that, the food tasted as bland as any white box meal she'd had before.

"I don't believe in fate, Aranya. I believe in making the best of any opportunity. And right now, I need to decide what to do with this opportunity."

"Kay was telling you the truth. Shangcorp is making it almost impossible for people to get out, but smuggling goods and people is what we're good at. If you help us, I promise you, we'll get you out of Shangcorp."

Lt. Wells studied the face of the woman who kept surprising her and, so far, hadn't let her down. The tiny figure who held so much sway in these regions. If she was to have an ally, she could do much worse.

Lily didn't believe in fate, but she always took advantage of her opportunities.

"Okay, Aranya. What's the plan?"

* * *

Going to take longer than expected, but everything is under control.

Capt. Davis wished he'd never received that message. No one who had everything under control would inform you of that. It was even harder to be angry at a faceless, nameless entity. This asset had come to him via another asset he had in Shangcorp. He had never met the first one, but they came with full credentials. The first asset vouched for the second asset and stayed on as the middleman to create some distance between all the parties. Davis appreciated all the precautionary steps taken, but wished he had a name and face to yell at. What the hell was the holdup?

But trustworthy assets were scarce, so he had to restrain himself.

Thanks for the update.

Staring at the picture of Lt. Wells on his DDU, he screamed, letting all his frustrations out at a face and name he did have.

| twenty |

The big nurse waited for Drake to finish his call before he spoke again.

"You look worried."

"No, I'm fine. Actually, that was my partner. He warned me to get out."

The hospital was quiet, no alarms or raised voices. Drake hoped it meant the security had not increased inside the building yet. "Can you tell me more about Aranya?"

Big Boy looked around nervously and motioned for Drake to come closer.

"Like I said, Aranya is the one trying to unite all the cells and have us working together. She is smart and elusive. I didn't even know it was her, here in the hospital, until she made contact. She's like a ghost. I'm sorry, but I don't think you'll find her if she doesn't want to be found."

Jimmy's words came back to Drake. "I need to go. There must be something? Please!"

Big Boy shrugged.

"Okay, what about your cell? Maybe someone there might know?"

Apprehension filled Big Boy's eyes. "I'm not sure they'll appreciate me sending a stranger over to them."

"Can't you vouch for me or something?"

"Sorry, but to be honest, I hardly know you. I don't know where you're from, but here in Lan-noi, it's hard to trust anyone. Anyone could be a spy or a mercenary."

"Mercenary?"

"Yeah, man. Mercenaries are all over the place in Shangcorp. They'll do anything for anyone for the right amount of credits. Look, I'm not saying you are any of those things, but again, how do I know for sure?"

Time had run out, and he had made almost no headway. He had one more shot at convincing the big nurse to help him before he'd have to go looking for Jimmy.

"My friend is a Penta Security officer. She is as anti-Shangcorp as any of you Believers. There is nothing more I can say to convince you to help me. But trust me, we are on your side."

The delivery was flawless. It was all bullshit, of course. He had no feelings or loyalties toward any corporation or territory. He doubted very much that Lt. Wells concerned herself with Shangcorp's policies either. But it was easy for people to believe in the "enemy of my enemy" cliché.

Drake turned and headed for the door. His HID pinged, and he pulled it out of his pocket.

"That's my number," Big Boy said. "I'll send you coordinates soon."

* * *

No one took any notice of him, and within minutes Drake found himself at the back door of the hospital. He opened it and carefully peeked out. A security hydro's lights flashed a little way up the road. The driver had parked it sideways across the road, blocking all traffic. He doubted they would notice him leaving the building. Drake stepped out, crouched down, and made for some cover. As he ran, he heard a noise behind him. Had they seen him? An orange ASR was running toward him. There was no point in hiding from it. It had him in its sights. Drake could not see any pulse weapons protruding from it. He braced himself, ready to catch it as it came for him, to throw it over the fence. But the orange ASR outsmarted him, coming to a sudden stop two meters away from him. Bending its rear hydraulic legs, it sat down. As it sat, three white dots danced in front of Drake's view. Jimmy.

"Buddy, where are you?"

"Hey! I see Seymour found you."

"Who the hell is Seymour?"

"Um, Seymour, ya know. He is sitting right in front of you."

The ASR stared back at him with his eye-like sensors.

"You stole an ASR?"

"No, he found me, ya know? I was walking and—"

"Jimmy! Later. I need to get out of here. There is a security hydro blocking my path. Where are you?"

"Not sure. I jumped on a hyperloop to get away from the security and got off at the first stop. I think I'm still in Lan-noi, ya know. It wasn't a very long ride."

Even a quick ride on the super-fast hyperloop could be hundreds of kilometers away.

"Okay, just stay there. Find out where you are and send the coordinates to me."

"Got it! Also, I think I know how to get you past the hydro."

Drake felt his HID vibrate.

"Install that file, then send it to Seymour. I'll send you his access codes."

"What is it?"

Jimmy's eyes lit up with pride. "Just a little code, ya know, to lock the officers inside their hydro for a few minutes. It will only work if Seymour is near the hydro, but as long as he is, the doors will stay shut."

"Brilliant, Jimmy. I'll just leave him there. No point in risking them getting out."

"Um, yeah, I guess that makes sense, ya know." Jimmy looked like he was about to cry.

"What's wrong?"

"Nothing, it's just, ya know, I kinda always wanted to have one. An ASR. Can you try to bring him back, maybe?"

After Drake's parents died, he'd lived a solitary life. He had no long-term relationships or partners. He knew tons of people, but he always kept them at a distance and preferred his own company. All he needed was his Hydrostar and the open road. Life was simple, and he was happy.

Then he met Jimmy Something, and everything changed. Now he had a partner by his side twenty-four seven. Drake couldn't recall the last time he had five minutes by himself. And now Jimmy wanted to add an ASR to the mix.

Drake looked at the pleading face floating in front of him.

It was a face he would take a pulse bullet for. Again.

"Whatever, Jimmy. I'll bring the stupid ASR. Just make sure you send me your coordinates."

Jimmy jumped up and down, making the visual go haywire as it tried and failed to track his face.

"Jimmy, you're making me sick. Stand still!"

"Oh, yes, sorry. Just a bit excited, ya know?"

"I gathered. Okay, I'll check in if I run into trouble."

Drake disconnected the call and opened the file that Jimmy had sent him on his HID. The HID wasn't the fastest piece of technology, and it felt like an eternity before the file was ready to be sent over to the ASR. Finally, with the ASR coded, Drake readied himself to get out of there.

Drake looked on as the little ASR ran up to the hydro, keeping in the shadows and using as much cover as it could. It appeared to have gone unnoticed, and it crouched down about two meters away from the hydro. It was Drake's time to move.

A low hedge ran along the road, up to where the hydro was parked. Drake knew that if the officers didn't look his way, he should be fine. He switched on his ARP and activated the ASR's camera to show him a close-up view of the officers in the hydro. It wasn't the best angle, but at least he could see the face of the officer closest to him. Drake had to assume the farther officer would monitor the road outside the hospital and the nearer one, the hospital. It was only a guess. He made the ASR view in his ARP smaller and started his run. Every time the officer moved his head, Drake fell to the ground and hid behind the small hedge. His entire plan relied on them being lazy and not using any sensors or thermal imagery. Once the officer looked away, Drake ran again, until he came to the end of the hedge.

Facing a three-meter gap to the hydro, Drake had to time his next move with precision. He waited almost five minutes for the right opportunity before crawling on his belly until he was right next to the hydro. His next goal was to cross the road and take cover behind a building. If the officers looked in their rearview monitor, they would surely see him, and although they were trapped inside the hydro, they could still call for backup. Even if he made his move when both had their eyes away from the DDUs in the hydro, he had no guarantee they would keep them there. He would need to keep their attention forward and focused.

On the small screen on his ARP, Drake saw the officer shift his weight toward his door. The hydro moved. He was trying to get out. Soon he'd realize that someone had trapped them inside their own vehicle. And he would surely see the ASR as he tried to figure out what was happening.

Gravel crunched as feet hit the ground. Drake's heart pounded in his chest. He lowered himself and saw two black boots facing away from him. The locking code hadn't worked!

"Jimmy," Drake whispered as the call connected. "I need you to send me a code or tell me how to operate this damn ASR. The door lock code didn't work."

"What's going on?"

"I'm stuck behind the hydro. I need a diversion. Can you make the ASR charge them, or something, to get their attention?"

Drake watched Jimmy work on his fancy HIC. His old, crummy HID vibrated shortly after.

"Use that. I'm sure it'll work, ya know."

Drake disconnected the call and opened the code. The strings of words and numbers made no sense to him at all. He closed the file and transferred it to the ASR.

He couldn't see it, but it clearly hadn't worked. The boots stayed in position.

Then he heard a noise.

"Hey! Check this out!"

A muffled reply came from inside the hydro.

"It's good, trust me."

Another muffled reply, but the hydro rocked, and Drake saw another set of boots on the ground. He realized, too late, that the officer might decide to walk around the back of the vehicle instead of the front. Drake would have nowhere to go. Panicking, he looked for an escape route. The boots moved away from him. He was pushing his luck, being so close to them, but he was safe for now.

"What is it doing?"

"I don't know!"

"Is it dancing?"

"Looks like it! I've never seen an ASR move like this!"

"Hang on, let me record this."

Time to go. Without looking back, Drake sprinted for the nearest building. He kept his head down, pumped his arms, and moved like never before. He rounded the corner and collapsed. He switched his ARP back on, connected to the ASR, and saw its point of view. What he saw was two officers crying with laughter at the dancing robot. Using his HID, Drake sent a new code to the ASR.

The ASR stopped dancing and ran away in the opposite direction.

"You go home now," one officer yelled.

Drake watched it run a few minutes and turn a few corners. He kept following it until he saw himself. He switched off his ARP, and the ASR came to a halt in front of him. It sat down and turned its head to the side, awaiting new orders.

"Don't be cute with me, okay? I'm not your boss, Jimmy is. Got it?"

Drake swiped his HID to find Jimmy's coordinates. Luckily, he was closer than Drake had feared. After making sure he had enough credits for the hyperloop, Drake searched for the nearest terminal and set off.

The ASR followed.

| twenty-one |

The plan had merits, but also multiple flaws. Kay ran over the details twice, and Wells made sure she took in all the information and asked questions when she needed to.

"So what do you think?" Kay asked her, having no more information left to give.

"To be frank, I don't think you can pull it off."

Miha and Kay looked shocked, but Aranya kept smiling.

"Luckily for us, then, that we have you," she said.

Wells laughed. "I think you are overselling me, Aranya."

"I believe with your experience and fresh take on things, we can overcome any obstacle."

Wells had to admire Aranya's optimism and faith. Or was it just sheer desperation and no other options? Wells thought back to what they'd told her about leaving Shangcorp and how difficult it would be for her without their help. Was she also desperate and facing no other options? Was she being optimistic that they would help her? She had never relied on anyone, yet here she was, putting all her faith in them helping her.

Doubt crept in, making her see things more one sidedly.

"The best I can do is show you the mistakes in your plan," she said, "and maybe offer some alternatives. But that's all. I'm not leading this mission. I'll tell you what to do, and then I'm out."

The only noises came from the operators manning the DDUs.

They were in a standoff. Kay, Miha, and Aranya wanted Wells to lead the campaign and inspire the other cells to do the same. Wells wanted to give them some pointers and get the hell out of there. Wells had nothing to lose, so she calmly waited for the others to speak.

Kay broke the silence. "I'm not sure that would be enough."

"Enough for what?" Wells knew exactly what he was saying but needed the words to be said. She wanted everyone to be on the same page.

"I don't think—we don't think it is enough for you to just help with the plan and then get a free ride out of here."

She knew it. This group of so-called freedom fighters had no real fighters at all and needed someone to do their dirty work for them.

"Okay then," Lt. Wells said, pushing her chair back and standing up. "I'm out of here. I wish you all the best with your plan. I need to get out of here, ASAP, so I best be going."

"Lt. Wells, you are making a grave mistake. We are your only hope of getting out."

Wells locked eyes with Kay. "And what's stopping you from asking me for another favor or more help once this mission is over?"

Kay's silence told her everything she needed to know.

"That's what I thought."

"You won't last two—"

"Enough!"

Everyone turned toward Aranya.

"Kay, stop playing games. Without her, we run a high risk of failure. This is the biggest operation we've ever attempted. If this fails, we'll lose many people, resources, and momentum. You know it. I know this was your plan, but it's time to hand it over to her. And listen."

Aranya turned to face Wells. She activated a DDU on the table in front of her.

"Here. I'm sending it to you."

Wells felt her bag vibrate and pulled out the old HIC. Names, contacts, coordinates. All the information she needed to get out of Shangcorp.

"It's up to you now, Lily. But that's everything we promised you, up front. The choice is yours."

Wells looked at Aranya's soft, pleading eyes.

She had not lied to her once and never let her down. She was also clearly the person making all the calls around here and the one who held all the power.

So why did Wells still not feel comfortable trusting her completely?

Was it the way she quietly manipulated people and pulled strings behind everyone's backs, instead of openly leading from the front?

Wells sat down and pulled her chair back in.

"If we are going to do this, we do this my way. Understand?"

* * *

The Believers were eager and ready to go. All Wells had to do was point them in the right direction. The sooner she did this, the quicker she could get out.

But first she had to do some work.

She asked for a secure DDU in a private room and some time alone. Aranya made it happen, and soon Wells stared at her reflection on the DDU screen. She shook her head at herself. "What are you doing, Lily?"

She had lost all contact with Penta and had been flying blind for months now. She was sure they would have made inquiries. They might even know where she was. In fact, they had to know. Their reach ran far and deep—even more in hostile territories. The only problem was, she had no way of contacting them. Her Penta-issued HIC had been damaged in the fight with Sammy Sanders, and her second unit only had limited functionality. Sure, she had gone overboard chasing Drake across the ocean and into Shangcorp territory, but as always, her results would justify her actions. Only, this time she wasn't so sure.

What had she achieved in chasing Drake? He'd given her enough information to secure an arrest warrant for Hector Delgado, the crime boss of sector fifty-nine. Instead of heading back to Penta and using the information, she'd sent the files to Penta headquarters and set off to, what? Rescue them? Instead, Drake and Jimmy were still on the run, Sammy Sanders had stabbed her and gotten away, and Bob Turner was most likely dead. It wasn't really a career highlight. Still, she hoped Penta would look at her exemplary list of achievements and not focus on this mess.

She activated the DDU and ran some code to ensure it was secure. The results came up positive, but she knew to still tread carefully. Her tech skills were proficient for her day-to-day duties but nothing spectacular. She could do more than the average civilian but knew her limitations.

The DDU patiently awaited her first command.

She typed in her first search string but didn't hit the *execute* icon. She looked at the screen and the two words on it.

Benjamin Drake.

She needed to know if he'd made it out of Shangcorp. She didn't blame him for leaving her behind. He was not a trained security officer. Seeing her lying in a pool of blood, he would have panicked. She could not hold that against him.

Benjamin Drake.

If he'd made it out, she would have one less thing to think about. But he was still here, in Shangcorp, she'd have to keep searching for him. There was no way that Drake and Jimmy could get themselves out on their own. She'd have to help Aranya, then find them before leaving Shangcorp.

Benjamin Drake.

She hit *execute* and watched the screen fill with results. She waited until it finished, then applied a filter to narrow the results down. The filter worked so well that the screen went blank. No results. She changed the search and made it more descriptive. A few results came up, and she applied some filters again. Only one piqued her interest. A person of interest that fit Drake's description, involving the open case of a multiple homicide outside of Kohsam. Not very helpful, but it told her something.

He'd never made it back to Penta.

Benjamin Drake had a record as long as her arm, and although it was all for minor infractions, they appeared regularly. If he was back in Penta territory, he would have done something reckless by now and popped up on her search. She would bet her life on it.

Which meant he was either dead or still here. Somewhere.

Lt. Wells cleared the screen. If he was still here after all these weeks, he would still be here in a few days. She had to put everything into helping Aranya, and then she could find him. She was a professional, and she had to make sure there were no distractions. So she pushed Drake to the back of her mind for now and focused on the job at hand.

Next, Wells searched for her own name. She needed to know if she was a wanted person or if anyone from Penta was looking for her. Shangcorp restricted DDU access of its citizens to within its borders. This DDU had better access than most, as she'd been able to find some results from Penta when she searched for Drake. But after searching for a few minutes for anything about herself from Penta, she gave up. The results were too filtered and restricted. Besides, it was more important to see if there were any mentions of her here in Shangcorp.

It seemed by smashing her HIC, Sammy Sanders had done her a huge favor. After failing to find anything, she reverted to a description search again, and found a few mentions of her as a Jane Doe in the hospital. From the articles, she learned she was practically dead when they brought her in, and she had been in a coma for days. Once she came to, they didn't know who she was, so she stayed a Jane Doe, as her HIC was malfunctioning and couldn't be used to identify her. Because of her injuries, the authorities wanted to question her. Currently, there was a bulletin out on her as a person of interest, with a photo attached. Any security officer worth their salt would find her in the system if she got detained for any reason.

Best make sure that doesn't happen, then.

* * *

"Aranya, could I see you for a second?"

Wells needed more access for her next task, but she was getting nowhere by herself. Until an obvious realization hit her. Right behind her, in the next room, sat multiple tech geeks, any one of whom could bypass the Shangcorp system and get into the Penta network. Aranya had shown that she would do anything to help, so Wells had no hesitation in asking her.

"Sure, Lily. How's the research going?"

"It's not. I can't get into the Penta Security network. Is that something they can do?" Wells nodded her head toward the people operating the DDUs.

"I don't know, but let's find out."

Wells grabbed Aranya's arm. "Aranya," she whispered. "I don't trust anyone. So please, be careful who you pick."

Aranya smiled and walked over to an operator. Wells couldn't hear what she said, but the operator stood up and came over to her.

"Lily, this is An. She can help you."

An glared at Lily from underneath her black fringe. "Hi."

She didn't wait for a reply and marched into the room Wells had been using. Wells followed and saw her already working on the DDU.

"So, what do you need? And be specific."

Wells appreciated the no-nonsense, straightforward approach.

"I need to contact someone at Penta Security, on a secure line."

"Sure. Anything else?"

"No, that's all."

"I'll call you when I'm done."

An turned her back to Wells and started working. Wells got the hint and went looking for Aranya.

"She's the best," Aranya said. "She'll get you anything you need. And you can trust her."

Wells hoped Aranya was right.

"Something I can't quite figure out is, who is in charge here?"

"Yes, I can see how a stranger might find it difficult to understand how things work here."

Wells nodded, hoping there was more to come.

"Kay was one of the first people to stand up against the corporation. He has always believed in a passive resistance. Strikes, protest, and such. Over the years, people have become frustrated with his lack of progress, but they still respect him as an elder. So my role is to guide the water in the right direction to fill the dam, and not build a new dam myself."

Thankfully things were as clear as mud now.

Someone cleared their throat behind Wells, and she turned to see the downturned face of An.

"I'm done. Just type in the person's name and your message and they'll get it."

An didn't wait for a thank-you or a reply and went back to her workstation.

Wells excused herself and went back into the room.

An had left the DDU open on the secure message app, and Wells got working immediately.

Captain Sturgis,

Please keep this message and its contents secure and private. I have taken every precaution on my end to ensure it's encrypted, but I have no guarantees.

First, I am still alive. I have some injuries that might need more attention once I'm back, but I am operational. I am still in Shangcorp, near a town called Lan-noi. Hopefully the information I sent through on Hector Delgado was enough to secure an arrest and a conviction. My apologies for not returning with the information myself, but I had to take care of two assets, Benjamin Drake and Jimmy Something. I believe they have proved their value in the past, and I thought I could extract them swiftly. But unfortunately I got injured and separated from them. I am again on their trail and hope to bring them, and myself, back to safety soon. I understand tensions are running high and that having a Penta officer in Shangcorp is not ideal, hence the private channel. I do not require any assistance at this stage, but would appreciate keeping this channel open in case things change.

Lt. L Wells.

She read the message once more before sending it. Captain Sturgis had helped her out when she went after Captain Santo, and she hoped he would be an ally again. He was a man with morals, something she didn't come across very often in Penta.

It was time to come up with a plan and lead this group of strangers on a complicated mission that had every chance of failure. It was hard enough to lead a group of highly trained professionals who knew exactly what to do and when to do it. Leading people she didn't know, and who did not appear to have had any training at all, would be suicidal. But she knew her chances of getting out of here alone were close to zero. She needed Aranya's help. Sure, she played hardball, and bluffed, but Wells needed to have the upper hand. If they knew she was relying on them, they would keep using her for more and more missions. She'd be stuck here forever.

The DDU made a noise, alerting Wells that a new message arrived.

It was Captain Sturgis.

Lt. Wells

I am not surprised to hear from you or that you are still alive. It also doesn't surprise me you are off on some harebrained mission you deem important. Let's hope you are right.

I cannot offer any official help. As you said, the standoff with Shangcorp will not allow it. We have people working inside the borders of Shangcorp, as I'm sure you know. I can set you up with one of them, but only as a last resort. They are being hunted down by Shangcorp Security, who have employed locals and mercenaries to help them. I do not want to risk exposing our agents, so please, only if it's crucial.

This line is secure, so use it again, if you must.

Stay safe Lt. Wells

Captain Sturgis.

Lt. Wells felt a surge of relief wash over her, knowing that someone out there knew she was alive and that she had open communications with them. It made her feel less alone.

With renewed hope, Lt. Wells got back to planning the new mission.

| twenty-two |

Drake got off the hyperloop and saw Jimmy sitting against a wall. He had his knees drawn up and his head hung down. Asleep. Drake stepped up to him and heard the ASR follow behind.

"Hey, buddy. Time to wake up."

Words didn't seem to be enough, so Drake nudged him with his foot. That seemed to do the trick and Jimmy woke up, startled and eyes wide open.

"Drake," he said, still sounding sleepy. "Seymour!" The ASR bounced forward and Jimmy smiled. "I thought I might lose you."

"I'm good too, thanks, Jimmy."

"Sorry, Drake. Just happy to see him, ya know."

Drake let it go. Jimmy looked happy, and right now, he was too.

"Okay, so what now?" Jimmy asked.

"Well," Drake said, pulling out his HID, "Big Boy gave me his friend's coordinates. I think we should go."

"Who's Big Boy?"

"The big nurse. The one who got his arm blown off."

"Oh, yeah. Him. Go on."

"That's pretty much it. We go to the coordinates and ask them to help us."

Jimmy stood up. "Do we know anything about these people?"

"No, not really, but it's the same group of people who helped Lily escape, so they must be trustworthy."

"Why?"

Drake was getting frustrated.

"What do you mean, why? They helped Lily, therefore they'll help us."

"But, ya know, why would they? If they are some underground resistance movement, why would they risk exposing themselves to foreigners?"

Confusion replaced the frustration. Jimmy had a point. Hours before Big Boy gave him the location of his friends, Drake's own friends had blown his arm off. All it took was one sob story to convince him to help him out. They had no information on these Believers, except that they'd helped Lily escape. Drake and Jimmy didn't even know why they'd helped her.

"Damn it, Jimmy. You're right. We don't know them. But I still think we should go. I don't see any other options."

"Show me those numbers again."

Jimmy copied the numbers into his HIC and brought the location up on a map.

"It's not too far away, ya know."

"No, it's not, but I don't see a hyperloop connection. It looks pretty remote, see?"

The coordinates Big Boy had given them sat in the middle of what appeared to be a jungle, with only one tiny road leading up to it. It wasn't that far, but with no hyperloop or highway to get there, or any vehicle to use, it could take them days, if not weeks.

Judging by their surroundings, this appeared to be the last hyperloop stop when leaving Lan-noi. The city lights were clearly visible to the left, and to the right, the hyperloop tube disappeared into the darkness.

They needed a vehicle.

Being on the outskirts of Lan-noi, they found themselves surrounded by a mixture of housing units and industrial buildings. Most of the bigger buildings had lights shining on the outside, but the windows appeared dark. The housing units were the opposite, with dark exteriors but lights shining from within.

Drake had to refer this one to Jimmy.

"Okay, buddy. What do you reckon? Any of these look like they might hide a hydro inside?"

"Let's go for a walk and get a better look, ya know?"

Jimmy bent down and typed a command on his HIC, which he then swiped over to the ASR. It jumped up and ran ahead.

"What's he doing?"

"Scanning. Checking for cameras, drones, and such, ya know?"

It seemed the ASR might prove useful after all. Drake nodded in approval.

The little orange robot stayed about fifty meters in front of them, continually scanning the area around it and sending the results back to Jimmy. The buildings all appeared run down, and the streets were in desperate need of repair. So it was no surprise that only a few buildings had any form of active surveillance equipment. Whenever the ASR sensed any, he would steer them clear of its range, making sure no one ended up on a recording somewhere.

"And?"

"A few of the housing units have hydros."

There was no honor among thieves, but Drake felt better *borrowing* a hydro from a company who'd have insurance and backup plans than a family who might rely on the hydro for their livelihood.

"I'd prefer one from a business, if possible."

"Sure." Jimmy kept looking.

The ASR stopped and seemed indecisive for a moment before turning down a narrower lane. Drake shrugged at Jimmy before they too turned down the lane, still following the ASR. The lane was a back route to the surrounding housing and industrial units. Most of the properties had high fences, with an occasional gate. Some fences had enormous holes in them, and others comprised interlocking wire mesh, both allowing Drake and Jimmy to look in and see the yards' contents. Most of the residential yards were tiny and had little in them. The industrial ones had a variety of things, but most seemed to use the back-yards for trash and storage.

The ASR kept to the middle of the lane, a sign that security was minimal.

A silhouette caught Drake's attention. A familiar shape, yet different. He walked closer to the fence to have a better look. Jimmy told Seymour to wait and joined Drake. The fence was one of the interlocking mesh types, which made visibility great. Between boxes and trash and a row of broken, rusted up hydro-cycles sat a relic. Something Drake had never seen in real life but knew the history of. Not this specific model, as most Shangcorp vehicles never made it into other territories, but the era.

The era that ushered in the end of fossil fuels and the new reliance on hydrogen. Before Nikolatec became the de facto manufacturer of hydro vehicles for half the world. A time of individual innovation when people had to convert their own vehicles into hydros. A dangerous time, too, with lots of deadly explosions, until Penta and most other territories banned hydro conversions. As always, it seemed Shangcorp turned a blind eye to the little things.

Like the old diesel truck conversion hiding behind the fence.

It looked forgotten and beautiful at the same time.

"Nah, looks like shit, ya know. Let's keep looking."

Drake didn't move.

"Seriously?"

He nodded at Jimmy.

"No way! That thing will kill us, ya know. It's a death trap!"

"That's the one, Jimmy."

"It's . . ." Jimmy threw his head back. "Argh. Okay. Seymour, come here!"

* * *

Drake found a small gap in the fence, barely big enough for Seymour to fit through. Jimmy gave him his instructions, and the ASR set off, scanning the yard, looking for any security devices or human activity. Jimmy had his ARP connected to Seymour and had a real-time view.

"Looks clear. I'll get him to go back to the truck and see if it looks operational. Which it won't be, ya know."

Drake ignored Jimmy. Seymour reappeared around the building and ran to the truck. Jimmy then commanded him to walk around it first, checking for any obvious damage or missing parts. Satisfied, he then had him crawl underneath the vehicle and inspect the underside and the drive train. After his inspection, Seymour came running back, sitting down in front of them, still on the other side of the fence.

"I hate to say it, ya know, but it seems to be in one piece."

Drake slapped him on the back. "Lighten up! It'll be a blast to drive. You'll see."

Jimmy's enthusiasm was still lagging Drake's. "Just because all the parts are there doesn't mean it will work, ya know?"

Drake was too excited to be brought down. "Let's find out then."

Drake made his way to where they'd slipped Seymour through the fence. The wire mesh was old and rusty, and Drake bent it upward to make the hole bigger. It was still not huge, but he crawled through. He walked over to the ASR and stood next to it, facing Jimmy through the fence.

"You coming?"

A sigh, one eye-roll, and some muttered words later, Jimmy crawled through the hole in the fence.

It was up to Jimmy to hack the truck's primitive operating system and unlock it. Taking longer than usual, because of the generational difference between the software in Jimmy's HIC and the truck's operating system, the door finally unlocked. Drake grabbed the door handle and pulled it open.

The smell escaping the cabin triggered a memory that was just beyond Drake's grasp. Something felt so familiar about the smell, but he could not place it. All he knew was that it made him happy.

Dust covered the interior, and Drake used his hands to wipe it away. He grabbed the steering wheel and made himself comfortable. The seats were old and worn in, but comfortable. The wheel, worn down and shiny, felt at home in his hands. Knobs and levers lined the dashboard, and a retrofitted DDU sat out of place in the middle of it all. Maybe Jimmy was right. Maybe this was a death trap. But if it had made it this far, it would go on for much longer.

Besides, Drake was in love.

He searched for a start button and had to look over every inch of the dashboard before he found it. It was slow work, as his ARP had to translate most of the words, and the symbols remained a mystery. He pressed the start button and got what he expected.

Nothing.

It was time for Jimmy to shine.

The truck was not a long-distance hauler and had no living quarters behind it, only a tiny cot. In the front, it had one bench stretching the width of the cabin. Drake slid over to the side, letting Jimmy sit in the driver's seat to do his thing. They both knew this was only temporary.

Jimmy stuck his head under the dashboard and started pulling at wires and making new connections. Occasionally he would come up, tap the DDU, shake his head, and duck under again. This went on for minutes before he came up again and said, "I think everything is connected, but it's hard to tell, ya know."

"Hard to tell, how?"

"Oh, the batteries are dead, ya know, so I don't know if it's all working."

"Why didn't you tell me earlier?"

"I was kinda busy, ya know?"

Drake clenched his fist and let it go.

"Okay," Drake recalled the old hydrocycles sitting next to the truck. "Looks like they might work on hydrocycles in here. Maybe they have spare batteries or a charger or something?"

"Let's have a look," Jimmy said, and jumped out of the truck.

This was another job for Seymour. While Jimmy set up the ASR for its newest mission, Drake found a place to insert the robot into the building. When Jimmy finished, he brought it over to Drake.

"I told you we should keep him."

"Yeah, yeah. He's okay."

Jimmy patted the ASR and gave it the command to go.

Detecting no security devices inside, it proceeded to the door, which allowed Jimmy to open it remotely. Seconds later, Jimmy and Drake stood inside the building with Seymour. Surrounding them were dozens of hydrocycles in different stages of repair. Most of them were small units, and all of them looked well used. They set off in search of a charging device.

It looked like a bomb had gone off inside the workshop. Hydrocycles, pieces of hydrocycles, and spare parts littered every available space. There didn't seem to be a logical order for anything. Drake and Jimmy kept up their search and finally Drake stumbled upon a row of batteries being charged.

"Jimmy!"

Jimmy ran over and surveyed the equipment.

"I've charged many a battery in my time," Drake said, " and I know these chargers look on the small side, but I was wondering—"

"If we could make one enormous super charger!"

Drake laughed. "Basically, yes."

Jimmy's eyes sparkled.

| twenty-three |

The classified file contained only logistical data—number of personnel, food supplies, armor issued, amount of ammo and weapons. There were no strategic plans included. But it was still an extremely valuable piece of information.

Captain Davis had nothing to do with the Mars campaign and had no clearance to access the files, but he had connections to enough people who knew people to get them. A few threats and some transferred credits later, the file was his. All he had to do now was send it via a secure channel to Captain Santo on Mars, to give him a heads-up. He also sent it to a contact at Shangcorp, as a gift. A little something that he could later collect on.

Davis checked his messages to see if there was any news on Wells yet.

A brief message awaited him.

Slight delay, but still on track.

He was hoping for something more concrete, maybe even a photo to confirm the kill, but at least he had an update.

Davis refreshed his message feed, hoping for a reply from Santo. It took fifteen minutes for a message to travel to Mars, and then the same for a reply. He knew he was being too eager, checking so soon, but he was keen to hear what Santo had to say about the file.

Davis had a feeling that Santo would be more than impressed.

* * *

The plan was simple. At a specific time and date, almost thirty cells from across the region would blow up a hyperloop tube in their area. Most tubes ran above ground in rural areas and only went underground in heavily populated areas, like cities. The hyperloop relied on the sealed tube to function, so a breach in the tube would be enough to shut it down. When a failure occurred, the hyperloop would shut down only the segment affected, and still operate where possible. A crew would then go out to the damaged tube and fix it. Being the primary transport for most people, the companies maintaining the hyperloops were extremely efficient. That's why the plan relied on all the cells hitting them simultaneously, to stretch the emergency and repair crews to their limits. It would most likely only bring the hyperloop to a halt for a few hours, but this was a show of strength. A warning shot. *Listen to us, or we will do it again, but bigger.*

Wells thought the plan was stupid and too simplistic to do any significant damage, but she also didn't want to get too in-volved. She was not here to lead a resistance. She was only here to help herself get home. As promised, she organized all the teams and gave everyone explicit instructions on how to pro-ceed. She also ran all the cells through a few worst case scenarios and gave them some options. To a casual observer, she would indeed appear to be a leader of the resistance.

Tomorrow morning, they would head out to their cell's attack point.

The door opened, and Aranya entered the small room. Wells was ready to sleep and was lying on her thin mattress on the floor.

"Hi, Lily."

"Hey."

Aranya went over to the other mattress on the ground and sat down on it. She removed her shoes and crossed her legs.

"I know we haven't really discussed it yet, but I am coming with you tomorrow."

It didn't surprise Wells.

Aranya still had the casts on her arms but had been using them more each day. Still, Wells didn't enjoy having a deadweight on missions.

"I'm not sure you'd be of much use, to be honest. Besides, your people need you. What if something went wrong out there?"

"The people need to see me, Lily. Unlike the corporations, we cannot be faceless. For us to succeed, the Believers need someone to follow. I hope you understand."

Wells reminded herself of the goal. She had no ill feelings toward Aranya, and didn't wish her harm, but if she insisted on going out on a dangerous mission, then so be it.

"And you are that person?"

"Not by choice, Lily, but fate has put me on this path." Aranya blushed, but Wells didn't see it reflected in her eyes.

Wells forced her eyes not to roll. "Well, for your people's sake, make sure you stay out of danger and follow my commands, okay?"

"Okay, Lily. I'm so grateful you decided to help us."

"You guys didn't really give me a choice."

"Sorry if we pushed you in a direction, Lily, but in order to get things done in Shangcorp, you sometimes have to do things you didn't think you were capable of."

Wells didn't like the sound of that.

Aranya sensed the tension in the room and laughed. "That sounded more ominous than I intended. I'm sure you haven't always played by the rules, working for Penta Security?"

Wells was all too familiar with the *whatever it takes* attitude to get a job done. "I guess. Best we get some sleep. We have a long way to travel tomorrow."

"Goodnight, Lily."

"Goodnight."

* * *

After a quick breakfast and a last-minute gear check, they set off for their destination. Kay and Miha stayed behind, forming the heart of the logistics team for all the cells. Aranya and Wells would communicate directly with them, and they would distribute the information to all the other cells and oversee their progress. Wells had the entire operation set up like she was doing a mission for Penta.

Outside the building, four odd-looking vehicles awaited them. Their front ends looked like a hydrocycle, and the back ends looked like a small hydrocar. The driver sat in the front and four passengers could squeeze into the back. Lily and Aranya climbed into the back of one vehicle that already had two other people sitting in it. Shoulders pressed against each other and knees touching, they barely fit. Luckily, Lt. Wells had been in her fair share of cramped armored vehicles before, and she made herself as comfortable as possible.

The little vehicle whined and shuddered and finally took off at a slow but steady pace. The noise inside the cabin was deafening. Wind came in through gaps in the paper-thin walls of the vehicle.

"If I knew about the transport, I would have amended the timeframe," Wells yelled.

"Don't worry, Lily. Bom-boms are our main transport in the rural areas. Once it's up to speed, we'll be fine."

"Bomb-bomb?"

"No." Aranya laughed. She spelled the word out. "It mimics the sound of the motor."

Wells tried to focus on the sound of the little motor pushing the bom-bom forward, but the road and wind noise drowned out everything else.

"I'll take your word for it."

Sitting right up against the rear window, only a thin film of plastic, Wells watched the road disappear behind them. The road cut through a dense forest and seemed barely wide enough for one hydro. Luckily traffic was light, and just like Aranya had told her, the only other vehicles that went past them were other bom-boms. As they did, Wells could hear the little motors—*bom-bom, bom-bom*. They seemed highly inefficient and incapable of doing any hard work, but Wells found them oddly endearing.

After three hours, the bom-boms stopped. Wells was glad to get out and stretch her legs. As a veteran of security work, she'd fallen asleep a few minutes after setting off. Any security officer knew that, especially on long missions, you slept when you could. No point in sitting around awake if your next rest might be days away. Lifting her arms over her head, she let her whole body lengthen. It felt good.

"We are halfway to our destination, Lily," Aranya said.

It was still early in the day, but the heat and the humidity made Wells's clothes stick to her skin. Lush green plants were everywhere, and for the first time in her life, Lt. Wells felt claustrophobic. Visibility was only a few meters, sometimes even less. Seeing anything through the thick vegetation was almost impossible. She switched over to her ARP, but with her HIC out of commission and her back up so outdated, its functionality was severely limited. She turned it off again.

"Let's grab some food," Aranya said.

The other Believers had gathered around a bom-bom, and using a small table, were rationing out white boxes. Wells lined up and grabbed one. Another rule was to never refuse food. It, too, could be the last for a while.

Everyone found a spot to enjoy their meal.

Aranya guided Wells away from the others and sat down on a rock. She set her meal on her lap and started eating.

"So," she said as soon as she'd swallowed her first bite, "how are you finding the mission so far?"

Wells had also found a rock and was already a few bites into her meal. "Same as any mission. Most of the time is planning and logistics. The actual mission is always the quickest part."

Aranya seemed to take mental notes. "Is there anything you would have done differently?"

Wells took two more bites before answering. "Yes, quite a lot actually, but time is not on our side."

"But hypothetically, if you had the time." Aranya's face beamed with innocence, but her questions were drifting into another territory.

"If I had the time," Wells grabbed a bite, "I would use smaller, maybe even two- or three-member crews. And hit more targets at once. To truly disrupt the system, I'd try to breach the tube in such a way as to trap some pods in between the compromised sections. The emergency crews would have to rescue the people first, before they could do any repairs. It would most likely take them a day or two, instead of hours. But it would mean more people, and more explosives."

Taking another bite, Wells kept her gaze on Aranya. She was smiling at Wells, but only with her mouth. Her eyes, her mind, were somewhere else. She blinked, and she was back.

"Such a strategic mind. It's a shame we didn't meet earlier."

Aranya closed her empty white box and made her way back to the others.

Wells sat a second longer, lingering over her last bite.

She knew Aranya wasn't being completely honest with her, and it didn't surprise her. They'd only met a few weeks ago. It would be naive to believe everything she told her. Wells didn't even trust the people she usually worked with a hundred percent. People always had their own little agendas and motives. Now that they were out of the hospital and Aranya was back in her element, between her people, she seemed stronger and more independent. She still tried to play the innocent victim, but Wells could see the act disappearing, little by little, day by day.

She knew that the real Aranya would emerge soon.

Standing between a group of people, Aranya was demonstrating something using her arms to explain. Everyone nodded as they followed along with her. The meeting ended and everyone walked back to their bom-boms.

"You ready to go, Lily?" Aranya called out.

In a few hours, you'll be done and on your way out of here. Don't get distracted. Stick to the mission.

"Coming!" Wells replied.

| twenty-four |

Death was imminent. Drake looked at the mess of wires and adhesive tape holding together the twenty or so battery charges. A loud humming sound complemented the vibration of Jimmy's concoction. Heat radiated from it. Drake knew it was only a matter of time before the whole thing exploded, and killed them.

"What ya think?" Jimmy asked, hands on hips, beaming with pride.

"Looks, uh, you know . . ." Drake gestured toward it.

"Yeah?"

"Well . . . Does it work?"

Jimmy pulled his head back as if he was smelling a foul odor. "What do you mean, *does it work?*"

"Sorry, I didn't mean to offend you, Jimmy. It just looks a bit—"

"How should I know?"

"You mean you haven't tested it?"

"No. They make these things to charge batteries. Why wouldn't they work?"

"Because you ripped them open and butchered their insides."

Jimmy looked at the buzzing, almost glowing now, pile of electronics. "Oh. Well, only one way to find out, ya know?"

He stepped closer to the bench, grabbed two wires, and positioned them on the old truck's battery. As the wires touched the terminals on the battery, a huge spark arced between them, and Jimmy went flying backward. He landed on his butt and sat shaking his head.

Drake stood stunned in silence.

"Oops. Maybe I should switch it off first, ya know?"

Walking in a zig-zag pattern, Jimmy made it back to the bench. It took him three tries to flick the switch into the off position.

"Jimmy, are you okay, buddy?"

Jimmy turned around to face Drake. His hair was crazier than normal, his eyes bigger and unfocused, and he had a twitch that made him smile erratically.

"I think so, ya know?" He turned back to the bench.

This time, with the makeshift charger unplugged, Jimmy reconnected the truck's battery. Squeezing his eyes almost all the way shut and scrunching up his entire face, he plugged the charger back in and flipped the switch. The loud buzzing quietened to a hum. Jimmy opened one eye and surveyed the situation. He opened the other eye and turned around.

"See? Nothing to worry about. Told you it would work, ya know."

"So you did." Drake said. Drake had to hand it to him—apart from almost killing himself, Jimmy had made it work. Some of the small LED indicators on the battery lit up, showing it was charging. Rapidly.

"How are feeling, buddy?"

Jimmy shrugged. "Okay, ya know. Been shocked a few times, so no big deal." He turned toward the battery. "All done! Let's get it in the truck."

Jimmy stood staring at him. "Oh. My turn, is it?" Drake stepped up and lifted the battery. It weighed a ton. "All good, buddy. I got it."

"Good. Cause with the shock and all, I'm not sure if I should strain myself, ya know?"

"I thought you were okay." Drake strained under the weight of the battery.

"Best play it safe. Let's go, Seymour." Jimmy led the way to the truck. Drake shuffled behind him with the heavy battery.

Sweat started pouring down Drake's face and back. Although the battery was heavy, it was more a result of the high humidity. The further they traveled outside of Lan-noi, and the closer they got to the jungle area, the more humid it became.

The battery went underneath the driver's side door. Jimmy had already pulled out the flat drawer that would hold it. Drake dropped it down on the drawer, reconnected the terminals, and pushed it all back into place. He made sure he secured the drawer's latch before jumping into the seat. Jimmy had already taken up his position, too. So had Seymour, on the bench between them.

"Nope. Nuh-uh. Not gonna happen," Drake said. "It can ride in the cargo hold."

Jimmy poked his head around Seymour to face Drake. "Please?" His hair was still wild from the shock and, coupled with his pleading eyes, it made it very hard for Drake to not cave in.

"Fine. He can sit behind us."

"Yes! Seymour, move to the back," Jimmy instructed the orange ASR.

It jumped into the back, and Drake gave Jimmy a look that said *anything else?* Jimmy just smiled at him.

"Okay, let's see if this worked," Drake said as he turned the converted hydro truck on. The DDU powered on, and Jimmy swiped through the menus to make sure everything was operational. Next was the big test. Would the truck start?

Silence fell in the cabin as Drake gripped the steering wheel, closed his eyes, and pressed the start button. The silence remained, as nothing happened.

"C'mon," Drake mumbled, and tried again. He knew the truck could have been sitting for a long time, and things might take a second to work their way through the system. He kept his thumb on the switch, quietly mumbling to himself. "C'mon. C'mon. C'mon . . ."

The entire cabin shook, and the low hum of the hydrogen engine filled the cabin.

Drake and Jimmy shouted out. Jimmy's was just pure happiness of achieving their goal. Drakes was an outburst of happiness, anger, and frustration. Things had not been going his way for quite a while now, but tonight they had a small victory. They still had much to do, but at least they had this. Something that made Drake feel normal again.

They finally had a truck again.

* * *

Jimmy had programmed the DDU to respond to the name Yolanda, the name Drake called all his trucks' DDUs. The truck was up and running and it was time to get on the road.

"Yolanda, run diagnostics," Drake commanded.

The outdated DDU flashed a bunch of schematics and numbers as it ran through all the pre-haul scans. A few things showed up that would need some attention soon, but for now, they were good to go.

"Still got those coordinates I got from Big Boy?"

Jimmy rummaged through his HIC. "Yup. Entering it now."

"Wow," Drake said as a green line appeared on the windscreen. Unlike the green lines he was used to, this one did not seamlessly blend onto the road as if painted there. Instead, it looked more like a line drawn on the windscreen, straight up and down, with no perspective to it. Luckily it was small and didn't take up too much of Drake's view.

"Told you. Piece of shit."

Drake shrugged it off. Even though the truck was tiny and old, and the tech outdated, he was still happier than he had been in months. He was in a truck, about to be on the road again. With his partner. What more could he want?

"Hydrogen." Jimmy's voice pulled Drake back to reality. "We're almost out. We'll need to refuel before we hit the road, ya know?"

Unlike his Hydrostar, which showed all the important telemetry on the windscreen, most of the data in the old truck was displayed on the small DDU and some gauges that were scattered about the dashboard. Drake foolishly took them to be decorative at first, but now realized they were all working. Even the one showing the hydrogen level, which painted a bleak picture.

"How much do you reckon it would take to fill it up?" Jimmy asked.

Drake did the math and knew they would not even come close to filling it up a quarter of what they needed. They were also facing another problem: a gray band of sky reached up from the horizon, slowly replacing the stars. Soon people would wake and start roaming the streets. It was time for them to leave.

"What's the plan?" Jimmy asked.

"We go. I'll figure it out." Drake pressed down on the accelerator. The old truck shuddered first before crawling forward. Drake carefully maneuvered it out of the yard and followed the green line to the nearest road.

"I'll search for a hydrogen station," Jimmy said. He had also fallen back into his role in the truck.

Drake had to concentrate more than usual, with the small, green directional arrows and lines appearing so out of place. Instead of following a flowing line on the road, he had to look at the corner of the windscreen to see what to do next. As he drove the old truck past the mix of housing and industrial buildings, he started to get used to it.

The arrows took them out of the neighborhood, and they turned onto a bigger road. It was no highway, but it was wider and flanked by jungle instead of buildings.

"How far is that hydrogen station?" Drake asked.

"There are a few, all of them about an hour away."

"Good. We've got enough hydrogen for an hour, and it will give us time to figure out how to pay for it."

The road snaked through dense jungle, and Drake felt trapped. With the road curving continuously, it felt like lush green trees and plants surrounded them on all sides. Up ahead, all he could see was the road bending away into more trees. In the rearview mirror—an actual piece of reflective glass, not a small DDU—was the same picture. Through his window, and Jimmy's, more green foliage. It was suffocating.

Jimmy came to the same conclusion. "Pretty dense, huh?"

"I feel almost swallowed up in it," Drake admitted. "It's like it's everywhere. I can't see more than a few meters in any direction!"

The local traffic didn't make things any better. Drake was driving much more slowly than he normally would have, feeling right out of his comfort zone on these roads. A few trucks, most of them older converted trucks like theirs, came rushing up from behind and impatiently tried to overtake them. The moment the tiniest gap appeared, they would take it, often forcing the oncoming vehicles to slow down or swerve.

The old truck's DDU was all but useless. By the time it issued a warning of a possible collision, the threat had already passed by. It got so out of sync that Drake had Jimmy disable it. He'd just have to wing it.

Another pest on the roads were these little three-wheeled hydrocar and cycle hybrids. They popped up from nowhere on a side road, barely kept up with the traffic for a few minutes, then disappeared again. Drake's nerves were shot. He'd always liked to drive his Hydrostar manually and enjoyed the feeling of being in charge, but right now, he would kill to have the latest Autodrive take over for him.

As Lan-noi drifted further and further away behind them, the traffic thinned out. The smaller three-wheeled pests became a rarity, and the other hydrocars and trucks they saw drove a bit more sensibly. Drake took a deep breath and spoke for the first time in minutes.

"Damn. I thought the highways around New Franco were a challenge in the little hydrocar."

Jimmy looked terrified.

"You can relax now, buddy. The road is much quieter now."

"A few times back there, I thought we had it, ya know?"

Drake couldn't agree more. "Okay, so back to our big problem. We need to get hydrogen. And fast."

Jimmy used his HIC to see which of the refueling stations was nearest. "Okay, seems there are a few stations around, mostly smaller ones, but that should be fine, right?"

Drake was more accustomed to the larger refueling stations he frequented on the highways back home. The kind that usually served ten to twenty trucks, with a small eatery attached to it. He would inevitably bump into someone he knew at those stations. It was only a few months ago since he last hauled, but it felt like a lifetime.

"You okay?" Jimmy asked.

"Yeah, all good. Just thinking. It's great that you have found hydrogen, but we still don't have any credits to pay for it."

Jimmy pulled a face that Drake used to mistake for him being constipated, but now knew he was busy scheming.

"Leave it to me," Jimmy replied.

| twenty-five |

Wells felt the bom-bom slowing down, and then centrifugal forces pushed her back against the wall as it took a sharp turn. It increased its speed, but only fractionally. Everything was shaking inside the cramped cabin, and Wells figured they had turned onto a dirt road. She saw the ever-observant Aranya watching her.

"I hope this dirt road means we're close," Wells said. The wind noise was quieter, but the road noise louder, so she still had to yell.

"We are."

Wells adjusted her seating position and tried to relax. Soon she was fast asleep again.

Until the sound of tires dragging on dirt and the feeling of her body being flung forward woke her. She looked through the back window and saw they had come to a standstill. Aranya was still steadying herself, but was already talking to someone on her ARP.

"I see. Sit tight. We'll be right over." She swiped her HIC, disconnected the call, and faced Wells. "We have a problem."

Aranya motioned for Wells to follow her and exited the bom-bom. Wells trailed behind her as she made her way to the lead vehicle. The driver leaned out of his window, waiting for them.

"Up there," he said, pointing up the road.

Wells and Aranya turned to look at the spot he pointed out. Wells wished she could access her ARP's zoom function, but she had a broken HIC and her backup was in her bag on the bom-bom. She squinted and saw what appeared to be a small hydro truck.

"I can't make it out. What's going on?"

Wells assumed Aranya did what she couldn't, as she swiped her HIC and presumably zoomed in on the hydro truck with her ARP.

"It looks like a hyperloop maintenance crew at our designated spot. We'll have to get closer to see more."

Aranya turned her ARP off and looked at Wells for direction.

"Did you bring a drone?" Wells asked.

"Yes, a maintenance one to place the explosives." Aranya guessed Wells's plan, and said, "We can't risk sending it, Lily. If they shoot it down, it will compromise the mission. I'm sorry."

Wells wished she had been more diligent. This mission was only a means to an end for her, and she knew she was rushing it. It was not her normal way of doing things. But her aim was to get out, not topple a corporation. Still, she blamed herself for not being prepared.

"Okay, then. We'll need to get closer. Even with my second HIC, I won't have the full functionality of my ARP. We need to get as close as possible to assess the situation and regroup.

You stay here. If something goes wrong, you can still get away. Pick two of your most trusted people to go with me. Make sure they're armed."

Aranya did not question or resist Wells's plan. She turned around and shouted out two names. Two Believers jumped out of the bom-boms and came over to them. Wells looked them over and couldn't find any reason to doubt their abilities.

"Okay," Wells said, addressing the two Believers. "It appears we have a maintenance crew up the road from us. We can assume nothing. We will approach with the assumption that they have weapons and consider them dangerous."

Wells thought this to be a fair approach, considering the tension between Penta and Shangcorp. People were calmer the further they traveled from the bigger cities, like Lan-noi, but she knew the news media would still do their best to scare everyone by only projecting the worst outcomes. Luckily, it seemed the people outside of the cities were less affected by the media's manipulation. The maintenance crew, however, would be from Lan-noi, and with all the panic there, Wells had to assume they would have pulse weapons.

"We'll cut through the jungle and follow a parallel line to the road. Flank them. Any questions?"

The Believers shook their heads.

"Okay, grab your pulse rifle, set it to stun for now, and get ready to move out in five minutes."

Wells turned back to Aranya.

"Did you know there would be a maintenance crew here today?"

Aranya looked shocked. "No! I swear, Lily, I didn't."

"Because taking out a part of the hyperloop and a maintenance crew in one attack would have a much bigger impact. Only, I did not sign up to kill civilians, Aranya. So . . . Did you know?"

"Lily, the crews are always working to keep the hyperloop running. The chances of us running into a crew were always high. I guess—I mean, I can see now that maybe I should have brought it up with you before."

Wells didn't like surprises on a mission.

"But," Aranya continued, "as you pointed out, it would be more effective to take out the tunnel and the crew."

"I also pointed out I'm not shooting civilians, Aranya."

The two Believers approached, but Aranya lifted a hand to stop them.

"I'm not talking about killing anyone. I'm suggesting we destroy their hydrovan and all their equipment. The crew will be free to go. It will take them hours to get back to base, and the maintenance company will be down a team. No one needs to die, Lily."

Wells had a hard time reconciling Aranya's words with the look in her eyes. Something told her she'd happily kill anyone to further her cause.

"As long as your people know we're not killing anyone."

"I'll make sure they know, Lily. Don't worry about it."

Wells wished Aranya's words and eyes would say the same thing.

* * *

Walking through the jungle was harder than Wells had expected. Within minutes sweat covered her entire body, running down her face and stinging her eyes. The heat was tolerable, but the humidity was unbearable. One Believer lead, using her HIC to navigate and stay parallel to the road, about twenty meters to their left. Every step, they had to either climb over something or duck underneath it. The maintenance crew were about a kilometer away, but Wells calculated it would take them at least an hour to get there at this pace. Having no drones or a functional ARP left her with few options.

The two Believers impressed her. They stayed quiet, observed their environment, and made steady progress. Aranya had said she would pick the best, and so far, it seemed to be true. The woman leading stopped and held up a fist. Everyone stopped. Using two fingers, she pointed to her own eyes, and then to something to their left. Wells followed her fingers and saw they were close to the hydrovan. Even if Wells's ARP worked, it would be no good. The jungle was too dense, and it would struggle to focus on the van. She estimated the van to be about fifty meters away. The distance, coupled with all the foliage, meant they should be out of hearing range, and only the best scanners should be able to pick them up. She hoped a maintenance crew out in the jungle didn't carry such a scanner as she shuffled closer to the woman leading them.

"Okay, this looks like a suitable spot to regroup. Can you pick up anything on your ARP? Body heat signatures, active scanners, anything?"

The woman shook her head, accessed her HIC, and focused on the crew. The other Believer held his position and scanned the area. They impressed Wells.

"It's faint, but it looks like a four-person crew. No active scanning. Weapons scan is inconclusive."

"Okay. Even if they are armed," Wells whispered, "We still have the element of surprise and cover."

Both Believers nodded.

"You," Wells said, pointing to the man bringing up the rear, "will be Team Bravo. We'll be Team Alpha. I want you to move another fifty meters further and wait for instructions. When I give the signal, we'll move in at converging angles, so keep your eyes open. Situational awareness is key."

Both nodded again, no confusion on their faces or body language. Wells had no doubt they had tactical training. Which meant they had to be ex-Shangcorp forces. This made Wells uncomfortable, but the fact that Aranya trusted them would have to be enough for now. Team Bravo silently moved along, and Team Alpha crawled forward, trying to get as close as possible to the maintenance crew. Wells tapped the woman on her shoulder, letting her know to stop. They were now about thirty meters away from the crew and could hear their voices. It also meant that the crew could hear any noise they made, so Wells put a finger to her lips to remind her teammate to be silent and tiptoe. They pushed forward to about twenty meters away. Wells leaned in close and whispered.

"Tell Team Bravo we are in position."

The woman sent a message via her HIC and a reply came back immediately. She held her arm up so Wells could read the reply. *Copy. In position. Awaiting Orders.* Wells nodded, and the woman dropped her arm.

One of the maintenance workers walked around the van and opened a side door. Wells got a good look at him. He appeared to be unarmed, and although the interior of the van was dark, she couldn't see any obvious signs of pulse weapons stored inside. After grabbing what he was looking for, he slid the door shut. Playing with some kind of tool in his hand, he walked back around the van.

"Okay," Wells whispered, "time to go. All targets are friendly. Go!"

Confident that they all spoke the same tactical language, Wells used the designator friendly to classify the crew workers as nonthreatening, unarmed, and not to be killed. She placed her hand on the woman's shoulder to hold her back a few seconds. Team Bravo was further back into the jungle than they were and would need a few seconds to catch up. Wells tapped the woman on the shoulder after waiting for what she hoped was the right amount of time, and they pushed forward. Taking their time, making sure they were stealthy, they finally emerged from the jungle. A second later, Team Bravo emerged and quickly took cover behind a fallen tree. Team Alpha ran to the hydrovan and kneeled next to it. Sitting behind the van gave them brilliant cover, but zero visibility. Team Bravo poked his head out and used the same two finger pointing gesture that the woman had used earlier. After pointing, he held up four fingers. He had visual on all four crew workers.

Wells took a deep breath as she berated herself again. This was the first time she had attempted a mission so unprepared. She had no cameras to toss around the corner to get a visual. There were no drones overhead giving her an overview. She didn't even have a working ARP. Wells took another breath and snapped out of it. No changing any of that now. What she had was two seemingly competent teammates and a pulse rifle. Things could have been worse.

Wells made eye contact with Team Bravo and waved her hand over her head. *Cover me.* He gave her a thumbs-up, which almost made her laugh. Although not the official sign used by Penta and most security forces, his intention was still very clear, if a little unorthodox.

She tapped her team mate on the shoulder, and they moved in unison around the van in the same direction the crew member had gone. This put them out of sight of Team Bravo but gave them a better attacking position. Wells stopped at the corner of the van and poked her head around. Four crew workers, all dressed in teal coveralls, were busy working on the hyperloop tube. Wells couldn't see any visible damage. This meant it was only minor, or that they were about to finish. Either way, she and her team would have to act fast. Bravo was still out of sight, but Wells knew as they approached the workers, he would cover them. Observing the workers one last time to confirm they had no weapons, Wells stood up and walked over to them.

"We're armed and will shoot. Put your tools down and get on the ground. Now!"

Confusion set in as the workers looked at Wells and then at each other. Wells realized that the workers' ARPs would have had to play catch-up, and had only translated the last part of her instructions, so she repeated herself.

This time they understood, and everyone slowly bent down and placed their tools on the ground, except one worker, who stood his ground and stared Wells down. Reading the situation perfectly, her teammate joined her, her pulse rifle aiming at the worker still standing.

"Please, we do not want any casualties. Drop your tools now."

He took a step forward instead. Wells did not know what kind of tool he was holding, but she did know that almost any tool could be used as a weapon.

"Okay, buddy, I tried to do this the easy way." Wells lifted her pulse rifle.

A loud crackle to her right grabbed her attention, making her turn her head involuntarily. Bravo had taken up a more offensive position and had clearly just fired his rifle. Wells pivoted her head back and saw one of the other crew members on the ground. Bleeding. In his hand, he was clutching a pulse pistol.

Wells had all her attention on the guy who didn't want to cooperate and did not know if the crew member with the pistol posed a threat or not. All she knew was that Bravo had deemed the use of lethal force necessary. The entire mission changed at that moment. Two of the remaining crew members fell to the ground in a show of surrender, but the other crew member took advantage of the diversion and charged Wells. He was on top of her in a flash, swinging the big metal tool at her head. She ducked in time and heard it making a whoosh sound as it swung past her head. She regained her balance and kicked him as hard as she could in the groin. Immediately, he doubled over, and Wells drove her knee into his face. She felt the cartilage in his nose collapse, and watched him fall backward, eyes shut, body stiff. He was out for the count.

"On me!" Wells yelled.

The other team members rushed forward and took up defensive positioning around her.

"What the fuck?"

Bravo looked at her defiantly.

"Why wasn't your rifle set to stun?"

He looked at his teammate instead of answering Wells.

"Talk to me right now, or I'm done." She turned to walk away.

"Aranya told us to use force," the woman said.

"No, she didn't. I was there. She agreed to no unnecessary force."

The woman accessed her HIC and showed it to Wells.

Casualties are a necessary evil in the battle for freedom. Use your discretion out there. The mission comes first.

Anger overwhelmed her, but this was not her first mission to go sideways. She composed herself and faced the two Believers.

"Switch your rifles to stun, right now," she ordered. "Then strip these two of everything but their clothes and have them carry their friend out of here."

Wells heard them mumble something, but she was already climbing into the maintenance van and heading back to Aranya.

| twenty-six |

The man exited the maintenance building and walked slowly over to one of the three-wheeled hydrocar-cycle hybrids. He got in, took his time to get everything started, and drove off. Drake waited until the noise of the little engine disappeared before turning to Jimmy.

"So? Will this one do?"

Jimmy nodded. "I think so. It's pretty quiet, ya know."

Jimmy put his hand on Seymour, who was sitting next to them on the ground, behind a bush.

"You're up, Seymour. Just do your best, ya know, and be careful." Jimmy said to the ASR. He entered everything he needed Seymour to do into his HIC and transferred it over. The orange robot stood up and ran over to the small refueling station. Every ten meters, it stopped and scanned, as per Jimmy's instructions. As it scanned, the results were displayed on Jimmy's ARP.

"So far there is only one heat signature and two low resolution cameras," Jimmy reported to Drake.

Seymour walked another ten meters and scanned again. The same information came through, and Jimmy relayed it again.

Nearing the first refueling pump, Seymour walked behind it and crouched down. Jimmy got to work on his HIC and after a few seconds said, "Done. I'm hooked into the surveillance system. It's not a very good unit they have here, ya know."

Jimmy finished up reprogramming the cameras. Then he pulled the little black square that Dina had given them out of his pocket and slipped it over his head. "Just to be safe, ya know."

"Be careful, buddy. If it feels wrong, abort and we'll regroup, okay?"

"I've got this, ya know. Walk in the park." Before Drake could reply, Jimmy sped off, running across the road and taking cover behind the same pump as Seymour. He took a moment to catch his breath before setting off for the small office with Seymour in the lead. The door opened, and they disappeared.

* * *

"On the ground! On the ground!" Jimmy yelled at the man behind the counter.

It had been months since he robbed a shop, but muscle memory quickly kicked in and he was flying on autopilot. Though the adrenaline made him shaky, he felt in complete control. By now, Seymour would have disabled the cameras, but Jimmy kept the mask on to be safe. The man was cooperating and was lying facedown on the ground.

"Give me the transfer code!" Jimmy yelled.

The man lifted his head and gave Jimmy a defiant look. This was usually the only sticking point. Handing over the transfer code would grant Jimmy access to all the day's earnings and the ability to transfer it to any HIC he wanted. The man would have been told by his employers never to do it, under any circumstances, even though they had insurance. On top of trying to keep their premiums low, they also had the opportunity to cash in on a death in the workplace payout if the employee got shot. So, win-win for the big guys again. A broken nose, either by a boot or a gun stock, would usually hasten the process a bit.

But that was old Jimmy.

"Fuck man, I don't want to hurt you, and I know you don't care about this place, ya know? So how about you just give me the codes and I get back to my family in Lan-noi?"

The man's expression didn't change.

"Don't do this, man," Jimmy pleaded.

It was clearly not his first time being held up.

"Dammit, man!"

Jimmy raised his gun and shot the man.

* * *

Drake saw the orange ASR run out the door. It sat down and raised one of its front legs. The signal. Drake left his hiding spot behind the bush and ran the fifty meters back to the truck. He'd left it in standby mode, so there was no delay in getting going. In less than two minutes from seeing Seymour, he'd parked the truck next to a pump. As Drake climbed out, Jimmy exited the building. His head was down, and his shoulders hung.

"How did it go? Everything okay?" Drake asked as he started the refueling process.

"Yeah, everything went as planned. Knocked out the cameras, but only after it captured me holding him up and telling him I'm from Lan-noi, ya know. When he wakes up, he'll call security and tell them about the failed robbery attempt. It'll take them hours before they realize there is hydrogen missing."

"So it all went to plan, then?" The tank showed half full.

"It didn't feel nice, ya know. The way he looked at me."

"Huh?"

"Like I was something disgusting, ya know?"

"You were holding a gun to his face, Jimmy."

"Do people find me disgusting?"

Drake could see Jimmy was hurting, but didn't know what to say.

"I'm not a bad person anymore, ya know? The things we do, it's only for survival, ya know."

The pump stopped as the truck's tank reached capacity.

"Jimmy, I know you're not a bad guy. Your past is not who you are. Your actions now are what define you—to me, at least. We've all done shitty things before. But we can't change that, now, can we? We can only try not to make the same choices again, I guess."

Realizing he still had the hydrogen connector in his hand, Drake replaced it in the cradle on the pump.

"Thanks, Drake. I'm really not a bad person, ya know. I'm really not."

"I know buddy." Drake punched his shoulder. "There is no way I would hang out with you if I thought you were. Now, how about we get out of here before anyone sees, okay?"

"Let's go," Jimmy said with a big smile and watery eyes.

* * *

The location of the coordinates Big Boy had given them was coming up fast. Having the truck full of hydrogen gave Drake a sense of calm and the confidence to push harder and drive quicker. Traffic had slowed down, and only the occasional lunatic came flying past them. How these people could drive so fast and recklessly was beyond Drake. It seemed rural Shangcorp didn't bother with speed cameras and drones. Or maybe the drones had all been redeployed to help with the standoff against Penta. The tiny green line turned into a small bent arrow. An approaching turn. Drake kept an eye out for the turnoff, expecting it to be small and not well signposted, as the road would likely be even smaller than the one they were currently driving on. And he was right. With almost no warning, a gap appeared in the jungle, with a road in the middle. Except . . . to call it a road was generous. Two lanes, with some grass growing in the middle, constituted their new route. Drake held on as he made the tight turn and clenched his jaw as the truck's brakes did the bare minimum to assist him. The truck went slightly wide, plowing through some plants, before Drake straightened it out. The humidity made him sweat profusely, and he wiped his brow.

"Sorry about that. Bit tighter than I thought," Drake said.

"All good," Jimmy replied.

Drake noticed Jimmy wasn't clinging on for dear life anymore when he drove erratically. The look of facing certain death still prevailed.

On screen, the navigation telemetry showed their destination to be only a few minutes away. There had been no housing units or any buildings since they left the highway, and the remoteness of the location alarmed Drake. He hoped Big Boy hadn't set them up.

The little green arrow became a turn symbol again, and as they rounded the corner, the road ended in front of a dilapidated structure. Drake stopped in front of it and looked around, keeping the truck on standby. There were no other roads in or out and only a single structure. To the side of the rundown building sat a hydrocar. It was a Shangcorp make, and Drake did not recognize it. It looked old but well looked after. He didn't see any other vehicles.

"Okay, buddy. This is it."

"Guns or no guns?" Jimmy asked.

Great question. Drake had hoped for this to be a friendly encounter and had given little thought to contingencies. Big Boy had seen Drake, Jimmy, Ziggy, and Dina at the hospital, but when Drake went back to talk to him, he was alone. There was a good chance Big Boy's friends were only expecting one person.

"I'll go in unarmed, and you can cover me from here."

"I got your back, partner." Jimmy lifted the Artie and slapped it.

Drake switched on his ARP and changed it over to broadcast mode. Jimmy did the opposite and now had Drake's point of view projected on his ARP.

"Good to go, partner."

"Okay, be ready. I've got no idea what I'm walking into."

Drake climbed out of the truck and started toward what looked like the entrance. Jimmy also exited the cabin, and climbed onto the back of the truck. This position gave him some elevation and suitable cover.

There was no DDU to be seen when Drake reached the door, so he knocked instead. He listened and heard faint footsteps approaching. He stepped back, making sure Jimmy would have an unobstructed view if needed.

The door opened.

A man that looked like a local eyeballed him.

"Joh said a *waigoren* might come around." It was the second time Drake had heard that word. He assumed it meant outsider or foreigner.

"If Joh is a big guy that works in a hospital, then yes, I'm the wai-thing."

"You alone?"

A loaded question. The guy could be nervous and all alone and scared of being overwhelmed. Or he needed to make sure there are no witnesses to whatever is about to go down. Joh's friend looked very nervous to Drake.

"Just me."

"Okay. Come in."

He stepped aside to let Drake in. Going inside would put him at a great disadvantage, as Jimmy could not cover him with his pulse rifle. Luckily, they were still connected by ARP, so Drake took the risk. He had to. This was his only lead to get to Lt. Wells.

Drake stepped into the dimly lit room, and as the door closed behind him, the business end of a pulse rifle greeted him.

| twenty-seven |

Dust and rocks flew into the air as the brakes grabbed onto the rotors and locked the wheels up. The van skidded a few meters before coming to a stop. Wells waited for the dust cloud to settle around the van.

And the red cloud of anger that floated inside her.

Wells climbed out of the van and walked around it. Aranya was still another few hundred meters away, but Wells knew that going in angry would not play in her favor. Not only was Aranya surrounded by her loyal followers, but she had a way of talking herself out of any wrongdoing and making it seem justifiable and honorable. Going in accusing her of not sticking to the plan would only backfire, Wells was sure of it. Best to calm down first and try to match Aranya's calm mood.

Wells kicked the side of the van as hard as she could before climbing back in. It took her less than a minute to reach the convoy.

"Lily, I heard what happened. I'm glad you're okay and that the mission was a success. We are so grateful to have you. I knew we couldn't do this without you." All the Believers bowed together with Aranya, in a show of respect for Lt. Wells.

She'd been right to calm down first. Aranya had come pre-pared for a screaming match, and she'd de-escalated the situ-ation even before it began. She knew she'd crossed a line, giving orders behind Wells's back, and her actions now confirmed it.

"We had a slight hiccup," Wells said. "Some confusion on a few details, but considering we are a new team, we did fine."

Aranya smiled with only her mouth. "I'm so glad Lily. You really are invaluable to us."

Lily smiled back.

"Once the rest of the team gets back, we'll regroup and continue," Aranya said, and turned to talk to some Believers.

* * *

It only took the two members that Lt. Wells left behind ten minutes to return. They looked sweaty and irritated. They im-mediately went over to Aranya to debrief. If this was a Penta mission, Wells would have been right there, taking everything in. But she wanted them to tell Aranya exactly how things went down, holding nothing back because she was standing there. Lt. Wells hated playing games, but clearly, Aranya didn't. Her gut told her to play along if she wanted to receive the promised help of getting out of here.

"Lily!" Aranya waved her over.

"If everything is ready, I think we can move out when you say," Aranya said as Wells walked up to her.

"Ready when you are, Aranya."

* * *

As instructed, the maintenance crew was nowhere to be seen when they arrived at the hyperloop. Some of their tools were still lying around, but there was no sign of the workers.

"You two. And you two," Wells said, calling over some Believers, "scan the area. Make sure there is no one around. Use your ARPs, but also do a visual check."

Wells doubted that an elite team of Shangcorp Security operatives would hide in these remote jungles, but she had been taking too many shortcuts lately. Something she planned on remedying. The two teams ran off in opposite directions, following Wells's orders.

Ten meters above them, a low humming sound turned into a *whoop-whoop-whoop* and a tremor shook the ground below. The sound grew louder, and the ground shook harder until it peaked and faded again.

"Seems the maintenance crew fixed the line before we got here," Lt. Wells said once the hyperloop passed.

This would please Aranya, as blowing up a broken tunnel would have been a waste of time. It would still have sent the same message, but the impact would have been greatly diminished. Aranya's face confirmed her suspicion.

The two teams returned, both confirming no activity in the area.

It was time to blow things up.

Wells walked to the bom-bom that was carrying all the explosives and opened the rear flap. The little hydro vehicle was a cargo-specific variant and had no seating in the back. Boxes filled with explosives took up the entire cargo space.

"You! Grab four people and move the explosives closer to the pile." Wells pointed to the vertical structure supporting the hyperloop tube.

"You two," she continued, "keep monitoring the area. Make sure no one approaches. Scan for any signals, as well. If anything pops up, tell Aranya or me." She looked around. "Who is the drone operator?"

A man approached Wells.

"Grab your gear and meet up at the explosives."

Silence fell, and everyone knew it was time to move. In unison, they all went about performing the duties handed out to them.

Aranya stood watching it all with a look of approval. She made eye contact with Wells and walked over.

"I wish I could have a hundred like you."

"Luckily for everyone, there is only one," Wells replied.

"I'm serious, Lily. A leader like you could change the lives of thousands of people. People who would follow you to the end of the world. You could make a genuine change here."

For the first time in days, Aranya's eyes matched her words. She believed every word she had said. Wells enjoyed seeing this side of her again.

"I can't. This is not my fight. These are not my people. I'm flattered, Aranya, I really am, but—"

"We've unloaded all the explosives," a man shouted right next to Wells, startling her.

"Thank you," she replied, restraining herself from putting a gag in his mouth.

Wells and Aranya made their way over to the team, awaiting their next orders.

"Who is the explosives expert?" Wells asked.

Two people stepped forward.

"Good. Start assembly of the devices and use all the hands available to do it quick."

Heads nodded all around and people set to work. Wells was no explosives expert but had worked with enough to know her way around them. But instead of lending a hand, she monitored the activities, supervising them, making sure it all went smoothly. She didn't know these people and had no intention of getting blown to bits by someone who didn't know what they were doing. Luckily, like the two people escorting her, the explosives personnel appeared to have had some serious training too. Their way of meticulously working on the devices reminded her of the teams she used to work with back home. The fear of being blown into pieces subsided, and Wells took joy in watching experts applying their craft.

After checking and rechecking all their work, it was time to place the charges.

The first few they did by hand, placing them a meter up on the pile supporting the hyperloop tube, ten meters above them. The rest were going directly on the tube on either side of where it met the pile. To do this, they'd need the drone.

The operator grabbed his gear and came over to where Wells and Aranya stood. Unlike the drones she'd seen in Penta, this model appeared ancient. The Penta operators could use their HICs and ARPs to maneuver the drones, and always turned about to be significant assets. But this operator had a separate control device to fly the drone. Wells hoped his skills were better than his equipment.

After loading the first charge onto the drone, the operator took over and, using his controller, lifted the drone off the ground. It struggled with the loaded weight, but slowly it made its way up toward the massive tube above them. Carefully, the operator maneuvered the drone to within an inch of the tube and set it to hover. Manipulating the hydraulic arms on the drone, he picked up the explosive device and attached it to the tube. He pressed a button to activate the explosive and returned the drone to the ground. A procedure he'd have to complete seven more times.

With two more to go, Wells felt a slight tremble in the ground. She strained to listen, and within a few seconds, she heard the unmistakable sound of an approaching pod in the hyperloop tube. If something went wrong now, lives would be lost. And that was not part of the deal.

"Stop the drone!" she yelled to the operator.

Wells's worst fear came true. The explosives were almost in place, and instead of stopping and letting the drone hover, the operator tried to rush the process and hastily mounted the explosive to the tube. As he moved the drone away, the explosive slipped down the pile, and he used the drone to prop it up. He stopped the explosive device from falling to the ground, but in the process, he accidentally pressed the activation button. With no time delay. Wells looked on as she saw the look of hopelessness on the operator's face.

The noise of the approaching hyperloop pod disappeared as the violence of the explosion took over all her senses, and the force flung her off her feet.

***

Darkness gave way to light and noise. Lots of noise. People screaming and yelling. Wells blinked and tried to focus on the voices. Although there was lots of noise, it sounded muted, like she was underwater. She shook her head. But it was pointless. It was not the first time she had burst an eardrum and she hoped it wasn't too severe. Heat made her aware that something was burning, and she quickly found the source. A few meters in front of her was the remains of the hyperloop pod, still in flames. The screaming and yelling voices came from within. Wells quickly surveyed herself for any injuries, but except for the ear and her chest, she seemed fine.

Wells jumped to her feet and accessed the situation. Three of the Believers, including the drone operator, had sustained massive wounds. They were dead. The remaining members were sitting or standing in disbelief, with a varying degree of minor cuts and bruises. Wells failed to see Aranya, but remembered that she was standing slightly behind her before the explosion. Wells turned around and saw her frail body on the ground. Bending down, Wells immediately found a heartbeat and saw breathing. That was good enough for now.

Running over to the surviving crew members, Wells started shouting orders as she approached them.

"We need to get those people out now! Find tools, guns, anything, and get in there!"

Everyone snapped out of it and scrambled around, looking for anything to breach the hull of the pod. The big tool that had almost decapitated Wells sat on the ground in front of her. Grabbing it, she inspected it to see if it would be of any use. Turns out, it was exactly what she needed. Wells found the power button and switched on the massive plasma cutter.

"Give me a hand!" she yelled as she ran toward the screaming. It gave her hope that the people were still alive, hearing their terrified voices.

Two of the Believers came rushing over, each with a metal pipe in hand. It was perfect.

"As I cut, bend open the hull. The moment it's big enough to grab people out, do it!"

The cutter weighed a ton, but adrenaline and years of lifting heavy weights in a gym helped her control it. Slowly, a ragged line appeared in the pod's hull. Wells wished she could go quicker, but she knew rushing it would only mean having to go back and redo it. Her arms were shaking, sweat stinging her eyes, but she held on tightly to the cutter, watching the cut grow.

Finally, it reached a stage where they could insert the poles and bend the hull open. Wells kept cutting as the Believers strained to open the side of the pod. A hand shot through the gap, grasping for help. As it flailed around, the arm ripped itself open on the rough cuts made by the plasma cutter. But that didn't stop the person trying to get out.

"Hurry! These people are dying!" Wells yelled out.

The two Believers, exhausted by now, didn't say a word, but forced their pipes deeper into the pod and pulled harder than before. They must have found a weak spot in the structure, for suddenly it snapped open, leaving an enormous hole. Immediately, people poured out of it, knocking all three of them down and trampling over them to get to safety.

Wells covered her head and crawled away from all the feet stepping over her.

A hand grabbed her by the shoulder.

"We need to leave now, Lily." It was Aranya.

Fatigued, injured, and shocked, Wells stared back at her, too tired to reply.

"The local security is almost here. They cannot find us at this scene. We must go."

Aranya pulled at Wells to stand up, but she didn't budge.

"Lily, please!"

Wells saw all the people huddling around, hugging each other, pointing fingers at her. Aranya was right. They had to get out of there.

"We're taking the van," Wells said. "I'm not sitting in the back of one of those shitboxes again."

| twenty-eight |

"Hey, now! I got these coordinates from Big—" Drake racked his brain to remember the name his new friend used only a few seconds ago. "Joh! That's it. Joh gave me these coordinates. He said you were friends?"

The door shut behind Drake, and his new friend came into view, taking a spot next to the gun wielder.

"We know Joh. We know him very well. But unfortunately for you, he is not our friend."

Drake tried to swallow, but his throat didn't want to co-operate.

"C'mon guys. The last few days have been really shitty, and Joh said to look you up for some help. What do you say?"

Drake knew Jimmy was watching all this and wondered what he'd define as an emergency before he came in shooting. The room didn't have any windows facing Jimmy, and Drake saw no way to reposition himself to give Jimmy a chance of a shot. The only option was for him to enter the house.

"Had a few bad days, huh?" The guy who'd opened the door faked wiping tears away.

So far, he didn't strike Drake as the most intelligent person in the room. Drake shifted his attention to the guy holding the gun. He had the same facial features as most people in the area, but unlike most people here, he was about as tall as Drake. He didn't seem overly muscular, and Drake gave himself favorable odds to take him down. If he could overpower him and take the rifle, he could take control of the situation.

"Okay, it seems there has been some mix-up here. What do you say we try to figure it out, eh?"

Both men laughed.

"What do you say we figure it out, eh?" the smaller man mocked him.

It dawned on Drake that Big Boy, or Joh, hadn't sent him here for reinforcements. This was a setup. How could he have been so naive? Believing a man who'd just lost his arm—because of him—was genuinely helping? Idiot.

"Okay. So tell me the deal here, so we can get this over with."

The smaller man stepped forward, right into Drake's personal space.

"The deal is, Joh owes us credits and told us he was sending a *waigoren* over to settle the debt. So it's your choice, really. Give us five hundred credits, or . . ."

Drake had no intention of rushing this conversation and waited for him to finish his dramatic pause.

"Or . . ." he said, pausing again, "we take your truck."

Drake knew there was no scenario where they would not kill him and take his truck anyway. The guy was just trying to get some credits first, before giving the kill order. Unfortunately, Jimmy still didn't see this as an emergency.

"Oh, is that all? Five hundred credits? Easy. Consider it done," Drake said.

The guy licked his lips.

"Okay. Swipe it over then." He held his dated HIC toward Drake.

"Ah, so, slight problem . . ." Drake watched the gunman, making sure he stayed relaxed. "All my credits are on an HID, in my truck."

The small guy gave the gunman a sideways look.

"And the guy who sold it to me encrypted it," Drake lied. "It's actually annoying having to scan my eye and use my password every time I want to access my credits, but hey, it is what it is."

Drake knew it would take them a while to get rid of the truck, so easy credits right now would be too appealing to pass. All he had to do was waste some time until Jimmy came in, or get everyone outside, so Jimmy could start being useful.

The small guy sniffed loudly.

"Okay. Tell me where the HID is and I'll go get it."

He could make this work. If Jimmy shot the guy as he opened the door, Drake would take down the gunman and regain control of the situation. Even if a fight broke out, Jimmy would surely be up to speed by then, and come help.

"Sure. On the bed behind the seat. Just lying there. Can't miss it."

The little guy gave him an intimidating look. "If he moves, shoot." He opened the door and left.

Silence settled in the room. Drake tried to see around the gunman and out the door, but as he stepped sideways, a grunt escaped him, and he waved the gun at Drake.

"So that's a no, then?"

If he couldn't see what was happening, he would try to hear. Focusing on the outside noises, he waited for the sound of pulse rounds crackling, or a rustle as Jimmy and the small guy fought. Any of those sounds, and Drake would jump into action. He imagined the process of the small guy walking to the truck, opening the door and leaning over the seat. He would rummage for a bit, but then come storming back. Somewhere between him entering the truck and rushing back empty-handed, Drake imagined Jimmy would step in.

Something should have happened by now, Drake realized. Minutes had passed, and nothing had happened. There were no pulse crackles. No rustling. And Jimmy hadn't come running in, saving the day. Something was wrong.

"Sure is taking his time," Drake said to the bigger man, blocking his view.

A wet, slapping sound came as a reply, and the man rolled his eyes skyward. Slowly, he tumbled forward, his head falling on Drake's feet. The back of his head was a gooey, red mess.

Looking up through the open door, Drake saw three people walking toward him from the truck. One of them was Jimmy.

The other two were Dina and Ziggy.

* * *

"I really should have charged you more," Dina said as she entered the room.

She walked over to a cabinet as Jimmy and Ziggy entered. Dina pulled a bottle out of the cabinet and drank straight from it.

"Wow! These mountain people always have the good stuff." She handed the bottle to Ziggy, who also took a gulp.

Drake looked at the dead man at his feet, then at Jimmy's smiling face, before turning to Dina and Ziggy.

"What?" Drake mumbled.

It was Jimmy who replied. "Hey, guess who rocked up as I was about to shoot that little guy out there?"

Drake assumed he was being rhetorical.

"Dina and Ziggy, ya know!" Jimmy waved his arm at them.

Clearly, it wasn't rhetorical.

Drake stepped back, and the leaking head thumped on the ground.

"I'm sorry—I mean, I'm really glad to see you guys again, but what the fuck?"

Dina took another sip from the bottle and handed it to Drake. He grabbed it, took a swig, and almost spat it out immediately. Whatever it was, it tasted like battery acid, and felt like it too, sliding down his throat.

"Hey! My turn, ya know." Jimmy held his hand out. Drake was all too happy to pass it along.

"Glad to see you too, Drake," Dina replied.

Ziggy just rolled her eyes.

"I thought you guys left?"

"We did," Dina said. "But we received a new contract and took it. Credits are credits, especially if war is coming."

Jimmy tried to pass the bottle back to Drake, but he shook his head.

"But why are you here? We're in the middle of nowhere. Literally. I do not know where we are. Why are you here?"

Ziggy shook her head and took the bottle from Jimmy.

"Because your friend from the hospital is our new contract, idiot."

* * *

It took Drake a few moments to process Ziggy's words. Dina, Ziggy, and Jimmy all had another round with the bottle, but Drake's head was swimming all on its own.

"I'm still confused. Who gave you this contract? Are you sure it's Lily you're after?"

"Yes, I'm sure," Dina said.

"How can you be? This doesn't make sense."

"When we left the hospital, we had no plans, but we figured the countryside would be calmer than the cities. We have no desire to get involved in this war, so we were looking for a spot to wait it out."

Dina pointed her head at the door, and Ziggy took a defensive position. Drake noticed she still had the silenced weapon she'd used at the hospital, which explained why he hadn't heard the shot.

"But everything cost credits, and since you gave me that crappy hydro instead of credits, we had to take a contract."

"A contract? What are you guys?"

"Bounty hunters!" Jimmy chirped in.

"I guess. Sort off. Let's just say our training and skills are in high demand."

Drake recalled how they handled themselves en route to the hospital and inside of it as well. Countless people and organizations would happily pay for services like that.

"Okay, so who gave you the contract?"

"I don't know," Dina replied.

"How can you not know?"

"I have done some work for this company in the past, and they contacted me. I'm sure they are just a middleman protecting someone else. So I really don't know."

Drake was still not following or understanding how they'd ended up in the same shack in the middle of a jungle.

"So you left us at the hospital, and then someone gave you a contract to come here?"

"Yes."

Drake was losing patience. Dina was being less than helpful, and he had a dead man's blood drying on his shoes.

"Dina, please," Drake pleaded.

A wide grin appeared across Dina's face before a chuckle escaped from her.

"I'm just playing with you, Drake. You look so serious today. Ziggy, doesn't he look serious?"

Ziggy glared at Drake.

"Okay. We are mercenaries. Ex-security. Most officials in Shangcorp are corrupt, so we figured, if we wanted to make some credits, we could either become like them, or leave the system and forge our own way. So we left. We pick up work through word of mouth, as we are very good at what we do. When you met us, we were lying low after a long contract that went bad."

Dina paused to have another drink.

"At the hospital, it was clear your friend wasn't there, so we left. No hard feelings, but this is my job, not a hobby."

"You made that very clear."

"Okay. Shortly after, we received a message. Again, I could tell you from who, but these people isolate themselves pretty good, and the name would lead you nowhere."

Drake nodded.

"Attached to the message were two pictures. The one was the one you showed us, and the other was the same person, but more official looking. The client wanted us to find and assist Lt. Lily Wells."

"Assist? Why?"

"I don't know, and frankly, I don't care. We have a code, and we never accept questionable jobs, but this one seemed easy and clean, so we didn't ask questions."

"Clean?"

"You know, not messy. Like your friend over there." Dina gestured toward the body on the ground.

"So why are you here?"

"When we received the contract, we were still close to the hospital, so we turned back. Figured you'd still be there, running in circles."

"We were, ya know?"

"Thanks, buddy."

"We saw you leave the hospital and followed you."

"Why didn't you just join us?"

Dina shrugged.

"It seemed you were on a trail, and we didn't want to interfere."

Drake pointed to the corpse, splayed out on the floor. "That looks like interference to me."

"I think you meant to say thank you," Ziggy replied from the door.

"I saw the path leading to the house, with no escape routes, and figured you might be in trouble. We pulled up and saw Jimmy. He confirmed you did not know what you were doing."

"You're welcome," Ziggy chimed in again.

"I had it all under control," Drake protested.

"Doesn't matter, now. We are here and can help you. The contract is to help her get out of Shangcorp. I guess you can tag along out of here with her. So, where is the lieutenant?"

Drake dropped his head. The blood on his boots was turning brown.

"You were right. I do not know what I'm doing."

| twenty-nine |

I will never forget those who walk beside me, and I promise you, I will reward your loyalty.

Captain Davis reread the message from Captain Santo.

I will reward your loyalty.

The most influential man in the solar system owed him. Davis shook his head in glee as he reread it again.

Poor and unambitious people scurried after credits, trying to amass as much as they could, before keeling over. They spent their worthless lives chasing something that, inevitably, meant nothing. A worthless existence.

Capt. Davis knew that the only thing that really mattered was power. Power was freedom. Power was control. Power was everything.

Being Santo's second in charge might not be the highest level of power, but it was a level few would ever achieve.

And Captain Davis was on track to do so.

He scrolled to the second message he had been obsessing about.

Almost done. Progress is slow, but positive. Will confirm the kill soon.

If not for the inspirational message from Santo, Davis would have ended the contract with the person in Shangcorp today and found a new one. Guns for hire were on every street corner, and with war coming and possible conscription, they would happily earn a few quick credits. The only reason he hadn't pulled the plug was that in all his years of lying his way up the ladder of corruption, he'd learned to keep things simple. Clever, but simple. With Santo playing Penta and Shangcorp off against each other, he had to focus on assisting Santo. Having a disgruntled killer out to get him because of a canceled contract was not worth the headache. If it meant Lt. Wells lived a few more days, so be it. Helping Santo, and getting recognized for it, was the primary goal.

Eventually Wells would die. And she would know it was because of him.

* * *

Aranya slid her sleeve down, covering her new HIC, and walked up to Lt. Wells.

"How are you feeling?"

Holding her chest, she looked up at Aranya. "Fine. I think my eardrum burst and my chest hurts, but I don't think the wound opened again. There's no bleeding, so I think it's fine."

"We lost some people today, but thanks to you, the mission was a success."

Wells felt blood rushing to her head and her muscles tensing up, ready to fight. "Success? We almost killed twenty civilians."

"Yes. I cannot argue with that, Lily. And I wish it had gone better, and that we didn't have three bodies to bury. But unlike the war everyone says is coming, we are already fighting one."

All this sounded like justifications to Wells. "How did the other groups go?"

"I checked my messages only a minute ago, and so far, it seems everyone had success, and no casualties on either side."

"Either side? Are you classifying civilians as the enemy now?"

"No, Lily, that was a terrible choice of words. You know that the leaders of Shangcorp are our enemy."

Lt. Wells wanted to put all this behind her as quickly as possible. The longer she stayed here, the more involved she'd get. Today had been a close shave, and if she'd had a hand in killing multiple civilians, she would never forgive herself. Aranya and her Believers were fighting a war that she had no place in.

"I need to get out of here, Aranya."

Aranya took Wells's hands in her own small hands. Hands with scars running all over them.

"Remember when we met in the hospital? Both of us broken. You chained to that bed. Prisoners. Look at us now, Lily. We are free, and one day all the people in Shangcorp will be free too. Don't you want to be part of that?"

A tear trickled down Aranya's face, despite her looking hopeful.

Wells wasn't buying any of it. She'd had enough.

Pulling her hands away, she said, "I'm done, Aranya. I've done my part. Actually, I think I've done more than my part. It's time for me to go."

"I'm going to try one more time, Lily. Stay. It might not be your people or your home, but you can do things here that you could never do in Penta. You can change history. The people will immortalize you. I know there is more for you here than back in Penta."

Aranya was right. There was nothing for her in Penta. When she'd chased down Drake and Jimmy Something, and uncovered Santo's plan to occupy Mars, she'd felt like she had her life back. Everything fell back into place, and afterward she tried to put Drake behind her and move on with her life. And it worked. Case after case, she ruthlessly went after and solved. Her life had meaning again, and everything she ever wanted was coming her way.

Then Drake came back.

In the middle of an investigation, his name had popped up, and he was right back in the center of her life again. Once more, she had to chase after him and Jimmy, but this time there was no glory at the end for her. Instead, all she'd received was a knife in the chest. Left to die alone in a foreign territory, lying on the side of the road.

She did not know if Penta would even take her back, considering she didn't have permission to be in Shangcorp. They might even arrest her upon reentering Penta territory. Maybe Aranya was right. Maybe her life there was already over. She just didn't know it yet.

"I can see you thinking about it, Lily. Why don't you stay the night, eat something, sleep, and then we can talk again in the morning? It's getting late, anyway."

Wells knew if she listened to Aranya, she might never see Penta again. Aranya had a way of manipulating her and those around her, and always seemed to get her way. She didn't strike Wells as evil, but there was something dark about her.

There was also something else about her. Moments of genuine friendship. Something Wells secretly longed for.

"I'm not going to change my mind, Aranya."

"That's fine, but you still need to rest before your journey back to Penta."

"Okay, but first thing in the morning, I'm leaving."

"Okay, Lily."

* * *

Lily Wells woke up in the same room she'd woken up in after leaving the hospital. The noises from the other room drifted in and it sounded like a busy morning. Wells grabbed her boots and looked for her bag, the one that contained her second HIC and some personal things. Strangely, it wasn't next to her bed, or, after a quick look, anywhere else in the room. She tried to recall where she'd put it the previous night. She remembered how tired she was after all the action of the day, and how she'd passed out as soon as they arrived back. Nothing else came to mind. She figured she might have dropped it somewhere in the building on her way to her room.

Wells grabbed the door handle to slide it open. The base was a typical rural Shangcorp dwelling and had little tech built in. Most doors, except for the exterior ones, had DDUs to operate them. Wells pulled the handle, but it didn't budge. Feeling embarrassed, she wondered if she was doing it wrong. It was a strange thing to admit, but she couldn't remember the last time she'd had to open a door herself. Didn't she open this door the last time she was here? Surely it was just stuck. She gave it a hard yank, but it stayed closed. She stood back and inspected the door and its rail to see if there was anything obstructing it. Nothing. The logical explanation was it had to be obstructed from the outside. Maybe a misplaced chair, or even the bag she couldn't find. She yanked on it one last time, then gave up.

"Hey! My door is stuck! Can someone open it, please?"

Wells took a step back and waited for the door to slide open. It didn't.

The noise from the other side continued uninterrupted. Something big had to be going down, having everyone so focused. She felt guilty for distracting them, but it was time for her to leave.

Stepping up to the door, she banged harder.

"Hey! Sorry, guys. I think the door is broken or stuck. Can someone quickly give me a hand?"

This time she stayed at the door and placed her ear on it, hoping to hear better.

A chair scraped the ground, and footsteps approached the door.

Finally. Wells took a step back again and waited to be released.

The door stayed shut.

"Aranya said to keep you in there until she returned. Please stop yelling and kicking the door." The voice sounded like An's.

"An, is that you? Where is she?" Wells yelled.

No answer came, so she kicked and banged on the door as hard as she could.

"Where is Aranya!"

"I told you to stop the noise. She'll be back soon."

Wells grabbed the handle and pulled as hard as he could. The door, like the building, was old but built to last. Pulling with all her might did not make it move an inch.

She collapsed back onto the makeshift bed.

Aranya had played her again. She'd lured her into staying, and now Wells had to consider that maybe she was her prisoner.

Pulling her legs up to her chest, she hugged them and laid her head on her knees.

No point in wasting any more energy. She'll need all of it for when Aranya returned, so she could kick her ass.

| thirty |

"Be careful!" Drake yelled at Jimmy.

The dead man's head banged against the truck's fender, and a sizable piece of scalp and hair stayed behind.

"Doesn't matter, ya know? He's dead," Jimmy said as he looked down at the mangled head hanging limply from its neck. He recalled seeing the tiny figure, head still intact, leaving the house that Drake went into. The little man had barely made it out of the house before a cloud of pink mist evaporated from him. It had taken Jimmy a second to realize what had happened, but as the man fell to the ground, he connected all the dots. Someone shot him. Jimmy spun around and switched his ARP to scan for body heat signatures. Two faint readings came back. He switched it back to normal and zoomed in. A huge rock filled his view. Which meant the shooter was behind it. Jimmy was a decent shot himself, but the rock was much further than he would trust the Artie to be accurate. Whoever had shot from behind that rock had to be good and well equipped. Keeping his ARP zoomed in on the rock, Jimmy slowly backed up, moving to the front of the truck to have some protection between himself and the shooter.

Once in position, he switched back to thermal, and watched the two readings slowly make their way toward him. Jimmy lifted his Artie to eye level and watched the two readings move closer. They were using all the natural cover and stayed well hidden behind trees and rocks. Not once did Jimmy have a clean shot. He switched his ARP back to normal and strained to see the intruders. Then one of them moved, and he had them back in his sights. They were getting very close. Close enough for him to see their faces. Faces he knew.

It was Dina and Ziggy.

Jimmy loved seeing people he knew, even if it wasn't always mutual. He put his Artie on the ground and stood up, waving. Dina kept moving toward him and signaled for him to get down, which he did. Jimmy crouched down and waited for Dina and Ziggy to reach him.

"Hey, guys! Funny seeing you here, ya know?"

Dina grabbed Jimmy and shoved him back behind the truck.

"What's the situation?" Dina asked.

"Where do I begin . . ."

"Jimmy. Right now. What's going on?"

"Oh, yeah, sure, ya know. Um, Drake is stuck inside with a guy with a gun, and I'm out here watching him and covering his back. Oh, shit—" Franticly, Jimmy scrambled to activate his ARP and regain visual on Drake. "Phew, seems he is still alive."

"Patch me and Ziggy in too."

Jimmy obeyed Dina and soon all three were watching as Drake made small talk with the gunman.

"Is there anyone else around?" Dina asked.

"No. Not that I know of, ya know."

Dina turned to Ziggy and nodded.

Ziggy jumped up, took up position in front of them, and fired her suppressed pulse rifle.

"Target down." And that was that.

Now, using his boot, Jimmy scraped the hairy scalp off the truck's fender.

"I'm sure dead people don't feel much, ya know?"

Drake was still reeling from having a gun in his face, then a body on his feet, and last, seeing Dina and Ziggy again. He was also trying to come to grips with having lost his only lead on Lt. Wells.

"Just ... never mind. Dina reckons a few meters into the woods should be enough."

The crushing heat and humidity made for slow work, and since Dina had made it clear that they weren't there to clean up Drake and Jimmy's mistakes, they still had to recover the bigger man's body, too. Shuffling into the woods, the shade brought some relief from the heat. Drake and Jimmy scuttled along a few more meters before Drake carefully put the body's feet down. Jimmy followed by dropping his end. Drake let it slide.

"We're so lucky the girls are back, ya know?"

Drake shrugged. Having extra hands and guns was great, but they had less of a lead on Lily than they'd had before. All the girls had been doing was following Drake and Jimmy around.

Drake sat down on a tree trunk. It must have fallen over years ago. Plants grew over and inside it. Jimmy came over and sat next to him.

"So that was a bust," Drake said.

"Yeah."

"I really thought we were getting close to Lily."

"Me too, ya know?"

Drake waited until Jimmy was breathing normally again. "Okay, I guess we better get the other body."

Slowly, they started the walk back to the house.

"So these guys had no information for us, ya know, but they knew Big Boy."

"Yup. So what?"

The sun stung their eyes as they left the darkness of the woods.

"Well, if they knew Big Boy, then maybe he knew something about these Believers, and maybe, ya know, there is some information that might help in the house."

There was some logic to this, but Drake feared it would be another dead end.

"Maybe."

Dina and Ziggy had made themselves at home and were enjoying some white box meals when Drake and Jimmy entered the house.

"You letting Drake do all the hard work again, Jimmy?" Dina asked.

"No, what do you mean?"

Drake stepped over the body to get a better look at the table. It wasn't the white box meals that grabbed his attention, but a portable Data Display Unit that sat next to Dina's meal.

"Where did that come from?" Drake asked.

"This?" Dina asked.

"Yes, Dina, obviously. Where did you get that?"

"You think we were sitting around braiding our hair while you went for your walk in the woods?"

Drake didn't bite.

"We searched this dump from top to bottom. Didn't find much of anything, except for this." She slid the DDU toward Drake.

"What's on it?"

Dina shrugged.

"I shoot things. But I figured your little friend over there might figure something out."

Drake looked over at Jimmy. "What do you reckon, buddy?"

Jimmy stepped closer and picked up the DDU. He flipped it over a few times, inspecting it.

"Should be easy. Looks like a generic model, ya know. Yeah. Shouldn't take too long. Just one thing, though."

Drake didn't like the sound of that. "What, Jimmy?"

"Could we have some of those white boxes first?"

* * *

After enjoying their meal under the watchful eye of a dead man, Jimmy grabbed the DDU and started hacking it. His tongue poked out of the right side of his mouth, a clear sign he was concentrating. Drake gave him his space.

"Seems we have some time, so how about you fill me in on the details, Dina? I'm still a little unsure how someone we worked with on a demolition squad is sitting here, supposedly ready to help our friend."

"You missed the part where we saved your lives."

"Feel free to include it in your story."

Ziggy looked up from her HIC and shook her head at Drake. *What is her problem?*

"I told you, Drake, we have a contract, and it's paying us to help your friend escape. It came through a third party, but my guess is, from doing this for a while, that it is someone in Penta."

"What makes you think that?"

"The wording. Some things sounded very, I don't know . . . Official. It makes sense for them to get her out. And the credits are substantial."

"If Penta is trying to get her out, maybe we can contact them and ask for more resources or help."

Laughing, Dina elbowed Ziggy. "This guy."

"Drake," she continued after the laughing subsided, "we're not the people you call when you want things done officially or have it linked to you. If we're involved, it means someone is breaking the rules somewhere. This might come from Penta, but no one there will admit it."

Another dead end. Drake wished, just once, that he could catch a break and figure out where Lily was.

"Done!" Jimmy yelled from the table.

Drake ran over to him. Dina and Ziggy slowly made their way, too.

"And? What did you find?"

"I just unlocked it, ya know? Let's see."

Jimmy started swiping around on the DDU, going through files, folders, and apps, trying to find anything that could be useful. Drake, Dina, and Ziggy all hovered over him, heads almost touching, trying to have a look too. Jimmy worked at an incredible speed, and Drake struggled to keep up. After twenty minutes of nonstop searching, Jimmy sat back.

"I don't think there is anything worthwhile here, ya know?"

It became clear after a while that the DDU had very little personal information on it and had most likely only been used to watch videos.

"Should we check again?" Drake asked.

All the faces told him he was wasting his time.

"Sorry, Drake," Jimmy offered.

"Hey, not your fault, buddy," Drake replied. He wished he could smash the DDU to pieces and vent some of this frustration. Instead, he said, "Okay, nothing else to do but get back on the road, I guess."

"And go where?" Dina asked.

"I don't know, Dina, but it's where I function. On the road is where my head works best. Something will come to me."

Drake gave Jimmy a reassuring look, and Jimmy replied with all his teeth.

"This is dumb," Dina protested.

"Hey, suit yourself. I'm not paying you anymore, so you can do whatever you want, or just follow us again."

"You haven't even finished cleaning here," Dina pointed to the body on the floor.

"Guess not. But I doubt anyone will come looking soon." The prospect of being on the road always invigorated Drake. "So come if you want, but we're out of here."

"And I'm taking this," Jimmy said, grabbing the DDU.

As they reached the door, Ziggy spoke up. "Did you see this?"

Everyone turned, looking at her. She was bent over, playing on her HIC as usual.

"What is it, Sweetie?" Dina asked.

"Check the news."

Dina activated her HIC and Jimmy, his new DDU.

"What are we looking for?"

"The report about the hyperloop explosions."

Everyone found the report and read it.

"It says it was an attack by Penta," Drake remarked.

"This is not a military attack," Dina replied. "This is a local, mobile group. Penta would have used long-range weapons, not small explosives on the ground. No, this was not Penta."

Drake read it again. "Why not? Aren't they at war?"

"Not yet, technically."

"But this could be them?"

"No, Drake. I'm telling you. This is a local group."

"Like the Believers," Jimmy said.

"Like the Believers," Dina echoed.

It was a stretch, but it was a lead.

"We need to go to the nearest attack site," Drake caught on.

"Exactly. If the Believers were responsible for this, then this might be our best shot at getting back on their trail," Dina said.

"So what are we waiting for? Let's go." Drake made for the door.

"Good work, Sweetie," Dina said, as she bent down and kissed Ziggy's forehead before following Drake out the door.

| thirty-one |

"Wake up! You need to go."

Sitting up, Wells did a scan of her injuries, ignoring the person standing at the door. Her arm seemed to have healed completely, but her chest still hurt. As she sat on the rags that passed for a bed, she breathed in deeply, feeling her chest expand, concentrating on her wound. It felt slightly worse than yesterday, but she'd had a rough day, blowing up structures and rescuing people. A dull pain on the side of Wells's head reminded her of her suspected ruptured eardrum. She hoped it wasn't too severe.

"Are you deaf? Get up!" the figure at the door yelled again.

Boots on, Wells rose slowly to meet the person face to face. She was glad when she realized she was a few inches taller. The face did not seem familiar to her, and she doubted he was part of Aranya's group, as he was in uniform.

Wells held her ground, staring the man down.

She watched his Adam's apple bob up and down as he swallowed hard, trying to keep his nerve. For the first time, Wells noticed the pulse rifle he clutched to his chest. Not very smart, buddy, Wells thought. It would take her two seconds to take the weapon from him if she chose to. But she didn't. If there was one uniformed person, there would be more. She was at a disadvantage until she had more intel. For now, the smart move was to play along.

The man regained some of his composure. He stepped aside so Wells could leave the room. She stayed close to him, inside his personal space bubble, as she brushed past him. She had to stay in his head, making him doubt his control of the situation. If he was second-guessing himself, it would allow her more time to make a move later.

Wells stepped through the door and into the operations room. Usually filled with Believers working on the DDUs, today it was empty. Not a single Believer to be seen. Not only did Aranya not have the guts to be here, but she'd also sent everyone else away.

"Keep walking," the man said in a muted voice.

She did, passing the empty workstations and then reaching the front door. It was closed, so she waited for her instructions.

The man reached past her and used the DDU to unlock the door. His pulse rifle hung loosely on its sling and banged against Wells. Her hand was close enough to curl around the grip and pull the trigger. His incompetence in leaving himself so defenseless gave Wells hope of a simple escape later. She hoped the rest of the team would be the same.

Bright sunlight blinded her for a second as the door slid open, and the man told her to move forward. Two armored hydro vehicles waited outside the house. Three uniformed personnel stood in front of them, pulse weapons drawn. Without her outdated HIC, Wells's ARP was useless, and she couldn't translate the wording on the vehicles. But looking at the uniforms, weapons and the logo, Wells knew these were local Shangcorp Security.

One guard opened a door, and Wells assumed it was for her. She needed to observe the new members of the crew and see how they behaved, so she waited. Everyone looked at her, waiting.

"Get in," the man said behind her.

Wells doubted he was in charge, but no one else spoke to make her think otherwise.

"No. Tell me where you're taking me first."

"Just get in."

"Make me."

No one moved, but a movement to the side caught Wells's eye. It was Aranya.

"Lily."

Apparently Aranya had the guts to be here after all, but Wells had nothing to say to her. She knew an apology was coming her way, justifying her behavior.

She was right.

"This was difficult for me. The last few weeks, I've come to see you as a friend. I have tried my best to convince you to stay and join our cause, but the more I tried, the more I realized you would never be a Believer."

"So your first thought was to hand me over to the authorities?"

Aranya shook her head.

"Of course not, Lily. I'm looking at the bigger picture. The greater good."

"How is handing me over to them the greater good? I thought they were the enemy," Wells said, jabbing her finger at the man holding the gun on her, confident he wouldn't do a thing.

"I fear you still don't understand how things work in Shang-corp."

"I know exactly how things work," Wells replied. "Who did you sell me out to?"

A tiny flinch of Aranya's eye told Wells she'd hit a nerve. "You still talk and act like you are in Penta, Lily." Aranya's voice had lost some of its tenderness.

"You didn't answer my question. Who bought you?"

Aranya's face couldn't hide her irritation anymore. "Let me ask you a question, Lily. I'm sure you've heard it before. If killing one innocent person meant you saved a thousand lives, would you do it?"

"I'm sure you've killed more than one innocent, Aranya."

Irritation gave way to anger. "Yes, Lily, I have. And every time, I save thousands. It's all for the greater good. We all must make sacrifices."

"And you get to choose who to sacrifice?"

Aranya's face changed again. She had a look of determination, or maybe self-importance. "Yes. As the leader of the Believers, the burden lies with me to make these decisions. So I make them."

Wells felt like she was seeing the real Aranya for the first time. "You gave me up to save yourself. Pinned all the blame on me for the explosions."

Aranya laughed. "Oh, no, Lily. We need the world to know we did that, and that we are to be taken seriously. You won't have to take the blame."

Wells thought she'd had it figured out, but suddenly, she found herself on the back foot. "Okay, you got me then. Enlighten me. If I'm not taking the blame, then why aren't they arresting you right now? You just gave them a clear confession."

"Still thinking like a Pentonian."

A feeling Wells didn't like took hold of her. Not fear, or hopelessness, but the impending sense of something bad and unknown coming her way.

"Sacrifice one for the good of the many," Aranya chanted. "Someone who has an interest in you paid me a vast sum of credits and a large supply of weapons to deliver you to the local authorities. So by sacrificing one, my war chest is full, and the Believers can achieve so much more."

"Who was it? What's their name?" Wells knew it was a long shot expecting an answer from Aranya, but she needed to know who to go after once she escaped from here.

"I honestly do not know, Lily. A third party facilitated everything. But I can tell you all the weapons arrived in sealed Penta Security containers."

This was not the answer Wells had expected. In her years rising through the ranks in Penta Security, she'd stepped on many toes and bruised a few egos. She never let it get to her, but now it seemed to have caught up with her. She tried to think of who had the clout to penetrate a small group of rebel fighters in a foreign territory and have her handed over. Some people at Penta didn't like her aggressive nature, and the list could contain many names. Figuring out who had done it would have to wait until she was back in New Franco.

"I've heard enough of your drivel, Aranya," Wells said, and walked to the armored hydro vehicle. "Please take me away from her."

* * *

Two vehicles, four guards, all armed.

Splitting the group into two was a smart move. If anything happened, the front vehicle could deal with it while the vehicle containing Wells could hunker down and defend itself. Having two vehicles increased their defensive and offensive chances. If Wells tried to escape or took control of the vehicle, the other team was still operational and could retaliate. It seemed, despite the small guards' meek temperament, that she was dealing with a professional outfit.

Even the cuffs they used were to the same standard as the electromagnetic ones used by Wells and other Penta officers. Slimline, and very effective, and close to impossible to hack. Given the lack of technology in the area, she'd half expected them to use rope.

Wells took a deep breath. The smell confirmed another observation—the vehicle was brand new too. Wells took a closer look at the guard next to her. New boots, shiny pulse rifle, latest model HIC. The vehicle in front looked brand new too. This was not a clever tactical move. They were out playing with all their new toys.

"When did you guys get all the new toys?"

"None of your business," the driver replied.

Sitting next to her was the same guy who'd pulled her out of her room. She might have thought that he was in charge, but it looked more likely now that he'd drawn the shortest straw.

"Nothing in this shithole is any of my business. I'm just making small talk, dickhead."

"Next peep out of her, put your fist in her face."

Wells doubted that would happen.

"The captain said to not rough her up, remember?"

"Don't tell me what the captain said, okay? If she runs her mouth again, close it."

Wells smiled and rolled her eyes at the driver. A faint smile from the guard next to her told her she had someone she could use later on.

"If I had to guess, someone recently made a huge donation to your office, and everyone received a pleasant bonus too."

Sliding his sleeve down, the guard tried to hide his flashy new HIC.

"What did I say about you talking?"

"I can only assume it was the same person who paid Aranya off."

This time, the driver said nothing. Because he had nothing to say. This was above his clearance level. He was just another grunt. Instead of admitting he didn't know, he stayed quiet. Which meant Wells needed to speak to the next person in line.

"Are we there yet?"

* * *

It didn't take long for them to reach their destination. As they entered a small town, Wells noticed poverty all around her.

Buildings that seemed on the verge of collapse still housed businesses. Most people walked the streets, and the only vehicles she saw were rusty bom-boms. The modern armored vehicles looked completely out of place.

The front vehicle swerved right and parked in front of another rundown building. Wells's hydro followed suit and parked next to it. The driver climbed out and walked over.

"Let's go," he grumbled as he opened her door.

Wells exited the armored vehicle and saw the other guard quickly run around the back of the vehicle to take up his position, guarding her. Once everyone was in place, they marched into the building.

None of the money they'd received from their benefactor had made it to the building. The inside reflected the sad state outside. Paint peeled from the walls, water stains decorated the ceilings, and the floor creaked. A small entryway gave way to a larger office, separated by a counter. A gate in the counter gave them access to the larger office. An officer standing behind the counter briefly glanced up from their DDU and pressed a button. The gate slid open to grant them access to the larger office. They passed through in single file and paused in the middle of the office. A door at the far end slid open.

"Our lucky charm!" the man, who had to be captain, proclaimed.

"Sounds about right. Seems you owe me a thank-you for getting you those new hydros."

The diminutive figure strutted over and bowed to Wells. "Thank you so much," he said.

Wells couldn't decide which she disliked more, his wispy mustache or his beady little eyes. She settled on the mustache.

"Now," the captain said, turning to his staff, "please escort our guest to her accommodation and make sure she has everything she needs to enjoy her last remaining days."

* * *

Local forces have secured asset (friendly). Will confirm kill in 48 hours.

At first, Davis had balked at the request to send the large amount of credits over, but he felt better about it, knowing where the credits went to now. He liked how his asset had isolated themselves and him by bribing and using local security. Brilliant thinking. An involuntary smile crept across his face as he imagined Lt. Wells sitting in a dark hole in the middle of nowhere. No one knew where she was, and she was going to die all alone. He wished his asset would have the locals kill her, but they were adamant that they needed a few more days and wanted to finish the job themselves. Davis guessed it meant they had a work ethic or something, or maybe a personal vendetta that he wasn't aware of, but either way, all that mattered was that in forty-eight hours, he would witness the end of one of the biggest pains in his ass that he'd ever encountered.

| thirty-two |

"It's so good to see the girls again, ya know?"

Jimmy was all smiles, looking back every few minutes to make sure Dina and Ziggy were still following them in the hydro Drake and he had stolen for them. The road was narrow, but luckily the traffic was light.

"I guess. I don't know. It still feels weird, doesn't it?"

Jimmy's face didn't agree with Drake.

"I mean, they didn't hesitate to leave us at the hospital, fending for ourselves, and now they are here to help?"

Mercenaries are only in it for the credits. They serve no company or leader, except for credits. Whoever will pay, they will obey. Dina and Ziggy fit the mold perfectly.

"I guess, but it's still nice to see them, ya know?"

There was no one else Drake could think of that he would want to have next to him if—or more likely when—the shit hit the cooling unit. Seeing those two in action was exhilarating and scary at the same time. If he had to choose a side, he would choose theirs every time.

"I'm glad too, Jimmy. It's just the timing feels weird."

"Yeah. Pretty good, right?"

It was too good. They'd admitted to tracking them and following them for days, but it still felt wrong.

"Just be happy. It won't hurt having them to help, ya know?"

Jimmy was right. With them on their side, their chances of getting Lily out of Shangcorp had increased tenfold. And that was the main goal—get out of Shangcorp. Who cared what Dina and Ziggy's motives were? They were a tremendous asset to have, and Drake knew they were better off for having them helping.

"I guess you're right, Jimmy. I'm glad they're here, too."

"I just hope . . ." Jimmy looked down at his fidgeting hands.

"What is it, buddy?"

"I just hope they don't take us drinking again."

* * *

Three dots appeared on the road in front of Drake, and quickly they merged into Dina's face.

"Hey. Everything good back there?"

"We're fine. Ziggy had a good idea where to start looking."

Dina told Drake the plan and hung up.

Drake looked at Jimmy and couldn't stop himself from laughing. "I'm sorry, buddy."

"What's going on? Why are you laughing? Drake, this is not cool, ya know? Tell me!"

A shudder went through the old truck's cabin as Drake had to downshift to make it over a hill. Once at the top, a small village appeared down the road. Drake steered the truck to the first building on the outskirts of town and parked in front of it.

"No. No. No. Please, Drake," Jimmy begged.

"I'm sorry, buddy, but the girls have a plan," Drake replied as he jumped out.

Dina parked the hydro next to them and she and Ziggy climbed out, stretching themselves.

"This will do," Dina said, as she took the lead and walked into the bar.

* * *

Luckily for Jimmy, the plan was not to get drunk with the two Slavor women. Instead, this was all about gathering intel.

Ziggy's plan was simple and had some logic behind it. When Drake was still hauling in New Franco and Penta, he would frequent bars. Life on the road could be very lonely, but bars were a place for haulers to connect. It became a virtual network for information and gossip. People talked, and even things you couldn't find on the Haulernet, you could uncover in a bar.

Ziggy's plan had merit. If it worked for haulers, it should work for rebel fighters too.

Every head in the bar turned when the four strangers walked in. After a quick inspection, everyone turned back to their drinks and minding their own business. A few lights tried their best to illuminate the place, but all they did was hide a dirty floor and the dirtier dealings happening at the tables. The place was only half full, and everyone looked local.

Dina grabbed a chair at an empty table and pulled it out. Drake and Jimmy followed her lead. Ziggy nodded to the back of the room and disappeared.

"I'll get the first round," Dina said, and walked over to the barkeep.

"This has to be the most depressing bar that I've ever seen," Drake said.

As if to make sure it was true, Jimmy craned his neck and looked around. "I'm not going to argue with you on this one, ya know?"

Like most buildings in this rural area, bamboo made up most of the building materials. Here it made up the walls, counter, and some chairs. The roof was some rusty sheet metal, and the floor was hard-packed dirt. Most of the people had tattered clothes on, and only a few wore shoes.

Dina returned, carrying four glasses of beer. As she sat down, Ziggy joined them, too.

"Here's the plan," Dina said, grabbing a glass and inspecting it before taking a small sip. "These people don't seem to have too much going for them, so an event such as the hyperloop explosions should be a talking point."

By now everyone had grabbed a drink and paused when Dina did to nod their heads.

"All we must do is listen in on some conversations and then get them to open up to us a bit. I'm sure a free drink will go far here."

"Ooh, we can use Seymour to listen to the conversations," Jimmy suggested.

"Nah," Dina shook her head. "He'll be more of a distraction. Not sure an ASR is an everyday occurrence here."

"Let's just enjoy our beers for a while and see what pans out," Drake said.

No one objected, so for the next few minutes, they all enjoyed their beers in silence.

Silence that allowed them to hear the other tables' conversations.

Most of it was out of reach of their ARPs and didn't get translated, but the tables nearest to them did. Especially the one right behind Drake. One of the people sitting at the table seemed to have had his fair share of beer already, and the volume of his stories increased by the minute.

". . . that's when I picked the little girl up and carried her to safety. Her mother was in tears, thanking me, praising me. But you guys know me. I'm not the kind who needs approval. Isn't that right, eh?"

"Did you hear that?" Drake whispered to Dina.

Smiling, she took a sip of her beer.

Drake grabbed his beer and went over to the table behind him.

"Sorry to interrupt, but I couldn't help but overhear your heroic story."

"I'm sure they could hear it all the way to Lan-noi," someone at the table said, making everyone snicker.

"It's all true," the storyteller said loudly, trying to drown out the laughter of his friends. "Every word of it."

A few more snickers and some eye rolls later, they moved on and resumed drinking. Most of the glasses were almost empty.

"I would love to hear it, if you don't mind. I work for a small news agency and stories like this always sell." Drake hoped he didn't need to see any credentials.

"You think they would use it?"

"Depends on how good it is."

The man looked less sure of himself.

"How about I go grab us all a round, and then we can get started?"

Drake left before he could answer or protest. After grabbing the beers, he returned to the table and placed a fresh beer in front of everyone at the table. No one objected, and they all looked at the storyteller to fulfill his obligation.

"Um, eh, okay, so, there I was, waiting on the hyperloop to go visit my sister in Lan-noi . . ."

"You're full of shit. The explosion wasn't even at the terminal," one of the other men chimed in.

"Well, obviously I know that, as I was still walking to the terminal when it happened."

The other man shook his head and drank his beer.

"Anyway, so there I was, still walking, when I heard the explosion." He looked at Drake for some reaction.

"Wow! That's crazy. Go on."

"It was. An enormous ball of flames came rushing toward me, and I had to drop to the ground to prevent myself from getting cooked."

"Most likely tripped over running away," someone at the table mumbled. This brought out another round of giggles.

"Maybe you would have, but I stood my ground," the man sneered at him. "Then, when it calmed down, I saw the pod on the ground. People were screaming and yelling, so I did what anyone would have done." He paused for effect and for a re-action from Drake.

"What did you do? Did you help those poor people?" Drake played along.

"Of course, I did. I'm not like these idiots, only worried about themselves. I jumped in and started pulling people from the wreck. Woman. Children. Even a few men. Helped them all." He took a celebratory sip of his beer, waiting for praise.

"Wow! Sounds amazing. A genuine hero," Drake said, lifting his glass to the man.

The man looked very pleased with himself. A local hero. Putting others' lives before his.

Doing such an amazing job, that he didn't have one scar, or one hair singed from the fire.

"Can we take a photo? Maybe outside? The light in here is terrible."

The man seemed even more impressed.

"I guess it makes sense. Put a face to the name. Think there might be a reward?"

"I'm confident you will get what you're owed," Drake replied, and led the way out.

* * *

"Okay, where do you want me?" the man asked as they stepped out of the rickety building.

He turned to face Drake, but instead saw Dina's fist flying toward his face. It made contact with his jaw, making his legs wobble and forcing him to stagger backward.

"What . . ." Confused, he held his chin.

"Okay. Time to tell the truth, buddy. What happened at the hyperloop?" Drake asked. Dina still loomed over the man.

"I told you, man. What's going on? Who is she?"

Before Drake could reply, Dina slapped the man across the face.

"Okay, okay," he said, now holding his chin and the side of his face. "What do you want? Just tell me. What do you want?"

"The truth. The news said that the only explosion that involved a pod happened far away from here, and I doubt you went there to board the hyperloop. Also, you don't even have a scratch on you. So stop the bullshit and tell me what you saw."

The man looked at his arms, that showed no signs of any heroic acts performed.

"I was there, okay? At the explosion. But you're right." He looked at his arms that betrayed him. "It wasn't the one with the pod."

Drake already knew this, but it was a good start, to come clean.

"So, what did you see?"

Shoulders dropped, all bravado gone, the man looked defeated. His moment in the spotlight was now gone.

"On my way to the hyperloop, I saw an explosion in the distance. At first, I thought it was Penta blowing things up. You know, the war and all. But nothing else happened, so I went to have a look. When I got there, there was a crowd of people and a massive hole in the tube. That's the truth."

"I believe you," Drake said. "Did anyone say anything? Did the people talk?"

"They all talked. It was a crazy thing to see."

"Yes, of course, but did they talk about who might have done it?"

The man looked at Dina, aware another slap or punch was coming if he didn't talk.

"Uh-huh. Everyone knows who did. It was even on the news."

"The Believers."

"Yes. So if you know that, can I go?"

Dina looked at Drake and shook her head.

"Almost," Drake replied to the man.

"But I told you everything I know!"

"There's one more thing."

The man swiveled his head between Dina and Drake.

"What, man? What is it?"

"Where can we find them?"

"Who?"

"The Believers."

The man looked relieved. "Sure, I can take you to them."

| thirty-three |

Illuminated by the bright fire they encircled, the men were easy to identify.

"Yup, that's them," said the storyteller from the bar.

From the safety of the darkness that the jungle provided, Drake observed the Believers. Alcohol was flowing freely, and they seem to be in a jovial or celebratory mood. Their clothes were dirty and tattered but didn't appear to be uniforms. No insignia or graffiti were visible to confirm their allegiance to the Believers. Old pulse rifles lay on the ground next to each person.

"You sure?" Drake whispered.

"Yeah. I know all three guys. Trust me, they are all balls-deep into this Believers stuff."

Drake looked at Dina to gauge her take on it. Her focus was still on the men surrounding the fire, making up her own mind. He needed her expertise on this, so he waited.

"Can I go now?" the storyteller asked.

"What do you think, Dina?" Drake asked her, ignoring him.

"We've been here for over twenty minutes, and no one else has arrived. By the way they are drinking, I don't think they are waiting for anyone else to show up. So I'd say we have three bogeys, all armed. That gives us a clear advantage. I think we let Big Mouth sleep, and then we split up, and take them."

"What do you mean, sleep? I've—"

Ziggy had already set her suppressed Artie to stun and shot the man before he could protest too much.

"I suggest you and Ziggy pair up, and I'll take Jimmy," Dina continued. "And since we are getting paid, let us do the work. Just back us up. Once we have them contained, you can have at 'em. Sound good?"

Drake could not see any reason not to agree to the plan from a tactically trained officer. "Sounds great. Jimmy?"

"Whatever you reckon, ya know." Jimmy swiped an instruction to Seymour and gave Drake a thumbs-up. "He'll keep an eye on him and warn me if he wakes up."

Drake had to admit that the little orange Automated Service Robot had been quite useful.

Dina gave everyone instructions, and using the cover provided by the jungle, both groups moved into position.

Everyone had their ARPs on and could clearly identify each other, as Dina had made them put identifiers on themselves. Drake didn't even know ARPs could do that, and looking over toward Jimmy's position, he saw the word *Jimmy* floating above his head. He quickly saw *Ziggy* too. He wondered what other tricks Dina had to teach him.

"Okay, listen up." Dina spoke to everyone via the cochlear implants that were part of their ARPs. "On my mark, we break cover and draw weapons on the bogeys."

No one replied, and everyone waited for the next instruction. The only sound in the night came from the three men laughing at the fire.

"Go!"

Bursting out of the jungle, all four had their weapons drawn and they yelled at the men to get on the ground. They yelled and screamed at the men, confusing and intimidating them. None of them appeared to have had any training as they scattered, fell over each other, and ended up on the ground. No one resisted or went for their rifles. Once on the ground, Jimmy ran over, as per Dina's instructions, and grabbed all the pulse rifles lying around. Ziggy moved in and tied their hands with thin magnetic bands. Dina and Drake kept their rifles on the men, shouting at them to stay down. Ziggy gave Dina a nod, and Dina told her to sit them up. Jimmy helped Ziggy, and two minutes after emerging from the jungle, all three men sat tied up on the ground.

"Sorry for doing this to you, but you were armed, and we had to protect ourselves." Drake waited a second to make sure the translators were working. Everyone's expressions changed simultaneously, so he knew they were on the same page.

"Okay. We are looking for people who belong to the Believers. And we've been told that you guys are Believers. Is that true?"

Either the alcohol or plain stupidity was to blame, but one guy got half up and tried to charge Jimmy. He didn't get far, falling over, but Dina still shot at him, barely missing, making a hole in the ground next to his head. From what Drake had seen, she'd missed on purpose.

"Please don't do that again," Dina said.

The man struggled to get back onto his back and took a second to sit up again. He glared at Dina but sat still.

"We don't need all three of you, so please start talking," Drake bluffed.

The man now glared at his two comrades, willing them not to cooperate. Clearly, he was the leader.

Drake nodded at Jimmy, who instantly shot the man. Seconds after struggling to sit up again, he was back down, sleeping on the ground.

"We stunned him," Drake explained it to the two men left. "So when he wakes up, he won't know what happened and you guys can tell him anything you want, okay?"

They looked relieved but still scared.

"Are you Believers?" Drake asked again.

This time Dina stepped forward, aiming her rifle at them. After making a hole in the ground next to the leader's head, they knew her pulse rifle would not make anyone sleep.

"Yes," they replied in unison.

"Great! Now all I need from you is to tell me if you've seen this person."

Jimmy came over and showed them the picture of Lt. Wells on his HIC. They both shook their heads without looking at each other. Their body language told Drake that they were telling the truth.

"You sure? Look carefully. You sure you've never seen this woman?"

This time they shared a look to confer, but still nothing.

Drake turned to Dina.

"Any ideas?"

"Ask them who the local leader is."

"Who runs the show around here? Who do you get your orders from?"

"Mister, we have nothing to hide from you. We'll tell you anything you want to know. Please don't shoot us."

Drake looked into their pleading eyes, saw their dirty faces and tattered clothes. These people had nothing. They were not a threat to them.

"Put down your guns," Drake said aloud. Dina gave him a quizzical look but obeyed. So did the other two. "Ziggy, take the cuffs off, please."

Dina nodded her head, and Ziggy obliged, but only after an exaggerated huff.

"Thank you," the man said, rubbing his wrists.

"Sorry for all this, but we really need to find our friend. She was last seen leaving Lan-noi with a group of people. We were told they were Believers. It's really important that we find her."

The man smiled at Drake, which made him feel like a dick for shooting at them and tying them up.

"Most people in the region are Believers to some extent. Shangcorp has squeezed everything they can out of us and the land. They have brought this upon themselves."

"You mean the bombings?"

"Yes. All of this. The uprising. Look at us. We have nothing left. What else are we supposed to do?"

"Who organized the bombings? Who supplied the explosives?"

"They sent it to us."

"Do you know who?"

The man looked at his sleeping leader and his friend, still cowering. Weighing up his options, he spoke up.

"We received the bombs directly from Aranya herself."

* * *

Aranya. The name had come up when Drake spoke to the big guy at the hospital, Joh. He called her the one who would unite all the Believers. The savior. And he said that she and Lily left together. But he also gave Drake the coordinates that led them to a place to be executed.

If the two stories matched about her being the leader of the Believers, there was a chance that not everything Joh had told him was a lie. Hopefully, it meant that Lily had left with Aranya. Which meant they would finally have a solid lead on finding Lt. Wells.

"Who is Aranya?" Drake played dumb.

The man looked puzzled, as if Drake had asked him what color green was.

"It's okay. We're just trying to find our friend, and someone told us she might be with this person, Aranya. Could you tell me who she is?"

The man nodded, satisfied that Drake was indeed clueless.

"She is the savior of the people of Shangcorp," the man said, echoing Joh's words.

It sounded like a propaganda slogan to Drake, but he kept that to himself. "Why would she supply you with explosives?"

"To start the revolution. To show Shangcorp that we've had enough."

The timing was perfect. Penta was positioning themselves at Shangcorp's borders, and the Believers were sabotaging it from within. This Aranya sounded like she knew what she was doing.

It also matched with what Joh had told him.

"Where is she?"

The man dropped his head and closed up.

"I promise you," Drake said, kneeling next to him, "we have no ill intentions toward her. We have no part in this war with Shangcorp and Penta. All we want is to find our friend and go home."

The man lifted his head and stared into Drake's eyes. "Are you Penta Security?"

The question caught Drake by surprise. "Uh, no. Why?"

Nodding his head toward Dina, the man said, "And those two?"

Drake turned around to look at Dina and Ziggy. Everything about them screamed security. Their stance, the way they held their pulse rifles, even their facial expressions.

"They have training, but we do not work for anyone."

"Do you think we have a chance?" he asked, facing Dina.

"Of what?" she replied abruptly.

"Winning."

"Against who? Penta or your rebellion?"

A smile of resignation took over the man's face and his body relaxed as he sighed. "It doesn't matter. Knowing that we stand a chance to better our lives and be our own people again would give us the hope we need to keep going."

Dina stared blankly back at the man.

"I believe with people like you and your friends," Drake said, "you stand a chance. I really do. I've seen the people here, and I think you will win whatever battle you face." Drake didn't know if he believed it himself, but he hoped it was true.

"Damn, Drake," Jimmy said, wiping his eyes.

Drake looked at the man, waiting for him to gather his thoughts and decide.

"Thank you," he said. "I hope what you said is true. I'll show you how to get to Aranya."

| thirty-four |

Time moves slowly when there's nothing to do, and Lt. Lily Wells hated not doing anything. Down time, or relaxation, was not something she ever needed or craved. Going to the gym or shooting range was her idea of winding down. Doing something, honing her skills, seemed like a better use of her time.

Sitting in a small holding cell, watching the guards play with their new pulse pistols, Wells could feel the tension build up inside of her. Being caged like this was her worst nightmare.

Sitting at a desk closest to her cell was the guard who'd woken her up in Aranya's compound. He seemed more reserved than the other guards and didn't join them in their boisterous play.

"Hey," Wells called out to him.

A quick glance was all she got.

"C'mon. Surely you're allowed to talk to the prisoner?"

He kept working on his DDU. She adjusted the translator strap around her throat to make sure he could understand her.

"What's your name? I'm Lily, but I guess you knew that."

No response, but Wells could see him tilting his head, actively trying to ignore her.

"Already played enough with your new pistol at home?"

Jaw muscles flexed as he bit down in an effort not to reply.

"I was a bit of an outsider in my team, too. Didn't bother me. But it can get lonely sometimes."

The guard stopped working but didn't look up or reply.

"Anyway, I just wanted to say, officer to officer, I thought you handled the situation back there better than your colleagues over there."

Nothing had really happened when they apprehended Wells, but she had little to work with.

"Thank you," came a timid reply.

"You've been doing this a long time?"

Looking up, he got back to work.

"Three years," he replied, looking at the screen. "It's not very exciting. Well, it wasn't till a few days ago."

Wells made sure the other guards were still playing and distracting themselves.

"You mean the explosions and catching me?"

The guard glanced over his shoulder to make sure no one saw him talking to the prisoner. Satisfied they weren't, he returned to working on his DDU. "Yes, and the new equipment."

"The rifles and the hydros?"

"Uh-huh. Would you believe before they arrived, we only had bom-boms?"

Nothing could have made Wells happier than hearing that. This was a small unit, not used to doing much more than taking the local drunks home and waving a finger at people who urinated in public. Maybe they had to investigate the occasional spat between neighbors, but they were not prepared to handle anything major, like a trained professional breaking out of lockup.

They might have received shiny new pulse rifles and powerful armored hydros, but Wells figured they did not know how to use them properly, if at all.

"So what's the plan? I mean, are you guys handing me over to someone or taking me somewhere?"

Another quick glance. "I can't say." Adjusting his chair, he tried his best to put his back to Wells.

"You don't know? Okay, I'll ask one of the other guys."

Wells waited a second before taking an exaggerated breath, readying herself to yell out across the room to the other guards.

"I *do* know," he blurted. "But I'm not even allowed to talk to you. So please be quiet and don't make a fuss."

Lt. Wells was used to taking orders. Most of her adult life, she had been told what to do and when to do it. She didn't always obey them, but she was used to receiving them. It was part of the job. From the right person, she would always entertain the idea of following them.

This guy was not the right person.

"Okay. I can see that you are very nervous about your friends over there coming over and joining us, so I tell you what—I'll behave and be as quiet as you want, if you tell me exactly what they have planned for me. If not, I'll tell those idiots playing with themselves that you've already told me what's going to happen. They seem like the shoot first, ask questions later types."

The guard was clearly an outsider. He looked over at the other guards playing and making noise. Wells could see a longing in him to belong. It was no coincidence that he'd been the one to go into the room and apprehend the villain. Considering their lack of training and experience, the other guards had most likely bullied him into doing it. If anyone might get shot at, best be him. Wells pitied him, but she didn't let it get in her way.

"Your choice. Talk to me or I get my answers from them."

"All I know," he finally replied, "is that tomorrow morning, someone is coming in to *handle* the situation. That's all I know, I swear. If you call them over, they'll tell you the same."

"What do you mean, *handle?*" Wells asked, already knowing the answer.

"I overheard the captain talking to someone. All I heard was him saying he'll keep you here till whoever arrives, and he promised not to do anything and let them handle it."

Wells racked her brain, trying to figure out who would come for her. She thought of all her conversations she'd had with Aranya. Since she was the one who sold Lily out, it made sense to have a connection with her. She remembered telling her about working for Penta, and chasing Drake and Jimmy, but that was about it. She'd never mentioned other names. There was no way that Drake or Jimmy were involved in this. She knew they were most likely still here in Shangcorp somewhere, but how could they be behind this? And the new hydros and rifles? Wells eliminated Drake and Jimmy from the list. Which left her with no one. She could not think of a single person she had wronged so badly that they would spend thousands of credits to buy a corrupt small-time captain and his security team to hold her prisoner.

She was wasting time and energy. According to the guard, she had until morning to figure something out.

It was time to escape this hole.

* * *

Fifteen hours and twelve minutes. That was all the time Lt. Wells had left on this planet. Capt. Davis looked at the countdown displayed on the biggest DDU in his office. Big numerals filled the whole screen, changing every second, counting down. He knew it would not happen the second it displayed zero, but they had planned the call for that time, and it gave him something to look forward to.

Davis leaned back in his chair, already savoring the victory.

I can't wait to see her face when she sees it's me.

| thirty-five |

Two guards patrolled the perimeter of the house, and another stood guard on the roof. An ARP scan confirmed that there was active surveillance surrounding the house. It wasn't a fortress, but it wouldn't be easy to gain entry.

Walking back to the parked vehicles where Jimmy and Ziggy were waiting, Drake spoke first.

"Can we do this? Without killing anyone, I mean."

Dina shook her head slightly. "You sure that is important right now? If we focus on getting to this Aranya person, and don't worry about casualties, it will make it easier, and our chances of success would increase. Worrying about who you can and can't shoot complicates things, Drake."

"Can't we just set all pulse weapons to stun?"

Dina shook her head once more. "Stun is not always effective, Drake. Sometimes it doesn't even do anything. We can't risk wondering if someone is down or not."

The dense jungle blocked out most of the moonlight, making their journey back to the vehicles slow.

Shooting at people had become part of his new life, and Drake had grown used to it. Maybe too much. The life of a hauler was violent at times, and he had been shot at more times than he could remember, but lately it felt like he was shooting at people almost every week. They were in a tight spot and had to move fast, so he understood the need to act quick and not make things more complicated than they needed to be.

"I just don't know if we need to kill more people to save one." Saying it felt wrong. Lily wasn't just anyone, but what he said was true. How many people would have to die so they could save her? What number was he comfortable with?

Dina stopped. "Drake, I'm a mercenary, not a monster. If I shoot you, the chances are very high that you deserved to be shot. These people, these Believers, have taken Lily hostage. It doesn't matter that they are fighting an evil corporation. They can still do bad things. Good people do bad things all the time. So if someone gets shot, it's because they made choices that led to us showing up at their door. I'm not here to take sides. I'm here to do a job. And that job is to get your friend out of Shangcorp."

Drake envied Dina's black and white outlook on life. It simplified so many things.

"I'm glad we're on the same side," he said as they set off again.

"Who said we are?" Dina laughed, punching Drake in the shoulder.

It took a lot of willpower not to rub his arm.

* * *

"Drake!" Jimmy yelled, and jumped up to greet his friend. Seymour followed and sat down next to him.

"So . . . It looks doable," Drake started.

"What the fuck does that mean?" Ziggy scowled at him.

"We have three confirmed bogeys, two patrolling and one on the roof, with multiple cameras, and possible bogeys inside." Dina clarified in Ziggy's language.

"Weapons?" Ziggy asked.

"Arties all around," Dina replied.

"Sounds doable, ya know?"

Luckily, Ziggy didn't stab him.

Dina looked down at Seymour. "Is this thing disposable?"

"Drake!" Jimmy yelled and stepped in front of Seymour.

"No. Why? What did you have in mind?" Drake asked.

"Strapping some explosives to him and creating a diversion. It's a good plan. You sure you want to keep it? It looks busted up."

Jimmy kneeled and hugged Seymour.

"Yeah, we can't blow it up," Drake sighed.

"Check this out!" Jimmy said, and swiped something at Seymour. The ASR jumped up and ran to Dina, who gave a step back.

"What's it doing?" she asked.

"Creating a diversion, ya know," Jimmy said.

The ASR fell to the ground, seemingly out of charge, only to jump up onto its hind legs and started the dancing routine Jimmy had given it to distract the Lan-noi security back at the hospital. Just like them, Dina and Ziggy couldn't help but laugh at its ridiculous moves.

"See!" Jimmy said. "You don't have to blow him up, ya know?"

Dina kept laughing. "This thing is as silly as you, Jimmy."

Smiling, Jimmy appeared to take it as a compliment.

"Okay," Dina said, gathering herself, "that will work too."

Jimmy called Seymour over, radiating with joy.

Everyone gathered around Dina as she laid out a basic plan for them to attack the house. She told Drake and Jimmy to grab their weapons and bring them to her. Drake grabbed his scatter-gun, and Jimmy his Artie.

"Okay," Dina began, holding Drake's gun. "This thing is bru-tal up close, but almost useless at any long range. That doesn't mean you can't use it. Even when you're far away, it's still a great deterrent, as it makes a lot of noise, and the enemy doesn't know what you're shooting at them. So use it to get close, keep shooting, and find cover. Also, always hold it like this."

Dina then showed Drake how to hold and carry the weapon more efficiently. He knew his way around pulse weapons, but the things she pointed out made sense and gave him more confidence in using the weapon.

Jimmy had fewer bad habits than Drake with weapons-handling, but Dina still helped him out with a few things. One could almost take him for a security officer, the way he handled the weapon now. Almost.

Dina eyed Drake from head to toes. "How're the ribs?"

Drake took a deep breath. "Fine. As long as I have this thing on." Drake tapped the graphene sleeve hugging his torso. "I'm fine. Don't worry about me."

"Okay, let's run through the plan one more time," Dina said.

"Hang on," Ziggy said. As usual, she'd been immersed in her HIC the whole time that Drake and Jimmy had been receiving instructions from Dina. "One of our contacts sent me a report of a foreigner being held in a local security lockup. The details are vague, but they mention it's a female."

"Where?" Drake asked.

Ziggy swept through her HIC, looking for the location.

"Small town. Not far from here."

"We have to go," Drake said to Dina.

"Hold on. We know that there is a link between Aranya and your friend, and we are right here. This new lead might be nothing and a waste of time."

"I know, but . . ." He had nothing else to say. His mind was racing with scenarios, trying to figure out which way to go. Dina was right. They were right here, at the place they intended to be, but if word got out of the ambush, the local security might clamp down and make it even harder to get Lily out of lockup. If they went to the local town, and it wasn't her, word might get back to Aranya of *waigoren* snooping around and she might up her defenses.

Somehow, his gut told him to go to the local town.

"We're sticking to the plan," Dina said, possibly seeing confusion in his face.

"I think it's her, Dina."

"I don't. And I hate to remind you, but I have a job to do. I can't stop you and Jimmy from going, but it'll hurt our chances of success if you do."

"But—"

"I'll go," Ziggy interrupted Drake. "I can handle myself and I know how to be stealthy. The plan will still work with three people. If it's a bust, I'll return immediately."

Drake snapped his head back to Dina.

"Okay, but the moment you confirm it's a negative, you return here, understand?"

"You know it," Ziggy said. She gave Dina a kiss. "I'll see you soon."

"You better," Dina said.

Drake, Jimmy, and Dina watched as Ziggy jumped into the old hydro and drove off into the night. Dina waited until the hydro's taillights disappeared before turning to Drake and Jimmy. "Okay, boys. Try not to die."

| thirty-six |

"ARPs on."

"Check."

"Check."

"Confirm visuals."

"Visuals on team, confirm."

"Yup, same, ya know. Got the visuals."

"Weapons live."

"Check."

"Check."

Nothing had changed at the house since their last recce. The two guards on the ground walked in circles around the building: one clockwise the other counterclockwise. The guard on the roof didn't seem to have any pattern to his movements and checked out different areas of the surrounding jungle at will.

"Okay, Jimmy. On my mark, you take out the top guard, and I'll take down the two patrolling ones," Dina said, reminding Jimmy of the plan. "Drake, you keep your eyes open for any other movement. Spread out."

Crouching and moving super slowly, everyone fanned out, making sure they didn't offer the enemy a single target to return fire to.

Waiting patiently, everyone watched the guards come around the opposite corners of the house. Jimmy lifted his Artie and acquired his target. Dina lifted hers and started tracking one of the guards. The guards were walking toward each other, about ten meters apart.

"Stand by," Dina ordered.

Drake watched the two guards nearing each other. He gripped his scatter-gun in anticipation.

Five meters.

Suddenly they stopped and looked up at the guard on the roof.

"Hold," Dina instructed.

The guards were outside of the ARPs' reach, and their conversation stayed between them. One guard on the ground turned back and disappeared around the corner. The other two continued chatting until an unfamiliar guard came walking around the corner. He stopped short of them and yelled something to his colleagues. The rooftop guard disappeared and seconds later, his replacement showed up. Everyone stood around, presumably waiting for the third guard to be relieved. Everyone seemed to yell at each other, and no one moved.

"What do we do?" Drake asked.

"Hold!" Dina replied. "They're too spread out, and we know there are more armed people inside now. Let it play out."

The conversation continued until another guard came running around the corner. He had a quick word with the last guard to be relieved, who shook his head and walked away, disappearing around the corner. The new guard held his hands up as if apologizing to everyone, and after another quick exchange, they all set off patrolling again.

"Jimmy, we'll give them one more lap and then we'll engage. Confirm."

"Got ya!"

Drake saw the two guards pass each other. Another short verbal exchange took place, but they kept on walking. They both disappeared around the building, and only the man on the roof stayed visible.

"Okay, Jimmy. Stand by."

It felt like an eternity, but eventually they both reappeared on their respective sides of the building. The new guard on the roof followed a more predictable back-and-forth pattern, making him easier to track. On his ARP, Drake saw both Jimmy and Dina raising their Arties and locking onto their targets. The two guards on the ground were now only a few meters apart.

This time, there were no interferences. The men kept walking until they passed each other, standing side by side for a split second. The split second Dina was waiting for.

"Fire!"

Two shots rang out from Drake's left, and four shots from his right. Dina had them switch their Arties to a single burst, for better accuracy, and had instructed Jimmy to take two shots per person. Almost simultaneously, all three guards fell. Unlike Ziggy's weapon, theirs weren't suppressed, and electric crackles filled the quiet night.

As the guards' bodies hit the ground, all three of them ran in a counterclockwise direction around the building and took up new positions across from where they had been. They stayed deep enough in the jungle to be invisible, but close enough to be accurate.

Huge lights flicked on and bathed the area in light, but the overgrown jungle did a great job protecting them. Six guards ran out of the house, all armed, looking around for the shooters. As the bodies were on the other side of the building, all the guards were now on the far side of the house from Dina, Drake, and Jimmy.

Jimmy accessed his HIC and sent a command to Seymour, who sat waiting in the jungle on the side of the house, in between the two groups. An electric pulse round crackle sounded from Seymour's hiding spot. Running five meters closer to Drake's group, Seymour played the audio file again. The guards who ran for cover after the first sound, now slowly made their way around the house, hugging it for cover. Seymour moved again and "fired" another shot. The guards paused, but hearing what sounded like the shooter retreating, regrouped, and two came running around the corner.

They fell dead within five steps.

Seymour doubled back and ran in the opposite direction, passing the guards until he faced their backs.

Dina, upon shooting the two guards, had immediately taken up position on the other side of the building.

Drake and Jimmy held their ground.

Seymour played the audio file again, ran and played it again.

Confusion took over the guards as they could hear the pulse fire but not see it. For a moment, the guards couldn't decide which way to cover. Then, gathering themselves, they did the sensible thing by splitting up. Two groups of two guards each went in opposite directions around the house.

Jimmy and Dina were ready and waiting. As both groups came running around their corners, they stopped them in their tracks.

"Hold positions," Dina said as silence fell.

Drake and Jimmy obeyed, sitting still, observing the building for any movement.

After two minutes, Dina spoke again. "Drake, you're up. Keep your eyes open."

It was Drake's turn. Jimmy and Dina had positioned themselves on opposite corners of the building, each covering two sides. If anyone came out, they would have a clear shot. Leaving the cover of the jungle, Drake ran toward the building and slammed himself against it. He turned his head sideways, but no one came running toward him. Looking up, he saw the first of the four cameras mounted on the outside. Quickly, he turned it into smoke and wires. Keeping close to the building, he ran to the next one.

"No movement. Stay alert," Dina informed everyone.

After shooting the second camera, he ran to the corner of the building.

"How's it looking?"

"All clear," Jimmy replied, having the best vantage point.

Drake turned the corner and made for the next camera.

Quickly, they were down to one camera. Soon whoever was on the inside would have no visuals on the outside, and they could breech the building.

Drake ran toward the last camera.

And straight into a guard. As he neared the camera, a door slid open, and before Jimmy could warn him, a guard stepped out, right in front of him. They collided, sending them both to the ground.

"Jimmy, do you have a shot?" Dina yelled over their connected ARPs, seeing what happened.

"Yes. No—uh, no. Fuck."

As they hit the ground, the guard rolled on top of Drake and started punching him. He hit the graphene cast and hesitated as he felt the rubbery material, and Drake threw him off. Drake crawled over the guard, trying to reach the scatter-gun, inadvertently blocking any chance of Dina or Jimmy taking a shot.

Drake's fingers scraped the scatter-gun's handle, but they had no time to grab on as the guard pulled him away. The guard was rolling away and dragged Drake with him. They were still a tangled mess, offering no shot to Jimmy or Dina. Drake gave up on the gun and refocused on the guard. Using his elbows, he pummeled the man's ear. The graphene restricted his movements, but it also protected him from the man's punches, which grew weaker with every throw.

Drake stopped and looked at the face beneath him. Eyes rolled back and barely breathing. He realized the man had had enough. Locating Dina's identifier, he grabbed the man under his armpits and dragged him toward her.

"What the hell are you doing, Drake?"

"Give me one of those magnetic cuffs you have," he replied, out of breath.

Dina grabbed one from her tactical belt and gave it to Drake.

"Your bleeding heart will soon be just that, Drake. A bleeding heart."

"He's out of the game, Dina. Did you want me to shoot him point blank?"

Dina's face gave him his answer. "Jimmy," she said, "we're going to use the door where Drake's mate just appeared from. Regroup."

Dina and Drake stayed put while Jimmy and Seymour made their way to them.

"Any sign of incoming traffic?" Dina asked Jimmy.

Jimmy scanned his HIC, accessing Seymour's advanced scanning sensors.

"Nothing showing up, ya know?"

"Okay. Drake, you're on door duty. You shoot them and slide them open, and we'll cover you," Dina confirmed everyone's roles again. "Once you open a door, hold your ground and let Seymour through. If the room is empty, I'll go in first, Jimmy in the middle, and you cover the rear."

They nodded in agreement.

"Let's move."

* * *

The lock on the door came apart as Drake fired a scatter round into it. A big irregular hole sat where the lock had been a second ago. Drake grabbed the rough edges of the hole and pulled on it, sliding the door open. It was a very basic door, and it had no emergency brakes or backup locks on it. Once Drake disabled the primary lock, nothing prevented it from sliding open.

Once the opening was big enough to fit through, Seymour burst through it, and scanned the next room. Jimmy was the only one tapped into Seymour's system and had to relay what he saw.

"Looks like a common room. Heating unit and big table. No heat signatures."

Dina nodded at him. "Go!" She made her way into the room, sidestepped, kneeled, and raised her Artie. Jimmy copied her as best he could. Drake had a good look around behind him before entering too.

"Clear," Dina confirmed once everyone entered the room. She looked at Drake and motioned with her head toward the new door.

Nervously, Drake approached it. The chances of another un-occupied room were slim to none, and he braced himself for what lay ahead. He raised his scatter-gun, and another lock bit the dust. He grabbed the hole and yanked the door open. As before, Seymour did not hesitate to charge in.

The room filled with electric blue light and sound. Drake threw himself backward, away from the door, and covered his head. He realized what he was doing and regained his com-posure. Sitting up, he aimed his scatter-gun at the open door and saw that all the pulse fire had stayed contained within the next room. Jimmy stuck his head around the door frame, giving everyone a view of the room via their ARPs.

DDUs filled the room, placed on benches creating multiple workstations surrounding an empty table.

Seymour sat cowering in a corner, behind a sturdy chair, attracting all the pulse fire. His one front leg had taken a hit and hung on by a few wires.

"Drake, the bastards shot Seymour!" Jimmy yelled out.

Before Drake could tell him to duck, the pulse fire was redirected in Jimmy's direction. Wood splintered in front of his face and made him fall over backward. He too composed himself quickly and sat up, Artie at the ready.

"Drake, make three holes in the walls for us!" Dina yelled over the noise.

Drake immediately understood her plan and shot three holes into the wall between them and the enemy. Dina ran over to a hole, jammed her Artie into it, and fired blindly. Drake quickly joined her. Seeing what the plan was, Jimmy ran over and joined too.

"Jimmy! You are the only one with eyes in there. We'll provide cover, but you need to take them out!"

Seymour was not in the best position, but Dina was right. He was the only one who had any idea where the assault was coming from.

Carefully, Jimmy repositioned Seymour and saw a pulse gun sticking out. Without hesitation, he started firing in that position until no return fire came.

Having one less pulse rifle shooting at them made an enormous difference in the noise level.

"I think there are only two more guns in there," Drake yelled at Dina. "Listen."

Dina stopped shooting for a second, listening to the cadence of the pulse rounds fired at them.

"I think you're right. Jimmy, can you see them?"

"No. They've pinned Seymour down, ya know. But I can try a scan?"

"If he can't face them, a scan will be useless," Drake said.

"Jimmy, decide, quick!" Dina yelled.

Drake saw the fear in Jimmy's eyes as he weighed up his options. All his decisions would involve Seymour being vulnerable and possibly destroyed.

"Okay! Okay!" Jimmy finally replied.

Drake and Dina kept firing at random intervals, keeping whoever was in the room busy. Jimmy worked on his HIC and swiped new instructions to Seymour. The little ASR hobbled out from his hiding spot, took another hit and fell down in the middle of the room. A tiny plume of smoke rose from his leg. The Believers ignored the broken-down ASR and focused their weapons on the holes in the wall.

"Scan complete!" Jimmy yelled again. "Dina, swap places with me."

Dina pulled her Artie out of the hole and stepped aside for Jimmy to take her spot.

"Okay. Hold still. C'mon . . . Almost . . . Yes!" Jimmy said, giving them a play-by-play as he shot at their assailants.

Dina gave Jimmy a pat on the shoulder and he stopped firing his pulse rifle.

"Listen," Drake said.

Everything went quiet. The return fire had stopped, and an eerie silence now filled the room.

"Jimmy," Dina began.

"On it," he replied. He accessed his HIC and did another scan of the room. "Empty. No heat signatures, ya know."

Drake grabbed the door and slid it open. Dina ran in first and took up a defensive position. Jimmy went in next and did the same, right next to Seymour. Drake went in last, walking backward, making sure no one surprised them from the rear.

The smell of burned plastic hung in the air, and Drake saw two bodies on the ground. He stepped over them and went over to Jimmy.

"Hey buddy. He did great."

Jimmy inspected Seymour from top to bottom. He let out a sigh. The second pulse cartridge had only grazed the top of his orange body, leaving a long black streak behind.

"Damn, Drake, that was close, ya know?"

"I know, buddy."

"He's fine. I can fix the leg, ya know. I programmed him to switch off when he reached the middle of the room, so if they scanned him, he would look destroyed. Then the moment they started shooting, I knew they wouldn't bother scanning him again, so I switched him on in low-power mode. The only thing that worked was his sensors."

"I'm glad your toy is fine, but we need to move," Dina said.

Drake helped up Jimmy, who put Seymour behind the chair again, out of harm's way.

A short hall led out of the room, with four doors leading off it. Judging by the size of the building, the rooms had to be much smaller than the first two rooms they'd encountered.

Dina seemed to read his mind. "These rooms are tiny. There can't be too many people in them."

"Agreed. We know there is at least one person in them," Drake added.

Dina nodded.

"Okay, we're sticking to the plan. Drake, take out the lock and if there is no return fire, open it and fall back. Jimmy, stay behind me, monitor the other doors and be ready to go when I move."

"Got it."

"Okay."

Dina nodded, and Drake squeezed past her and made his way to the first door. The lock evaporated as he pulled the trigger. He fell back against the wall to cover himself and waited. No sounds came from within the room. He grabbed the newly made hole and slid the door open. Without hesitation, Dina breeched the room and took up position in the middle of the floor. Jimmy saw her go in and followed. Drake kept his position and watched the remaining three doors.

"Clear. Let's move."

Dina came rushing out and took up a position next to the opposite door. Drake moved to the other side of the same door and Jimmy took up Drake's old position. Dina nodded, and he blasted the lock. No sound came, so he slid the door open, and Dina and Jimmy quickly cleared the room.

In seconds, everyone was in position for the third door. Drake removed the lock and waited a few seconds. Again, no sound came from within the room, so he grabbed the ragged hole and pulled on it.

And screamed as a pulse round pulverized the tip of his pinky finger. Grabbing his hand, Drake saw that a third of his pinky, everything above the first knuckle, was missing.

The door remained shut, as he'd had no time to pull it back before someone altered the look of his hand.

Dina, standing on the opposite side of the door from Drake and closer to the hole, poked her Artie through it and fired into the room. After a few seconds, she stopped and removed her pulse rifle from the door.

Holding onto his hand as tight as he could, Drake tried not to make a sound, as he knew everyone was trying to listen in on the room. The urge to yell and swear always made the pain feel less, but he knew he had to suck it up. All three tilted their heads, trying their best to hear any signs of life.

"I'm hurt. I won't shoot back. I need help."

The voice took everyone by surprise.

"Fine. I'm sliding the door open. When it's open, throw your weapon through. Any funny business and we're coming in shooting!" Dina yelled.

"I understand."

Dina nodded at Drake, who curled his injured hand into a ball and grabbed the hole with his other hand. He closed his eyes as his fingers went into the hole, praying he wouldn't lose any more digits. Nothing happened, so he pulled harder. The door slid open and a pulse rifle crashed onto the floor at Dina's feet. She kicked it aside and walked in, Artie at the ready.

Jimmy followed, and Drake stuck his head around the frame to see what was happening.

A tiny figure sat on a makeshift bed, blood covering her lower half. She had a soft smile and looked completely out of place in between all this violence.

Drake was wrong.

"My name is Aranya, and I think I'm dying."

| thirty-seven |

Ziggy parked the old hydro and made sure it wasn't visible from the road, breaking off some branches and covering the rear. She stood back and surveyed her work. Only someone who went looking for it would spot it.

Satisfied, she set off on foot. The small town was another kilometer away, and the walk would only take her a few minutes. She'd decided against driving into town, as most people around here drove bom-boms or small hydrocycles, and she did not want to attract any attention. Sticking to the side of the road, she could scamper into the bush if a bigger vehicle, like that of a security force, came past. Every few meters, she did a quick scan to make sure she didn't miss anything approaching her in the dark.

Up ahead, the first buildings appeared. Ziggy stopped and did another quick scan. A few heat signatures came up, but not much technology. Satisfied that these buildings would statistically not prove a threat, she pushed on.

As she neared the first housing unit, she went into stealth mode. Carrying an automatic pulse rifle would cause anyone who spotted her to raise the alarm. From here on in, she would stay in the shadows and use as much of the surrounding cover as she could. The town didn't seem to have many residents, and Ziggy found it easy to evade the ones she came across by using her ARP and hiding. She was making slow progress, but being inconspicuous was more important than speed.

Night had fallen, and unlike bigger towns, this one didn't have a great number of streetlights. Scattered at random intersections and corners, the outdated lampposts did their best to illuminate a small radius around them. Most buildings had some illumination of their own, but sizable dark patches loomed everywhere. Sneaking around would be a breeze.

Nearing the center of town, Ziggy paused when she saw two shiny new armored vehicles parked on the street. The building in front of them was rundown, like most in the area, and had a DDU sign above the door displaying one word: SECURITY. She'd found her target.

The building had better lighting than most around it, but there was still enough darkness for Ziggy to make it all the way to its walls without detection. She hunkered down and activated her ARP once more. Modern buildings had all kinds of tech preventing people from scanning through the walls and invading the occupants' privacy, but Ziggy guessed, by the look of the buildings in the area and the one next to her, that tech would not be a feature here. And she was right. Scanning for heat signatures, she easily picked up seven unique signatures. One further away, three concentrated together, one close to the front entrance and two more near each other. An educated guess would put the prisoner alone or with one guard. If it was up to her, she would make sure someone monitored the asset, so Ziggy placed her bets on the two heat signatures closest to her.

Having established a headcount and rough layout of the interior, it was time for action.

Calmly, as if she belonged there, Ziggy walked through the front door. The heat signatures turned into faces as she saw the group of three standing around to one side, and one of the single ones at a counter at the entrance. Her assumptions had been correct.

"How can we help?" asked the officer behind the counter.

The three officers standing around turned and looked at Ziggy. She knew the pink hair and heavy makeup always attracted attention, but around here she stood out even more than usual.

"Yes. I need to speak to whoever is in charge of the prisoner."

The three guards were out of earshot, but they kept their attention on her.

"And what is the nature of your inquiry?"

Ziggy hated the part where she had to be nice to people to get what she wanted, instead of taking it by force. This felt like so much more work.

"Of course," she said, smiling through gritted teeth. "I may have some information regarding the person you have in your custody. I'm confident your superior would be very interested in what I have to say."

The guard at the desk gave Ziggy a look that said "I have nothing better to do."

"Follow me."

A small gate in the counter slid open and Ziggy followed the guard past the three officers staring at her to a closed door at the other end of the building. No alarms went off, and no one did a body search. These people were either very trusting or completely incompetent. The officer announced them at the door via the DDU, and as they waited for a reply, Ziggy observed the rest of the building.

It was quite small. Beyond the entrance was the counter, and behind that were a few workstations. An open door to the side revealed a common area, and a closed door next to it had the symbols for a bathroom above it. The opposite wall had two doors, but no signage. She knew from her scans that one of them had the prisoner in them. The only other door was the one behind them, which slid open.

"Come in!" a voice commanded.

The officer waved Ziggy in and disappeared. Ziggy waited for the door to slide shut before approaching the man.

"Hi, I'm here to pick up my friend."

The man stroked the few hairs that lived on his upper lip. "Your friend, eh? And who says we have your friend?"

Ziggy opened her coat, pulled out her Artie, and shot him. His eyes were almost as big as the hole in his chest.

"Don't waste my time," she said to his corpse as she left the room.

* * *

Having a suppressor on her Artie meant that it muted the sound significantly, but not entirely. As she left the office of the recently deceased chief, one of the three guards that stood together came over to see what the noise was.

"Everything okay? We thought we—" Ziggy cut him short with a pulse round in the neck. The man fell to the ground, clutching the wound, blood spraying everywhere.

She knew where Lily was, and she'd tried to do this the nice way, but these people were just slowing her down. Artie still raised, she mowed down the other two officers, who hadn't even realized what was happening and died with their arms still crossed.

The officer at the counter saw Ziggy and sprang into action, diving over the counter and taking cover behind it. Ziggy did not know if the officer had a pulse weapon and proceeded with caution. She also had to watch the side door, as she knew there was one more guard in there.

Using a workstation as cover, Ziggy kneeled and fired a few rounds over the counter and into the front doors. Keeping her sights on the counter, she waited for return fire, but none came. Assuming the guard did not have any weapons, and not wanting to waste too much time trapped in the building, she ran toward the counter and vaulted over it. She landed on her feet, but immediately went into a roll for a few feet and ended up in a kneeling position facing the guard, who sat hugging herself.

"Throw me your weapons!" Ziggy shouted.

"I don't have any. I don't have any. Don't shoot me."

The woman started crying, and a quick scan confirmed she wasn't lying.

"Okay, get up. If you hesitate for a second to comply, I'll shoot you. Understand?"

The woman nodded her head.

"Okay. Open that door." Ziggy motioned with her head toward the door she believed led to the holding facility.

"Yes. Yes, I can do that." She stood up and almost ran to the door, forcing Ziggy to pick up her pace to keep up.

"Slow down," Ziggy said, as the officer was already accessing the DDU next to the door.

Ziggy walked back a few steps and took cover behind another workstation.

"Okay, now open it."

Nodding, the woman finished entering the code into the DDU, and the door slid open. A volley of pulse rounds came flying through the open door, as Ziggy had expected. The woman fell and covered her head with her arms.

Another volley came through the door, but Ziggy didn't retaliate. She waited as a third wave of pulse rounds came flying over her head. Still, she waited. A faint scraping sound told her the shooter was moving, and she knew they would poke their head out soon to see why no one was shooting back. Ziggy sat up, took aim at the door, and waited.

A head appeared, as she knew it would, and she greeted it with a pulse round between the eyes. The guard tumbled backward, and Ziggy entered the room.

"Lily?"

The prisoner looked at her but didn't say anything.

"I'm with Drake and Jimmy. They are going to be so happy to see you."

| thirty-eight |

Blood flowed through Aranya's fingers and soaked her clothes. She looked pale and weak.

"Where is Lily?" Drake yelled at her. He felt guilty, considering her condition, but if she knew anything, she had to speak up now. While she still could.

Aranya exhaled heavily, but didn't answer.

"She's dying," Dina said as she shoved Drake out of the way. "Lift her clothes and find the wound."

Drake scrambled back to Aranya and did as Dina told him. Blood was everywhere and he couldn't see where it was coming from.

"Here," Dina mumbled, biting down on a medical packet. She rummaged through her backpack and handed Drake a sealed pouch. Taking it, he ripped it open and found a medical grade, high absorbent micro towel. As he started wiping Aranya's abdomen, the blood disappeared into the towel. Blood smears still covered her skin, but her wound was now easily identifiable.

"Found it!"

Dina bumped into Drake as she moved into position to see the wound. She still had the package in her teeth, and pulling down on it with one hand, tore it open. She took the synthetic skin out of the package and slapped it on the wound.

"Keep pressure on it," she instructed Drake.

"Jimmy!" Dina turned around and found him. "Find me some water."

"I think the synth-skin is working," Drake said.

"Looks like it, but we need to get some blood in her."

Jimmy ran back into the room with a bottle of water.

"Open it," she said, and waited for Jimmy to turn the cap. Once he had, she took a small packet and emptied its contents into the bottle. After shaking it, she gave it to Drake.

"What is this?" he asked. The liquid had turned a deep brown color and was thickening.

"We need to hurry. I'll keep her mouth open, and you make sure all of that goes down her throat."

"Huh? But—"

"Go!"

Dina pulled Aranya's head back and pulled her jaw down. Drake opened the bottle and started pouring the brown liquid down her throat. Dina pinched Aranya's nose, forcing her to swallow if she wanted to catch a breath. Every time she gasped, Drake stopped, and once Dina gave him the nod, he poured in more liquid. It felt more like torture than saving a life.

Drake waited until the bottle was empty before asking Dina again, "What was that stuff?"

Dina leaned Aranya back against the wall and turned to Drake.

"It's a protein that shocks her body into producing blood quickly. It's more complicated than that, but I never listened. All I know is, it works. In five minutes, she'll be ready to talk again."

Drake, Jimmy, and Dina all collapsed to the floor. Dina grabbed something out of her bag and tossed it to Drake. "For your finger. How does it feel?"

Drake caught and then opened the small packet of synthetic skin.

"It hurts like hell, but I'll survive," Drake replied as he applied the synthetic skin to the end of his now much shorter finger.

Aranya's breathing had slowed down and become more rhythmic and deeper. Soon her eyes fluttered, and she opened them. It took her a second to take in her surroundings and the unknown faces around her.

"Thank you," she said, after regaining some composure.

"Don't thank us. We're the ones that shot you," Dina stated.

"Aranya, my name is Benjamin Drake and I'm a friend of Lily Wells. We are trying to find her, and you might be our only hope."

Aranya smiled at Drake. "Ah, Lily. Such a leader. So inspiring. I wish things could have turned out better."

"What do you mean? Is she okay? Where is she?"

Staring into Drake's eyes, Aranya took her time. "Do you believe in the greater good, Mr. Drake?" Her breathing was still labored, and her words came out as a whisper.

"Sure." Drake guessed it was what she wanted to hear. His whole life had revolved around the next contract and the next bar. He lived day to day, by himself and for himself. He had never thought about things like the greater good. But things had changed in the last few months.

"To me, and all the Believers, the greater good is all that matters. Until we gain our freedom from Shangcorp, we cannot be individuals. We must act as one." Aranya stopped, out of breath.

Drake failed to see what this had to do with Lily. "We're all one. I get it. Where's Lily?"

Aranya touched the synth-skin and flinched. Some of the color had returned to her face. "Lily had a choice. Help the Believers and stay with us, or leave and go back home."

That meant that Lt. Wells would be well on her way to Penta by now. Given the choice to be anywhere in the world, or at Penta chasing bad guys, Drake knew Wells would always pick Penta in a heartbeat.

"All my pleas for her to stay were in vain and she left."

Time for them to do the same. If Lily was already out of here, then they had to go as well. The borders were about to close, or could already be closed. If she was on her way, he knew she would make it back home.

"If she's already gone," Drake turned to Dina, "we need to go, too."

"She's not gone yet," Aranya said behind him.

"You said—"

"The greater good, Mr. Drake."

"Is she okay, ya know?" Jimmy pointed to his head.

Drake was wondering the same thing. It seemed the blood loss was causing her to babble. "What about the greater good?" He was readying himself to leave.

"Lily was about to leave when I received a very generous offer to hand her over to the local authorities."

Drake froze.

"A local security chief contacted me and offered me weapons and credits in exchange for Lt. Lily Wells. The greater good, Mr. Drake."

Drake kneeled in front of Aranya, grabbed a handful of her clothing, and pulled her face close to his. "Where is she?"

"She is a very capable woman, I've learned, so I have no fears for her safety," Aranya replied.

"Answer my question!" Drake spat.

Aranya's faint smile faded away. The reflection in her eyes became dull. She was slipping away.

"Dina, give her more of that brown shit," Drake yelled, and turned back to Aranya. "Where is Lily?"

A hand rested on Drake's shoulder, and he shook it off.

"Where?" he yelled, and shook Aranya.

The hand returned and gripped him tighter. "She's gone, ya know."

The eyes that stared back at Drake had no life left in them. They were looking at something beyond him, something the living couldn't see.

"She was never going to make it, Drake. Her insides are most likely all scrambled. The synth-skin was only to keep alive for a while longer."

Relaxing the muscles in his hand, he let go of Aranya's clothes and watched her body slump against the wall. Slowly, she leaned over and gently slid to the floor.

"We didn't learn anything," Drake said, head down.

"If she sold Lily out to a local chief, maybe it's the same one Ziggy went to, ya know?"

All the shooting and questioning had consumed his attention, so much so that Drake had completely forgotten about Ziggy. "Jimmy, you're right. It must be! Dina?"

Dina looked at Drake and shrugged. "Could be. She should be there by now. I'll call her."

Dina swiped her HIC, activating a call on her ARP to Ziggy.

Drake watched her staring off into space, waiting for the three dots to merge.

After a minute, Dina gave up.

"She's not answering."

"Why?" Drake asked.

"How should I know?" Dina shook her head.

"Let's just go to her, ya know?"

There was nothing left for them to do here. They'd shot most of the DDUs to pieces and everyone was dead. Almost everyone.

"The guard outside!" Drake recalled the man he'd refused to shoot. "Maybe he knows which security picked her up."

"Worth a shot," Dina said, and made for the door.

Drake stood up, wiped his bloodied hands on his pants, and gave Aranya's body one more glance before heading out of the room. He wondered who would rise to fill the void she'd left.

Dina and Jimmy had already located the guard by the time he reached them. Sitting against a tree, he looked like he was just waking up.

"Hey buddy. My friend here really—and I mean really—wants to shoot you. I've asked her to wait because I think you might be useful. Please prove me right."

One eye had swollen shut, and he had a busted lip. The look he gave Drake did not seem cooperative. Drake pushed on. "Okay. Our friend, her name is Lily, she was some kind of prisoner here. Tall, almost my height. Do you know who I'm talking about?"

One eye bobbed between Dina and Jimmy and then back to Drake. He nodded.

"Okay, great! Now, do you know what happened to her? Who took her?"

His good eye surveyed his interrogators once more, before nodding again.

"Who was it?" Drake asked.

This time, the eye looked around on the ground as he weighed up his options. It didn't take him too long to realize he didn't have that many.

"It was the guys from Kronwei," he said, still eyeing the ground.

"That's where Ziggy went!" Jimmy shouted.

Dina and Drake looked at each other.

"Let's go," they said simultaneously.

| thirty-nine |

"Dammit," Dina said as she disconnected the call on her Human Interface Console.

"Still not picking up?" Drake asked.

Dina shook her head. She was sitting next to Drake in the truck, close enough for him to see the tension in her neck muscles. "She must be close to Wells and not able to speak."

Drake knew she was talking to herself, not him, trying to reassure herself that Ziggy was okay.

"Hope so, ya know," Jimmy piped in from the back, where he sat on the small bed, working on Seymour's leg.

No one said anything for a while, and Drake concentrated on following the tiny green arrow on the screen.

"How's his leg?" Drake asked finally. He didn't really care about the orange Automated Service Robot, but he knew it meant a lot to Jimmy. Besides, it had proven itself to be useful more times than Drake was willing to admit.

"Almost there, partner. Once we get back to New Franco, I'll give him a proper service, ya know."

Drake saw Dina scrolling through her HIC, checking messages and noticeboards, looking for any news or mention of Ziggy.

"I'm sure she's fine, like you said," Drake tried to reassure her.

"I've known her for almost ten years now, Drake. We've been through a lot. I know what she's capable of. I don't think anyone in this region is a match for her," Dina said. She paused and scrolled on her HIC again. "I just wished she would update me."

A yellow rectangle with the word Kronwei popped up on the windshield. They were now within the village's limits. A cluster of lights up the road confirmed they were indeed close now.

"So what do we do?" Drake asked. "I mean, do we go to the local security?"

"Pull over," Dina replied.

Drake slowed the old truck down and found a spot to park on the side of the road.

"I still believe she is fine, but we need to look at this pragmatically," Dina continued. "If the local security somehow detained her, we might face a hostile situation when we enter. Having no communication at the moment, I think we should operate under the assumption that Ziggy and Lily are being held captive."

Drake and Jimmy nodded their agreement, waiting for the new plan.

"Okay, Drake, you'll enter the building first, unarmed, and I'll judge the situation via your ARP. Jimmy and I will then come in once I have a good reading on the entire scene. So make sure you look around and keep talking."

"Okay. A few things . . ." Drake replied. "Why do I have to be the one going in unarmed? And what do you want me to talk about? The looming war with my people?"

"Because you are the shittiest shooter between us three. And you can talk about whatever you want. I don't care."

Drake decided not to reply. Not that he didn't have plenty to say, but because Dina was right.

"Okay then, let's go get them," Drake said, and pulled out onto the road again.

* * *

Drake's heart was pounding in his chest, reminding him of his not quite healed ribs. He was about to see Lily for the first time in months, but that was not the sole reason for the adrenaline spike. Climbing out of the truck, he would have attributed his clammy palms and racing heart to the fact he was about to see her, but as he neared the entrance to the security building, his heart raced for a different reason.

Big, ragged holes littered the door. Holes like the ones he'd made with his scatter-gun, only smaller. These holes were the aftermath of a gunfight. The moment he saw them, his heart started pounding.

"Dina, what do I do?"

Sitting behind the truck, Dina and Jimmy watched Drake, ready to move if needed.

"Can you hear anything inside?"

"No," Drake replied.

"Does your ARP have scanning abilities?"

"Yes."

"Okay, then scan for heat signatures."

It was the obvious move, and Drake felt slightly annoyed that he hadn't thought of it before asking Dina what to do. Accessing his HIC, he found the scanning settings and ran a body heat scan on the building. Drake's HIC and ARP units were outdated, glitchy, and in dire need of replacement. The results wouldn't be as accurate compared to if Jimmy did the scan, but Drake didn't want to waste any more time in swapping places or debating Dina about each person's tasks.

"Okay," Drake started, as he scanned the building. "From what my crappy unit can do, I can only see one person in there. The others could be out of range, but still inside, or Lily is alone, and Ziggy hasn't arrived yet."

"Don't speculate. Stick to the facts," Dina replied.

"Okay, I can see one person."

Drake kept scanning, waiting for Dina's next command.

"Go in. We've got you covered."

A DDU next to the door had the word *door* displayed on it, and Drake pressed the screen. Slowly, and loudly, the doors slid apart, revealing the interior of the security office to Drake. The doors came to a stop.

"Guys . . ." Drake started, but didn't need to finish, as Dina and Jimmy were already standing next to him.

* * *

For a second, the interior of the security office looked normal. Rundown and grimy, but normal. Then, beyond the counter that separated the civilians from the security personnel, the scene changed. As Drake observed the office, he spotted three bodies on the ground. All three were in uniform. Then he saw the open office door, with another uniformed person. This guy sported a big hole in his chest. Turning his head, he saw another officer lying on the ground. He was laying across a doorway, resting his head in a pool of blood. Next to him sat the only active heat signature in the building.

Dina approached the female officer sitting on the ground, hugging her knees and crying.

"What happened?" she asked with typical Slavoric empathy.

The woman looked up at her, eyes swollen from crying, cheeks wet, but didn't say anything.

Dina slapped her across the face. "What happened?"

She had her attention now.

"A woman came in and killed everyone."

"Just like that? Walked in and killed everyone?"

Drake intervened. He positioned himself next to Dina and offered the lady a kinder face.

"Can you please try to be more specific? We are looking for the person who you had in custody. Do you think you can tell us exactly what happened?"

"I work the front desk. This lady came in, saying she had information regarding the person we had detained. I took her to see the chief. Next minute, she started killing everyone." She shot a look at Dina, anticipating another slap.

"And the prisoner? What happened to her?"

"She, I mean the woman who came here, took her. I overheard her saying she was a friend and that Jake and Jimmy would be happy to see her."

"Drake and Jimmy," Drake corrected her. "Do you have any idea where they went?"

The woman looked at Dina and shook her head.

Drake stood up and walked into the holding cell. Old fashioned iron bars split the room in half. On the side where he was standing stood a small workstation, and on the other side was a small bed. A gate in the bars stood open, and Drake entered the cell. He tossed the thin blanket on the bed, but there was nothing of Lily in this room. He made his way back to Dina and Jimmy.

"Okay, we know they were here and can't be too far away," Drake said.

"They could have gone in any direction," Dina said as she tried her HIC again.

"We can just track them, ya know."

Drake and Dina snapped their heads toward Jimmy.

He smiled back at them.

"Jimmy, what are you talking about?" Drake asked.

"When we stole the hydro, and I hacked its DDU, I also installed a tracking app. It's something we used to do in New Franco, ya know. A way of keeping score of the hydros we stole."

"So you can track the hydro right now and tell us where they are?"

"Yup. If you want, I can do it now, ya know."

Drake bit his tongue and nodded at Jimmy. "If you could, please, buddy."

Still smiling, Jimmy accessed his HIC. "Got 'em."

* * *

The tracking app led them to a location on the outskirts of town. They still had another hundred meters to go when Dina grabbed Drake's arm.

"Stop the truck."

Drake pulled to the side of the road and put the truck on standby.

"What's going on?"

"Something's wrong, Drake. Ziggy should have called me by now or answered my calls. It feels wrong."

"I feel the same. I didn't want to say anything back there, but why did she shoot everyone?" Drake replied.

"I assume they shot first." Dina's face never revealed much, but Drake could see the worry in her eyes.

"I'm sure they are fine, Dina, but let's play it safe, then. What is our best option?"

Dina mulled it over. "No. I'm being paranoid. She's just completed the mission successfully. I'm sure she is planning on connecting with us soon. Maybe her HIC took a shot. We're wasting time speculating. Let's go in and find out."

Drake liked that idea. He couldn't wait to see Lily's face again.

Leaving the truck where it was, they walked the last few meters to the location. The road seemed very narrow, and Drake didn't want to risk getting the old hydro truck stuck. It only took them a few minutes to reach an old building that looked abandoned, save for the low light glowing from inside.

"After you," Dina said.

"Thanks, Dina. For everything," Drake said, and opened the door.

After months of worrying about her and wondering if he'd ever see her again, she was sitting right in front of him.

Bound to a chair, with Ziggy's pulse rifle pointing at her head.

| forty |

"As promised. Lt. Lily Wells."

Capt. Davis's eyes grew bigger as the pink-haired woman stepped aside to reveal Lt. Wells sitting on a chair, hands and legs bound. A gag muted her, but her eyes projected pure hatred toward the DDU in Davis's office.

"Finally, your day has come. You messed with the wrong man, little girl. Always strutting around, thinking you are so much better than all of us. And then almost getting me arrested for helping a friend? Nah. Not this guy. I make the rules now. Not you."

Davis took a sip of his traditionally distilled whiskey to calm his nerves. Seeing her helpless and at his mercy sent his heart rate through the roof. *Don't have a heart attack now.* Hand still shaking, he took another sip of the scarce and almost priceless liquid. As much as he wanted her to die, he didn't want to rush the moment.

"The only thing making me happier than seeing you die to-day is knowing my face will be the last one you ever see."

Davis emptied the glass, ignoring the heartburn that was burning in his chest.

It was time for Lt. Lily Wells to die.

* * *

"I'm with Drake and Jimmy. They are going to be so happy to see you."

Wells surveyed the woman standing in front of her, trying to connect her to Drake and Jimmy. She certainly fit the type Wells imagined them to associate with. Pink hair, scars on her neck and face, dirty long coat. She seemed their type.

"How do you know them?"

The woman seemed surprised by the question. "We really need to get out of here. I'm sure someone will be here soon."

Wells looked at the dead guard lying at her feet. She wished he had listened when she told him to stay put and not go out there. He didn't deserve this.

"Maybe, but I still need to know who I'm trusting with my life here."

The guard's pulse rifle was on the ground, but out of reach.

"Okay. I met them at a work site a few months ago, and they asked me to help them find you. We got separated a few days ago, but I've already told them to meet us at a rendezvous point. We really need to get going."

The guard's blood reached the woman's boot and pooled against it.

"Mind if I take this?" Wells leaned over, reaching for the pulse rifle.

"Nah, grab it and let's go." The woman turned and made for the entrance.

Wells grabbed the pulse rifle and followed her outside.

"I'm Ziggy," she said as Wells reached her.

"I'm Lily. But I guess you knew that."

She gave Wells a smile and motioned with her head to get going. Wells followed her, and the two made their way to the edge of town. Ziggy turned off the road and moved branches around to reveal an old junker.

"Get in," Ziggy said as she climbed in.

Wells jumped in the passenger side, holding her gun casually in her lap, but pointing in Ziggy's direction.

"Hold this," Ziggy said, handing Wells her pulse rifle.

Interesting move, Wells thought. Handing over her gun made her seem trusting, but it also occupied Wells's hands and made it more difficult for her to use her own weapon. Holding two rifles in the constraints of a hydrocar's cabin made her clumsy and would slow her down. Wells repositioned herself as best she could.

After running the start-up procedure, Ziggy reversed the old hydro out of the bushes and onto the road. She put it in drive and drove back into town. As they passed the security building, Wells noticed no one had come to investigate yet. Ziggy kept driving and soon they reached the other side of the small village. She took a turnoff and followed a small dirt road until it ended in front of an abandoned building.

"I know. Looks shit, right?" Ziggy said as she parked the hydro.

"I just came out of a holding cell, so I'm not complaining."

Ziggy smiled at her and held her hand out for her gun.

So far, Ziggy hadn't done anything to make Wells believe she had an ulterior motive, but Wells did not know her at all, and her story about Drake was super flimsy. Handing her the weapon back would take away any advantage Wells had held.

"I've got it," Wells said, and opened her door.

"Don't be silly," Ziggy said and grabbed the pulse rifle out of her hands.

Wells could not get a read on this woman.

"This way," Ziggy said, and walked around the corner of the building.

Standing on the far side of the hydro, Wells had to move quickly around it to catch up to Ziggy, who had disappeared. She half ran, rifle pointed to the ground, knowing it was a mistake to let Ziggy out of her sight.

She was right.

Rounding the corner, Wells saw the electric blue muzzle flash of a pulse weapon. There was no time to react.

You idiot, she thought as gravity pulled her into a black oblivion.

* * *

Waking up from a pulse stun is never fun, but Wells was grateful that there were no bright lights in the room to compound the headache she already had. As she waited for her eyes to focus, she felt her breathing restricted to her nose. She tried to remove whatever it was blocking her mouth, but her arms stayed put. A quick test proved her legs to be immobilized, too. Giving up for now, she scanned the room.

A DDU sat on a table in front of her, and the rest of the room seemed to be empty. Wells turned her head as much as she could, but couldn't see anything else. The only other door opened, and Ziggy appeared.

Ignoring Wells, she accessed the DDU that sat in front of her. As she stepped away, Wells could see that she'd started a call and was waiting for the recipient to pick up. Ziggy took a spot next to Wells and waited for the guest to appear.

"As promised. Lt. Lily Wells."

Wells looked at the man on the screen. He seemed extremely happy to see her. Her mind was still reeling from the stun earlier, and she failed to recognize him. He seemed vaguely familiar, but she doubted she knew him very well. She realized he had a Penta Security uniform on and instinctively noticed his rank. Captain. She had worked with her fair share of captains in her career, but still she struggled to place the vaguely familiar face.

". . . and then almost getting me arrested for helping a friend? Nah. Not this guy. I make the rules now. Not you."

As he ended his little monologue, Wells's mind fog cleared and all the pieces fell into place.

She waited for him to finish, not really listening to his words. She'd heard him speak before and knew she wasn't missing much.

Wells looked at Ziggy and motioned her head upward. She didn't know how else to signal to her to remove the gag. Luckily for Wells, she caught the gesture.

"Do you want me to remove the gag or shoot her?" Ziggy asked in a completely emotionless tone.

On the screen, Davis licked his lips and poured himself another drink.

"Let her have her last say." She knew he wouldn't be able to resist hearing her beg for her life.

Ziggy grabbed the gag and yanked it out of Wells's mouth.

"Thanks."

Wells's mouth felt dry, and she took a second before speaking.

"I'm sorry, but you clearly know me and here I am with no idea who you are. Have we met before?"

Wells watched Davis's face turn bright red. The anger he felt manifested itself visibly, and he could do nothing to hide it.

"I know you know me!" Veins were now visible, too.

Slowly shaking her head, Wells peered at the ground, faking a deep thought.

"Nah, I'm sorry. Maybe you could refresh my memory."

If she could scan his biometric telemetry, Wells was confident she would see a man on the verge of having a stroke.

"I know what you're trying to do! It won't work. I have you now. I win!"

Wells tilted her head and shook it slowly, showing she was still at a loss.

"Okay. I guess you win . . ." Wells stopped herself. "Sorry, but this is going to bug me. What was your name?"

Davis threw his glass at the screen, and Wells saw his image disappear as the glass must have knocked over the DDU in his office. The image came back, closer than before, his red face filling the whole screen.

"Kill her! Shoot her! Now! Just shoot her!"

Wells looked at Ziggy and saw her contempt for the unhinged man on the DDU.

Without a word, Ziggy lifted her pulse rifle and aimed it at Lt. Wells's head.

"Now!" Davis screamed.

| forty-one |

A voice kept yelling from a nearby DDU, but Drake's focus was firmly on Wells and the gun pointing at her. Drake kept waiting for a third person, the actual bad guy, to show up and for Ziggy to aim her pulse gun at them.

But the only bad guy in the room seemed to be Ziggy.

"What's going on?" Drake asked the obvious question. He felt Dina moving closer behind him.

"Ziggy?"

Ziggy stepped forward, gun still pointing at Wells. Drake raised his scatter-gun at Ziggy. He wasn't sure what was happening, but he knew she had her weapon pointed at Lily's head.

"I'll shoot you in the face if you don't drop your gun right now!"

"Drake, don't," Dina said and put her palm on the scatter-gun's barrel, pushing it down.

"Dina, what the fu—" Drake stopped as Dina gave him a pleading look.

"C'mon, Dina. If it wasn't for those two idiots, you'd be taking the highest offer, too." Ziggy said, and Dina turned to face her.

"What is she talking about?' Drake asked.

"Tell him, Dina."

Drake looked at Dina, waiting for an explanation.

"When we took the contract, there were two jobs. From different origins, but for the same target. One wanted to rescue the lieutenant, the other wanted to capture and kill. The second one paid much more."

"So, you took both jobs?" Drake wondered if he had his gun pointed at the right person.

"No! I swear, Drake, we agreed to take the first one."

"*You* decided to take the first one, not me," Ziggy replied. "You made an emotional decision because of him."

"What does she mean?"

"I told her we were taking the first job because you were a friend, and I didn't want to betray you."

It was the closest Drake had ever seen Dina to being emotional.

"Dina, you know this makes more sense, right? She means nothing to us. I mean, she's Penta Security, for crying out loud."

Dina still had her hand on the scatter-gun's barrel, but took it off. She shouldered her Artie, barrel still pointing down, holding it in the ready position.

"Ziggy, this is not what we agreed on. You are making a mistake. Step away from her and let's get out of here."

The man on the DDU was still yelling, but no one paid him any attention.

Ziggy moved sideways, placing Wells between herself and the others. "This is what we do, Dina. Pick the highest paying contract and move on. Why aren't you with me?"

Dina seemed to struggle to find the right words. "We know these people, Ziggy. We can still make a small fortune finishing the first contract."

"They don't care about us. No one does. We need to take care of ourselves." Ziggy raised her suppressed Artie to eye level.

Dina and Drake raised their pulse weapons in response.

"Dina, I will shoot her, I swear!" Drake yelled.

He wished he had an Artie and not the scatter-gun. The chances of him hitting only Ziggy and not also Wells were slim to none. But he had no choice other than calling Ziggy's bluff. He knew, though, that it was all up to Dina to take her out. All his hope was on Dina choosing him over a ten-year relationship. Maybe Jimmy could take the shot. Except, Drake realized Jimmy wasn't in the room.

Dina looked at Drake. *Trust me.*

"Put down your weapon, Drake," she instructed him. He looked into her eyes and laid down his gun, leaving him completely exposed. Jimmy was missing, and he didn't have a clean shot to take at Ziggy. He had no choice but to trust Dina.

"Ziggy, let's go," Dina said as she lowered her Artie. "You and me. Let's just walk out of here and go."

Ziggy immediately trained her pulse gun on Drake. "No. This contract will set us up for years. I'm doing this for us, Dina. How can you not be on my side on this?"

An orange flash zoomed by Drake, distracting him for a second. Ziggy also took her eyes off Drake as Seymour sprinted into the room and ran straight for her. Smoke was already billowing out of his repaired leg, but he kept running toward her. As he approached her, he dipped down and braced for a jump. Wells must have seen this happening, as she swung all of her weight to the side and toppled herself over. Ziggy sidestepped the jumping ASR, and it crashed into the wall, falling into a motionless pile. Slightly off balance, she returned her gaze to Dina, who had her Artie back up to eye level and her finger on the trigger.

"Sorry," she said as the blue electric crackle sent a pulse cartridge hurling toward Ziggy.

The impact was high on her left shoulder and sent her spinning backward, falling right next to Seymour. Blood poured out of the wound, and she lost her grip on her pulse rifle, sending it rattling to the floor.

Drake jumped into action and kicked the gun away. Dina came rushing over, medi-pack at the ready.

"You didn't put it on stun," Drake yelled out, surprised.

"I know," Dina replied. "I told you I never trust it."

Jimmy came running into the room.

"Where were you?" Drake asked as he opened the synth-skin pack. He tore a small piece off and stretched it over his injured finger.

"Dina shoved me outside as we walked in, and I knew it meant she had a plan, ya know. I heard what was going on, so I grabbed Seymour and sent him in as a distraction. Where is he?"

Drake pointed him out, and Jimmy scrambled over to the ASR.

Dina opened a bottle of water and added the protein sachet to make some of the brown blood-growing proteins for Ziggy to drink. Wiping the blood away from the wound, Drake applied the rest of synth-skin and saw Ziggy take a deep breath. She was alive, but unconscious.

"When you're all done, can someone please help me?"

"Lily," Drake remembered the overturned chair and Lily still strapped to it. "I'm so sorry, here . . ."

Helping her sit up, he got to work on freeing her arms and legs. Once done, he stood back and waited for her to stand up.

"Almost fell asleep," she said, standing face to face with him.

Drake didn't answer. He couldn't. Nothing he could say would tell her how happy he was to see her. How sorry he was to have left her. How he blamed himself for her being stuck here in Shangcorp. All the words he knew were useless to him.

"Hey, Lily!" Jimmy yelled from the corner of the room, where he was already fixing Seymour.

"Hey, Jimmy."

"I'm . . ." Drake's tongue and brain stopped working again.

"It's fine," she replied. "We can have a long and detailed discussion later and you can answer all the many, many questions I have, but we need to figure out how to get back to Penta ASAP."

Ziggy moaned, and they both turned their attention to Dina, who was holding her in her lap.

"Go. She'll be fine. We'll figure this out. But you need to go, Drake."

"You sure? I'm kinda pissed off at her. Aren't you?" Drake asked.

Dina looked down at Ziggy and stroked her hair. "Oh, I'm angry, believe me. But she did what I taught her to do. So where does that leave me?"

Jimmy came walking over with Seymour limping behind him. He grabbed Wells and hugged her. "I knew we'd find you, ya know."

"I'm glad you did, Jimmy."

Seeing Jimmy and Lily embrace almost brought out the waterworks. He had never felt like this toward anyone, never mind two people. Drake knew they still had a daunting journey ahead, trying to get back to Penta. Their escape was far from done, but at least they were all together now.

"Okay, we have a truck outside. Let's go." Drake went over to Dina and crouched down next to her. "I know you only did it for the credits, but I appreciated you choosing the first job."

Dina shrugged. "I thought it'd be easier, that's all." She gave him a knowing smile.

Drake stood up, ready to leave.

Wells held her hand up. "One more thing."

She grabbed the DDU that had Davis's face on it.

"What's happening?" he asked.

"What's happening, Eugene, is that I'm coming for you." Wells threw the DDU against the wall.

"Now we can go," she said, walking out of the room.

Drake happily followed her.

FROM THE AUTHOR

Thank you for purchasing and reading my book. These days, reviews are crucial to the success of a book, so if you enjoyed what Drake, Jimmy and LT Wells got up to, please take a second and leave a review or rating. Not only would I greatly appreciate it, but it would also make a huge difference.

If you wanted to stay up to date with news and upcoming books, feel free to join me on Facebook or Instagram, and subscribing to my newsletter.

Until next time!

Eric

https://www.facebook.com/erickrugerwriter/
https://erickruger.com.au/join-us
Instagram - @erickrugerauthor

The Adventure Continues

www.ingramcontent.com/pod-product-compliance
Lightning Source LLC
Chambersburg PA
CBHW031954130726
47904CB00013B/1497

* 9 7 8 0 6 4 8 9 7 5 4 4 1 *